PRAISE FOR RACHEL VAN DY

"*The Consequence of Loving Colton* is a must-read friends-to-lovers story that's as passionate and sexy as it is hilarious!"

—Melissa Foster, *New York Times* bestselling author

"Just when you think Van Dyken can't possibly get any better, she goes and delivers *The Consequence of Loving Colton*. Full of longing and breathless moments, this is what romance is about."

—Lauren Layne, *USA Today* bestselling author

"The tension between Milo and Colton made this story impossible to put down. Quick, sexy, witty—easily one of my favorite books from Rachel Van Dyken."

—R. S. Grey, *USA Today* bestselling author, on *The Consequence of Loving Colton*

"Hot, funny, and will leave you wishing you could get marked by one of the immortals!"

—Molly McAdams, *New York Times* bestselling author, on *The Dark Ones*

"Laugh-out-loud fun! Rachel Van Dyken is on my auto-buy list."

—Jill Shalvis, *New York Times* bestselling author, on *The Wager*

"*The Dare* is a laugh-out-loud read that I could not put down. Brilliant. Just brilliant."

—Cathryn Fox, *New York Times* bestselling author

Cheater's Regret

ALSO BY #1 *NEW YORK TIMES* BESTSELLING AUTHOR RACHEL VAN DYKEN

The Consequence Series

The Consequence of Loving Colton

The Consequence of Revenge

The Consequence of Seduction

The Consequence of Rejection

The Wingmen Inc. Series

The Matchmaker's Playbook

The Matchmaker's Replacement

Curious Liaisons Series

Cheater

The Bet Series

The Bet

The Wager

The Dare

The Ruin Series

Ruin

Toxic

Fearless

Shame

The Eagle Elite Series

Elite

Elect

Entice

Elicit

Bang Bang

Enforce

Ember

Elude

Empire

The Seaside Series

Tear

Pull

Shatter

Forever

Fall

Eternal

Strung

Capture

The Renwick House Series

The Ugly Duckling Debutante

The Seduction of Sebastian St. James

The Redemption of Lord Rawlings

An Unlikely Alliance

The Devil Duke Takes a Bride

The London Fairy Tales Series

Upon a Midnight Dream

Whispered Music

The Wolf's Pursuit

When Ash Falls

The Seasons of Paleo Series

Savage Winter

Feral Spring

The Wallflower Series (with Leah Sanders)

Waltzing with the Wallflower

Beguiling Bridget

Taming Wilde

The Dark Ones Saga

The Dark Ones

Untouchable Darkness

Stand-Alones

Hurt: A Collection (with Kristin Vayden and Elyse Faber)

RIP

Compromising Kessen

Every Girl Does It

The Parting Gift (with Leah Sanders)

Divine Uprising

Cheater's Regret

CURIOUS LIAISONS, BOOK 2

RACHEL
VAN DYKEN

SKYSCAPE

SKYSCAPE

This is a work of fiction. Names, characters, organizations, places, events, and incidents are either products of the author's imagination or are used fictitiously.

Published by Skyscape, New York

www.apub.com

ISBN-13: 9781477819975
ISBN-10: 1477819975

Cover design by Shasti O'Leary Soudant

Printed in the United States of America

To Melody. Without you, this book would have been a nightmare. Thank you for all of your insight!

Prologue

Rain dripped from my chin as I banged my knuckles across Thatch's fancy apartment door.

Over and over again.

Like a crazy person, I smacked my hand against it. Tears mixed with water from the outside streamed down my cheeks.

I was "that girl."

The one who went to her boyfriend's apartment late at night, a complete hot mess of emotional chaos.

"Thatch!" I hit the door a third time, my palm stinging from the contact.

Finally, it opened.

Thatch was shirtless and shoeless.

His jeans hugged his body in a way that should have been illegal. Then again, he was a plastic surgeon—perfection was kind of his thing.

Anger surged through me and then . . . insecurity quickly replaced it. Brooke, the girl I had found him kissing, was taller than me, more athletic. She had stripper hair, the kind that just screams extensions, and her face was flawless. Probably along the lines of what Thatch was into. And her body? Let's say it was made for sin.

And looky here.

A sinner.

In my entire life, I had never been more aware of my wet black band shirt or my holey boyfriend jeans.

My navy-blue Converse sneakers squeaked when I shifted from the left to the right foot and back again.

"What?" He cocked his head to the side. "It's late."

I frowned. Seriously? Why is he treating me like I'm the one who just got caught cheating? "I . . ." My voice was hoarse from crying. "I'm sorry for running away. I just . . . I was upset." His face was like stone. No smile, not even any anger, just a chilly indifference that had me wanting to wrap my arms around my suddenly freezing body. "I want to try, Thatch. I . . ." My voice was barely a whisper. "I love you."

I held my breath.

He didn't say it back.

In fact, he didn't say much of anything for a few moments.

Moments that felt like hours.

Finally, he pressed his fingers to his temple and then shrugged. "We're done, Austin."

"But—"

The door clicked shut in my face with the finality of a gunshot.

Chapter One

Austin

"Fire!" Someone had shouted the word loud enough for me to jolt awake in a full-on panic. Heart hammering against my chest, I quickly assessed my bedroom for flames or smoke.

Pink walls. I *hated* pink. Pink walls summed up just about everything you needed to know about me. Namely, that my life wasn't mine to control. I had pink walls because my mom liked soft colors and wanted my room to look feminine.

And the old One Direction poster with asshole Zayn on the front of it? Well, that's what normal teenagers had on their walls, right? At least, that's what my father said, since we always had to please the voters. And when the local news did a story on our house, it was a huge hit. Look at the all-American straight-A student and her normal high school room! Yay me. So the walls were pink, and I was staring up at One Direction.

Damn you, Zayn, damn you to hell!

I shook my fist in the air. Partially because I was still pissed at him for leaving, but mainly because I was so pissed at myself for allowing others to control me.

I blinked up at the white ceiling, my eyes finally dry after so much crying. No tears left, I sighed.

No fire.

No heat.

Just. Nothing.

I blinked again. Had I imagined someone shouting "Fire!" at me? Was I really that exhausted?

"Oh look, you're awake." My best friend, Avery, breezed into my childhood bedroom with a plate of chocolate chip cookies in one hand and a glass of wine in the other. "I was afraid you were dead."

"What?" I yawned, stretching my stiff arms over my head. Pieces of chocolate fell onto my face as I opened my clenched hands. Huh, imagine that, I still had some. "Why would I be dead?"

"You smell like it." She scrunched up her nose. "And word on the street is you've given up showers and decided to stop shaving your legs." She held up her hand.

"What? What are you doing?" I squinted and tried to focus. "Why are you holding up your hand?"

"Girl power. High five." She closed it into a fist. "Or do we bump?"

"Why are you here? In my room? Isn't it Monday? Don't you have work?" After Avery screwed her boss—literally—and found her happily-ever-after with her childhood friend-slash-nemesis, she'd been moved to a different department, one that needed so much organization, I almost felt sorry for her having to put in so many hours. Between both of our schedules, we'd barely seen each other in the last week.

"Saturday." Avery rolled her green eyes. "It's Saturday, Austin, as in, the weekend." She picked up a half-eaten granola bar and made a face. "Is this all you've had today?"

I snatched the bar away from her and almost growled. "Mine."

"Wow, your transformation is complete. You've turned into a hairy beast with smelly hair and . . ." She narrowed her eyes. "Dear God, you have Cheetos in your hair."

"Really?" I perked up.

"No!" She smacked my shoulder. "See! This is what I was afraid of! This is what you do when you get sad! You revert back to your junior high self." Her eyes leveled me with a knowing glare. The one that was ever present during the tumultuous high school years when my then boyfriend, Braden, had literally slapped a piece of bread out of my hand during prom night because he said it was going to make me fat. Thinking about him gave me hives.

Avery sighed. "Are you stashing junk food in your bed?" She pulled back the covers to reveal my shame. "MoonPies in your nightstand!" Her movements were too quick.

"No, don't!"

Too late. She could barely get the drawer open as chocolate MoonPies spilled over onto the floor.

"Austin." Avery shook her head slowly and held out her hand. "Give me the Mountain Dew."

Braden had hated Mountain Dew.

That's why I bought stock in PepsiCo the minute we broke up.

"I have no idea what you're talking about," I sniffed while trying to move the unopened soda farther under my pillow.

"One!" She held up a finger. "Two!"

"Stop counting! I won't be threatened in my own room!"

The room I still lived in while I finished grad school.

The room that reminded me of all the things that drove me to want to go to grad school in the first place.

"Three!" Avery launched her body across mine, using her nails to scratch my arm as she dug under the pillow and swatted the Mountain Dew onto the floor. "Oh, Austin, they put formaldehyde in these things!"

I clenched my eyes shut. "Just go away."

"No. I'm not leaving—and not just because you're trying to pickle your body with this . . . Look, it's been a month." She pointed a judgmental finger at my can of soda. "You need to get over him."

Him.

Because I refused to say *his* name.

Because saying his name was just asking to be haunted by the feel of him, his rough hands running all over my body, the way he kissed like he was going for the gold, or the way he never, ever, let me leave his side without squeezing my hand and kissing me across the lips, gently as if to say, *Hey, just wanted to touch you.*

The dreams were bad enough.

The memories?

Worse.

I refused to think about him during the day, because that just gave him more power, but my body had different ideas at night, when the darkness blanketed me in a quiet loneliness that threatened to choke me to death.

Everything was perfect.

And then it just. Wasn't.

Damn it.

The tears came again.

Of *course* they did.

My chest was sore. Like an idiot, I rubbed it, but nothing made the heartache dissipate. Add school stress to the mix and I was an exhausted hot mess, barely able to function without sobbing my eyes out and drinking lots of coffee so I wouldn't fail at life . . . or my classes.

School stress, I knew I could manage. I always did.

Family stress, it was always there.

Exhaustion? Well, that was typical for a college student.

But the whole Thatch situation? That's what sent me over the edge. That's what kept me up at night. That's what made it so that when I turned in my last project, my professor gave me the number to the UW counselor hotline.

Thatch.

Why? Why was I so unlucky with guys?

He was *supposed* to be a really hot one-night stand. We'd had an agreement, and then everything changed. You'd have to be insane not to want more of that man after one night. And when that one night turned into another, then another, and things got serious on my end, when I confessed how I really felt, he should have made a run for it! That's what cock-sucking cheaters did! They made a lame excuse about how it was "fun" and then ran in the opposite direction with their tail between their legs. But what did he do instead? He said, "Let's try."

Let's.

Try.

As in, let's be more than sex partners every other Saturday when I wasn't up to my ears in research and when he wasn't scrubbing in on some lame-ass boob surgery.

Try.

So try we did.

And it worked.

And it was awesome.

Until it wasn't.

Until the leopard took a good hard look in the mirror and thought to himself, *Gee golly gosh, I really do miss those spots! Damn it! I can't be tamed.* Insert Miley Cyrus lyrics here.

End of story.

No happy ending.

Because the leopard let a girl, who was not me, maul him with her mouth in front of me, hours before confessing that he'd been feeling *apprehensive* about our arrangement.

What? Like we signed a contract or something?

That should have been my first clue.

Instead, I ignored it, and walked in on him kissing my best friend's sister.

And then, after all the tears on my end, when I went to his apartment the next day and said I wanted to really try to make things work.

He said no. And broke up with me. With *me.*

As if I were the one who did something wrong! When I was willing to forgive and forget—willing to move the hell on! Because I liked him. An irritating voice panging inside my chest cavity, a voice also known as my heart, had other feelings, strong ones, feelings that reminded me how tender he'd been toward me, how loving, how caring. How pissed off he'd been when I told him about my parents' lack of affection, and how nurturing he'd been when I confessed how badly school was stressing me out.

Fine. I loved him.

Had loved him.

Had.

I still couldn't even look at my navy-blue Converse sneakers or favorite boyfriend jeans without bursting into tears. I'd worn them the night he'd broken up with me and quietly closed the door in my face.

The sound of the door clicking shut may as well have been a gun going off.

The pain was probably the same.

I knocked. Over and over again.

Finally, one of the neighbors threatened to call the cops. I hadn't even realized I was sobbing until I got into my car and glanced in the mirror.

He'd broken me.

And he hadn't even looked sorry.

With a loud sigh, Avery pushed Snickers wrappers out of her way and sat on my bed, putting her hand on my lap. "It will get better, I promise."

"No," I sniffled.

"Would it make you feel better if I told you that I took a can of spray paint to a few of his signs downtown and gave him boobs?"

I started laughing. "Yes."

"No can do. I'm pretty sure they send you to prison for that kind of shit, but I did manage something even better."

I perked up.

"Oh, I see that look of revenge in your eyes, and I like it. I can work with revenge. What I can't work with is Sad Austin. I hate Sad Austin, she's no fun, and I say this because I love you, but Sad Austin's going to give Awesome Austin diabetes one day." She pulled out a bag of Skittles from the foot of the bed and dropped it onto the floor.

"Those aren't mine," I said defensively while my mouth watered with need for the sugary, sticky candies.

"I forgot you still have an imaginary friend who sneaks into your room and litters it with junk food."

"Hey, that excuse worked when I was eight! My parents totally believed me." Probably because for the most part they ignored me. I was to be seen and not heard, and when the time came for me to do my part for Daddy and his campaigns, I memorized cute little speeches and made sure to wear dresses that were only an inch above my knee. My parents loved me—they just had an odd way of showing it.

"That's called 'enabling,' sweetie." Avery patted my hand and stood. "And I refuse to do that. So, Sad Austin has got to go. The first step is admitting you have a problem, and you"—she pointed to the adjoining bathroom—"have a problem. You smell like cheese."

"But I love cheese," I whispered longingly. "I could go for some cheese right now." Where the hell was my Gouda when I needed it!

"Not the good kind, Austin." Avery scrunched up her nose.

My shoulders slumped.

"Austin," Avery began, using her serious voice, the one that said she was done with kid gloves and was ready to pull out the big guns, "you're smart, motivated, a kick-ass friend, and you're only a few months away from graduating with your MBA!" I nodded. She was right. She knew my hot buttons. There was a reason I was trying like hell and working my ass off. "Besides, do you really want to be like your mom?"

And there it was.

The knife twisting.

I recoiled.

A loud sigh escaped between my lips. Avery didn't take it at all as a sign to stop talking before I burst into tears or smothered her with a pillow.

"She gave up everything for your father. Her education. Her interests. Now look at her."

Yeah, my mother was a perfect Stepford wife with a tight smile. The perfect trophy wife. The perfect everything.

All modeled after my father's idea of perfection.

I shivered.

That could not be my future.

"You don't want that, do you?"

"Thatch wasn't turning me into that," I said defensively. Even though a small part of me knew that if I was willing to overlook cheating this early on in a relationship, then I had already lost a part of myself, an important part. I frowned. "What the hell!"

Avery jumped back.

I clenched my fists. "I was going to take him back!"

Her eyes widened.

I cleared my thoughts with a shake of my head. That bastard! I was going to sacrifice my pride for him! And he shut the door in my face!

In. My. Face.

"What's this revenge you speak of?" I asked, feeling the best I had in weeks, probably because I suddenly realized I wanted to be angry at him, not sad because of him. I wanted to cut off his balls and feed them to piranhas while he watched.

"First." Avery moved my hand away from her arm—apparently, I'd been squeezing her skin between my fingers. "My arm isn't his face. Second." She grinned. "I got Lucas drunk and got dirt on Thatch, so much dirt that I turned into a dirty little girl and—"

I covered my ears.

"Just making sure you're listening." She winked. "Let me put it this way. When a guy screws you over, cheats on you, and you're the one in bed eating all the calories and hating life? Well, we don't get sad, we get mad."

"Madness is insanity. It's not actually anger, Avery."

"'Anger' doesn't rhyme with 'sad'—work with me here." She clapped her hands in front of my face. "Okay, I've breathed through my mouth enough—go shower before they send in the hazmat people."

I rolled my eyes. "Stop being melodramatic."

"Your mom found a mouse yesterday."

I let out a snort. The only time my mom came into my room was to steal my clothes. The ones she fought tooth and nail to fit into. Spin classes were her addiction—then again, she had a sweet tooth too, so she had no choice but to take a daily class in order to stay perfect.

For my perfect father.

For our perfect family.

I gagged.

"So?"

"In your room. I'm pretty positive it died from Cheetos consumption."

"You're lying."

"It had a bloated stomach. We had a funeral for it and everything."

I rolled my eyes at her clear exaggeration and slowly walked toward the bathroom, stopping once I was at the door and turning to whisper, "Thanks, Avery."

"For what?"

"Kicking my ass."

"Oh, that part comes later." She winked. "Just remember . . . revenge can be sweeter than"—scrunching up her face, she made a circular gesture around the room with her arm—"whatever the heck you have going on in here."

I nodded and shut the door.

She was right.

I was going to destroy him.

And when I was finished?

His heart was going to be shattered and scattered—just like mine—just like mine still was.

Chapter Two

Thatch

"I'm sorry, what the hell did you just say? You were mumbling."

Lucas covered his mouth with his hand and said something under his breath about being drunk and a turkey.

"You did what with a turkey?" I shook my head. "Because you really don't want to know what I'm thinking right now."

With a sigh, Lucas dropped his hand and took a long sip of coffee. We'd been sitting at Starbucks for the last five minutes while he mumbled about needing to tell me something important.

I checked my watch. "Look, I have surgery in an hour, so if you could just"—I lifted my hands in the air—"be normal, for one second, that would be fantastic."

He'd been my best friend for four years, and the best wingman a single guy could ask for. Until he put a collar on his dick and gave his girlfriend, Avery, the leash.

Pain sliced through my chest.

I ignored it.

Heartburn.

Regret.

Really it was all the same.

"I may have gotten drunk," Lucas finally said. His dark eyes darted between me and the coffee cup, then back at me. "And . . . said stuff."

"Lucas Thorn." A woman, probably one of his many exes, walked up.

"Not now," he said in a bored voice. "I don't have a list anymore." He was referring to the list of women he picked from—women he used to date and cheat on, all the while telling them it wasn't cheating if they were aware it was happening.

So basically, on a scale of one to ten, Satan would have been a ten, Lucas would have been a nine point five—ask any of the scorned ones.

One hissed in our direction once—I half expected her to throw holy water in his face and demand he burn in hell.

The woman looked between us, said under her breath, "Still a bastard," and stomped off.

"You got drunk," I repeated, completely unfazed since the man would always have women falling all over themselves for his attention. It was his thing. It would always be his thing. "And said stuff."

"Important stuff." He winced. "Shit, I'm just going to come out and say it."

"Thank God."

"I told Avery about you."

I froze, opened my mouth, then froze again. "And when you say you told her about me, I'm assuming you don't mean you told her that I used to have a pet pony and a fish named Spike?"

"I thought your dog was Spike?"

"Spike died. You mean Muggles."

"Ah!" Lucas snapped his fingers. "And yup, that's it, that's the confession, she knows things." His nervous expression said a hell of a lot more, but I didn't have time to question him about whatever the hell type of drug he was taking to force him to admit he told Avery I had pets when I was young.

If anything, all my past revealed to anyone was that I wasn't a complete jackass, since I actually knew how to take care of animals when I was a small child; ergo, I was capable of taking care of actual human beings.

Not that I wanted to.

"I'm not completely comfortable with the way you just lowered your voice and then pointed at me like you were Harry Potter casting an unforgivable curse," I mumbled to my shifty friend.

"I would never Harry Potter you," he said in a calm voice. We both took Harry Potter very seriously.

"Thanks, man. Good talk." I stood and yawned. I would do anything—illegal even—for more sleep, but lately, a certain woman haunted my dreams, and business had been good, not that I was complaining, but it was causing me to burn the candle at both ends. "God, why does every woman want implants that can cause severe back issues?"

"Are you seriously complaining about touching breasts all day?" Lucas gave me a completely shocked look, one that made me doubt my own sanity.

"Yeah." I slapped my face with my free hand in order to wake myself up. "It's boring as hell, I'd rather do a rhinoplasty."

"A nose." Lucas rolled his eyes. "You'd rather do a nose than breasts. Are you feeling okay?"

"Fine," I snapped at him. I rarely snapped. "Was that it? You just felt bad for telling Avery stuff about me?"

"Yeah. That was it." He rocked back on his heels. His shifty eyes did not make me feel good about our conversation, yet I had no choice but to ignore the tingling feeling in my gut that warned me, somehow, the universe had shifted.

The tingling continued all the way to my office.

And started again when I punched the button for the third floor and waited for the elevator to ascend.

When the lights flickered above me as the elevator came to a jarring halt, I muttered out, "This is bullshit."

I refused to be superstitious because my best friend was having an off day and decided to include me in it. I stepped over the cracks in the slate floor as I made my way past my office and into the OR. Before I washed my hands, I kissed the hammer necklace on my neck and tucked it into my scrubs.

Everything was fine.

It was going to be completely and totally fine.

◆ ◆ ◆

Holy shit.

It wasn't fine.

It was far from fine.

The patient didn't die—thank God. But the procedure that should have taken ninety minutes took three hours. It would have been helpful if she had let me know she was on blood thinners.

She could have bled out.

For breasts.

We typically never risked surgery if the patient had a history of blood clots and was on a blood thinner—but apparently, she wanted to risk her life just so she could look better in a swimsuit. I was being harsh. But by not telling me about her medical history, the patient had put her life in jeopardy.

I pulled off my scrubs, opened the door, tossed them into the laundry bin outside of my office, and shut the door again.

Something felt wrong, weird. I was still on edge after talking with Lucas and I had no idea why, though I had a suspicion of what the cause probably was.

Miserable. I was miserable. And I knew the misery was of my own making, but it didn't make it hurt any less.

I swore and blindly reached into my office closet for my clothes.

And reached again.

And one more time, because in the last two years since leaving residency, my clothes were always in the same spot.

Always.

I turned around to actually face the closet. The wooden hanger was empty.

Completely empty.

"Son of a bitch!" I yelled. Where were my clothes? I'd changed in my office like I always did before surgery and had hung them up. I glanced around the room for something to cover up with.

And came up empty.

Whatever. I'd just put my scrubs back on.

But when I opened the office door and poked my head out, the bin was gone.

They never took the bin until the end of the day.

Shit, I was losing my mind.

Okay, Thatch, think.

Exhausted, I rubbed my face with my hands and tried to come up with an option where I didn't have to walk down the hall completely naked.

Because I was.

Naked.

I refused to wear underwear during surgery.

It was one of my rituals.

I liked to be as comfortable as possible. I listened to rap music while I gave people nose jobs and breasts, and I free-balled.

"Shit."

I called the receptionist. At least someone could bring me a new set of scrubs.

It went to voice mail.

When I looked down the hall again, it was empty. Like my entire office was in a cult and had been suddenly taken to the mother ship.

I quietly closed the door and prayed that I'd left my gym bag in the closet. I pulled open the door to find no gym bag. But folded neatly on the ground were a pair of spandex bicycle shorts and a yellow biking competition jersey.

They sure as hell weren't mine, but what choice did I have?

Biting back a curse, I pulled the shorts up to my knees and winced—they were so tight around my thighs, I wouldn't have been surprised if my dick suffered severe blood loss. Hah, wouldn't Austin just love that! The cheater, her words not mine, could no longer get it up because he put on bicycle shorts that didn't fit because someone stole his damn clothes!

Maybe my clothes disappeared because I was new around the office; so far, unlike the other new surgeon who joined the practice at the same time, I hadn't undergone a hazing ritual. My reputation for doing the best breast augmentations in the city made me highly sought after, and I fielded a lot of offers before picking this practice, which promised to fast-track my partnership. It helped that I was young and, according to the other partners, "easy to market"—thus our clinic's ad campaign featuring my face splashed all over park benches and buses in the Greater Seattle area.

"Damn it!" I shimmied into the shorts with a snap, the spandex molded against my dick like a second skin—it wasn't a good look.

Next, I pulled the jersey over my head and grimaced at myself in the mirror. Well, at least I wasn't naked anymore! Though on second thought, naked would probably have been better than the skintight competition gear. I was going to have a hell of a time taking this shit off.

I tugged at my long blond hair in irritation. I really needed to cut it, especially now that Austin was out of the picture. She'd been obsessed with my hair. Just another reminder of what I lost. Though can you really say you lost something when you're the one who refused to find it? I smoothed down my hair one last time, then opened the door and poked my head out to confirm that no one was around to witness my walk of shame.

I quickly left my office and prayed that the storage closet where we kept extra scrubs would be open.

Locked.

The one across from it was locked too.

Ten minutes later.

And I'd tried every damn closet in the place.

And I was still dressed like fucking Lance Armstrong.

Parts of me were clearly trying to break free.

As if on cue, my dick twitched painfully.

People wore this shit? For real? And sired children?

I slammed my fist against the wall in anger. I was exhausted from surgery, still panicked that it had almost gone so wrong, and all I wanted was to finish out my day and go. I quickly snatched a nearby clipboard to cover my crotch and continued trying doors down the hall. Where the hell was everyone?

Finally the conference room door opened—I knew there would at least be someone in there who could hint at where one of the partners must have hidden my clothes—jackasses.

"SURPRISE!" The room erupted into laughter and cheers, scaring the shit out of me and forcing me to walk into the room—in my Lance Armstrong drag. Only I was twice the guy's size, so it was like stuffing a sausage into a miniature hot dog bun.

I had to grit my teeth to keep from swearing. Making matters worse were the crotch stares I was getting from two of the nurses—both of whom had made it painfully clear on more than one occasion that they wanted a quick screw.

"Well, it looks like someone doesn't need a penile enlargement after all," a familiar voice called out with a chuckle.

And then the crowd parted.

"Austin." I said her name with venom, not longing. I refused to show weakness when it came to the girl with pale skin and dark brown hair with golden highlights.

The girl I destroyed.

The girl I still wanted.

The girl who had the brass balls to try to make me into someone I would never be.

The girl who got away.

She was a brilliant and terrifying woman in expensive clothing; she looked innocent enough—she wasn't.

Then again, neither was I.

Austin stood, cake in hand. "We just thought it would be fun to surprise you on your special day."

The hell? "My special day," I repeated at an utter loss. Why was she in my office building?

"You've been recognized by the city of Seattle for your exceptional work in plastic surgery." She grinned, waving a plaque in front of my face. "I came by myself to deliver it." She winked. "Daddy wanted to, but you know how busy he gets."

Even though she was smiling, her eyes looked empty. I knew that smile. I just never thought I would ever be on the receiving end of it. Was it me? Or was it lingering sadness that her father was once again too busy for her—but never for free publicity? Wait. That made no sense. Why the hell wasn't he the one bringing me the award rather than his daughter, the woman I couldn't stop thinking about? "So, on behalf of the mayor of Seattle, I present to you . . ." Oh hell, cell phones stood at attention, taking pictures of me with the plaque. In spandex. "The Best of 2016 Award for you and your staff!"

My body twitched.

I couldn't help it.

She'd said "staff."

"What an honor." I kept my voice even, because it was rare for someone my age to receive an award of this caliber, but she was ruining it with her presence. Ruining what should by all means be a huge moment for a plastic surgeon.

"And how cool is it that the picture going into the newspaper will have you in your gear for the big race!" she said loudly as a camera flashed.

I stepped away from her while my staff began to chatter about the award and how great it was to get one at such a young age, and just out of residency. As excited as I was about the award, I knew it would put more of a target on my back—which just meant more stress.

"Big race?" Apparently, all I was capable of was repeating everything she said. "Big race for what?"

Austin pointed to my shirt. "The Seattle to Portland Classic, of course. I mean at least that's what it says on your sleeve here." Her fingertips grazed the shirt and then fell to my skin before she pulled away and smirked. "I bet you're just dying to get on that bike." She drew out the word "bike" while a cold sweat started trickling down my neck and into my spandex shorts, which meant I was going to have to be buried in them since it would be nearly impossible to get too-tight sweaty spandex off my body without chopping off my legs.

I stared her down. Hoping my glare would get her to shut the hell up about my clothing or the fact that she'd said "bike."

"You're doing the classic too?" Troy, one of the doctors I worked with, walked into the room and grinned. "Hey, we should train together!"

Shit.

"I uh—" Was it hot in there? I tugged the tight jersey, irritated that it made a sucking noise as it plastered itself against my chest again, and I tried to think of an excuse.

"Oh, that's such a great idea! My father's going to be doing the race as well—maybe all of you guys could go on a few long rides together." Austin winked at me. "Some of those rides can be brutal. Why, I've even heard of cyclists getting hit by cars."

Troy laughed.

I felt myself pale as a choking fear wrapped around my neck in the form of visions of dismemberment by a semi.

"That's not common," he said reassuringly as he patted my back. "Had I known you were into cycling, we could have trained for the race this week together. Eh, next time, right?"

"Yeah," I croaked, flashing him a fake smile. "That sounds fun."

Death? Getting hit by a car? Sign me up.

He left me alone with Austin.

Her eyebrows arched as she gave me a mocking smile. "Gee, Thatch, you think they're going to let you keep your training wheels on?"

She kept staring and smiling.

And then it occurred to me.

That tingling feeling.

Lucas's confession.

Son of a bitch!

Lucas told her!

She burst out laughing. "Don't worry, Thatch, just wear a helmet!"

"That's it." I gripped her by the elbow and tugged her away from the party. The hall was silent except for the click-clack of her high heels against the slate.

Once we were in the safety of my office, I slammed the door and glared. "What the hell do you think you're doing?"

She lifted her chin.

God, I'd always loved how pretty she was when she was angry.

"And how the hell do you know about"—I coughed and averted my eyes—"that?"

"That," she repeated as she advanced on me. Damn it, I hated how tall she was—it made it hard to antagonize her. "Meaning the fact that you can't ride a bike?"

"Fucking hell." I tugged at the ends of my hair again, my one and only nervous habit. "What else did Lucas tell you?"

"Ribbit, ribbit."

I stumbled back against my desk. "You bitch!"

"It's not like I'm an actual frog. No need to get your panties in a twist, or in your case, really, really tight spandex." She scrunched up her nose. "Those shorts really don't do the little man downstairs any favors, do they? Maybe I should have gotten them in a bigger size, but wouldn't you know? They were completely out of extra-large."

"Wait, what?" I ignored her insult and held her gaze, my heart thundering in my chest while anger pounded through my blood. "You? You did this to me? You set me up!"

"Gee, I wonder why I would do that." She tapped her chin. "And no, it's not like I planned on seeing you. Trust me, if I could avoid you forever, I would, but considering our best friends can't keep their hands off each other, we're stuck together." Her smile was cruel; hurt laced her features. "Besides, you know how my dad sometimes makes me do these things for the press. Plus, he's been really busy lately, so . . ." She straightened, but I didn't miss the hurt flash across her face. "An opportunity presented itself, and I took it."

Yeah, I just bet he was *busy*.

"Just like an opportunity presented itself for you to slit the tires on my car?" I countered.

Her lips twitched.

"It's not funny."

"It's kind of funny."

"Do you even realize how expensive that was? The towing? The new tires?" I roared.

Her façade broke as she sucked in a breath and looked down. I knew I'd hit my mark; she knew I was paying off student loans while she was still living at home with her rich dad, who had the city at his fingertips.

My guilty conscience reminded me that even though she seemed to have it all, at home, she was lonely—and ignored. I pushed the irritating emotion away and hung my head.

Besides, there was so much she didn't know.

I was too tired to deal with her.

Too exhausted to attempt to figure out the mess I'd created for both of us. We were in that weird stage when you slept together, broke up, and still had the same friends, making it impossible to ignore each other.

"I've done nothing to earn this level of"—I waved my hands in the air—"crazy, even from you."

Austin's pretty head jerked to attention. "You insulted me. Embarrassed me. Humiliated me. Kissed another woman, and then dumped me. After cheating on me!" She yelled "cheating" so loud, I was sure people could hear her from space.

I refused to feel guilty. It was for the best. That's the lie I told myself, and it was the lie I was going to stick with. "What the hell do you want, Austin?"

"Revenge." She grinned. "But I thought it would only be fair if I warned you first . . . Gives you more of a fighting chance." She rose up on her tiptoes and wrapped her arms around my neck. "And I'm always fair."

I kept my arms pinned at my side even though all I wanted to do was press my mouth to that sweet spot on her neck and wrap my arms around her waist.

She'd been an addiction.

One that nearly destroyed us both.

One that threw me off the path I'd sworn to stay on for years.

"Revenge, hmm?" I whispered, almost grazing her soft lips and trying to act calm when my brain was going a million miles a minute. "Sounds dirty, and if I remember correctly—you're all vanilla."

Her eyes widened with hurt.

"Plain," I repeated, hating myself even more. "Young." She jerked back. "Inexperienced." She backed away as if I were firing actual shots at her. I pursued her, pinning her against the wall. That's it, keep her angry. It's the only way. "Immature . . . and without any sort of direction. Try your damnedest to get your revenge, Austin. Hell, what else would I expect from a girl who's only twenty-two? Because that's what you are, Austin, a girl." I deserved to be slapped. "And here I thought I made myself so clear. I want a woman."

Tears filled her eyes. "What happened to us?"

I refused to answer that loaded question. What happened to us, indeed? Every time I wanted something out of my reach, I had a sinking feeling I was going to get burned. And this time, I was right. But I wasn't just burned, I was wrecked, completely destroyed. I just never expected the fire to be so hot—or the ramifications to be so life-altering. "Have fun with your little revenge plan, just leave my car alone next time."

"I'll try, but you know I love the soft leather seats."

The memory of us kissing in my car slammed into me, her hungry lips as she pressed her body against mine, my obsessive need as I tasted her skin, stripping her clothes as fast as my hands would let me. It was always that way with her. The leather seats were nothing compared to the way she felt beneath my fingertips, and then she'd pressed her ass against the horn by accident, causing us to erupt in laughter just as someone shouted at us to get a room. I'd never experienced the type of relationship that held laughter, sex, and friendship—until Austin.

"We had fun," I finally said in a detached voice.

"Tell me why we broke up, and I won't do it," she answered, crossing her arms.

She only thinks she wants to know.

It was on the tip of my tongue to say something.

To end her misery.

To make her smile at me again—not with the empty one reserved for banquets and ribbon cuttings, but the smile she used to give me when it was just us. God I hated the hurt in her eyes more than I hated the emptiness.

"The 'why' won't make you feel better," I said as the silence between us stretched for miles, making me feel older than my thirty-two years. Did she see the slight twitch of my hand? The intense need my body had to touch her? Did she know that my heart, stupid messed-up thing that it was, still beat for her?

No.

And she never would.

"Fine, your funeral." She was back to being saucy and dangerously close to making me want to kiss her again.

I barked out a laugh. "Yeah, okay." Austin wouldn't hurt a fly, though a small part of me was slightly worried about just how drunk Lucas had gotten. It wasn't like I had a lot of secrets. Another part of my brain alerted me that yes, she had in fact slit my tires, but she'd been pissed; this was different.

It's not like Lucas got drunk and confessed anything worthwhile, right?

My hand twitched at my side.

She knew about the biking and the frogs.

Did that mean he told her about my . . . *phobias*?

No. Impossible.

With a sigh, she dug into her purse and tossed me a key. "Locker number six, bottom floor."

"Bottom floor?"

"Your clothes." She gave me another empty smile. "They might be wrinkled, though, and before I forget—" She launched herself at me, fusing her mouth to mine. "Congratulations on the award."

I was too stunned to do anything but lick my lips like a masochistic bastard—and let out a moan at how good she still tasted—better than I remembered.

Like candy.

If she hated me? Wanted revenge? Then why the hell would she kiss me?

I only had to wonder for a few seconds.

Until I opened the door to head down to the bottom floor for my clothes and felt my mouth start to itch and my throat tighten.

Chapter Three

Austin

I covered my face with my hands and peeked through the space between my fingers as I looked at a picture of Thatch scratching his face. "Avery, you said it was a minor allergy!"

We were sitting on a park bench in downtown Seattle, enjoying the best clam chowder I'd ever had while birds flew over us, begging for scraps.

I didn't share food.

So I was really ready to wage war against those things if need be.

I clutched my soup closer and elbowed her. "Avery?"

"Hmm?" She was busy texting Lucas, probably explaining that she was going to be late for dinner because she almost killed his best friend.

That sucked. She got a fancy dinner date, and I was scarfing down soup and trying to keep animals from taking my sloppy seconds.

She stared at her screen with a dopey grin on her face.

I grabbed her phone and sat on it. "You aren't even listening!"

"Sure I am, minor allergy, all true." The problem with best friends? I could be sitting on her phone or peeing in front of her and it still wouldn't faze her. She'd just fish the phone away from my naked ass and use that same hand to grab a Pringles.

"Avery!" Oh no, his skin was going into full rash mode, and angry red bumps started appearing around his mouth. If I were a horrible human being, I'd admit it looked like herpes. Instead, I said, "It looks like his face was lit on fire."

"It probably was—that pesky soy allergy's a bitch."

I threw up my hands. "I don't want to kill him!"

I wanted revenge! Not a death on my hands!

I mean, I would be lying if I said I didn't often dream about him getting hit by a car, but in my dream, it was almost always a really slow car, driven by a slow grandmother, and he had a few scratches and got what was coming to him.

"Oh." She seemed disappointed at this information, like a true friend hell-bent on making you feel better about an ex. When she'd encouraged me to eat all of the sushi and soy sauce, then gargle with the rest of the bottle for good measure, I didn't think it would even do anything to the guy!

Sighing, I leaned against the cold park bench and looked at the picture his receptionist had sent us. Thankfully, it had only taken a few bribes to get the woman to join our side—and once we told her the dirty details, she couldn't wait to join Team Austin and stick it to her boss—even though she did admit that he was the easiest doctor to work with.

Easy my ass!

This was war.

Casualties were all part of the game.

I scrunched up my nose and looked at the picture again.

Apparently, it was possible to still look damn sexy even with an ugly face rash.

His blond hair kissed his toned and tan shoulders, and his high cheekbones just made me want to practice with my sculpting kit on his face.

The guy's bone structure was downright irritating.

"He wouldn't tell me why." I slumped against the bench.

"Told ya so." Avery was still texting.

"I even gave him an ultimatum. Tell me why you cheated, why you broke my heart when things were going so great—I mean . . . I wanted closure, an answer, anything!" I threw my hands into the air and almost chucked my phone at Avery's face.

"Take a deep breath," Avery instructed. "What you wanted was for him to say he was sorry."

My stupid lower lip trembled as I croaked out, "Yeah, maybe."

It wasn't still supposed to hurt this bad. I was beyond that stage, right? I did the crying-and-eating-my-feelings thing, and now I was pissed. Except, I'd actually seen him today, and all those emotions surged to the surface the minute he'd walked into the room. It felt like his piercing eyes saw right through me even though I'd arrived at his office in my best armor. A pencil skirt and sexy blouse with heels. I'd been prepared. But one could never be prepared for Thatch. He was muscular, tall, model gorgeous, and smart. The smart part really burned, because it just meant he had so much in his favor. I had always been the smart one, and then Thatch came into my life—gorgeous, perfect, intelligent Thatch—and he'd stolen my heart.

Avery's voice made me jump in my seat. "You wanted him to say he was stupid, that he messed up, that Brooke-the-bitch accidently fell across his face, and he had no choice but to kiss her because Obi-Wan Kenobi was whispering in his ear that if he didn't return the kiss, the Force would leave planet Earth."

"STOP USING *STAR WARS* REFERENCES!"

"I can't help it." She slumped. "Lucas is forcing me to watch all of them . . . He put me on sex hiatus until I'm done."

I patted her shoulder.

"The point," she said, thrusting her hand into the air, "is that he couldn't give you the answers you needed or wanted. Ergo"—she held out her other hand and winked—"we make him pay."

"But not for long," I said quickly. "I'm not that immature."

She gave me a knowing look.

"What?" I shook my head. "I'm not. I'm an adult, and adults don't get even when their ex-boyfriend sticks his tongue down someone else's throat at their best friend's fake engagement party." Actually they did, but I was trying to sound like a responsible adult and not a psycho who wanted to inflict pain on his man parts, no matter how good they actually looked in those stupid spandex shorts.

We were quiet, and then Avery said, "Well, when you put it that way."

"Whatever happened to the white picket fence?" I stood. "Or the cute dog? Or getting married in college! Whatever happened to a man keeping it the hell in his pants!"

"Amen, sister," a woman said under her breath as she breezed by me.

"Thank you!" I called after her, and turned back to Avery. "Seriously. What happened to the dream?"

"The dream?" she repeated with a confused stare.

"The dream!" Did she really not get it? "Going to college, finding the love of your life, dating, getting married, having kids, struggling with bills, camping trips because you can't afford to go on vacation! What the hell is wrong with society? I just want to eat hot dogs with my future husband and watch Netflix!"

"I don't think camping trips are really my thing. Not that kind of dreamer, and hot dogs?" Avery patted my knee.

I shoved her hand away. "But the point is this, somehow, along the way, it's like men have decided that it's okay to stick their prick wherever they want and not suffer the consequences. And I'm sick of it! I'm tired of dating someone, falling for him, and then having him leave me because I'm the problem!" I kicked the dirt with my shoe. "I'm the NORMAL one, Avery!"

She winced.

"I mean not now. Now I'm angry, so you can't count this against me."

She stared at me for a minute, then gave me a single nod. "That's fair."

"He's going to pay." I thrust my hand into the air. "And I know just how I'm going to do it. He thinks a face rash that looks like herpes is bad? Well, by the time I'm done with him, he won't forget the name Austin Rogers!"

"Good for you!" Avery stood and gave me a high five. "Just don't kill him."

"Hah, he should be so lucky."

Chapter Four

Thatch

My face was on fire, and my entire office was still in an uproar over the award. News had already traveled about the big race I was supposedly doing with Troy and the mayor, which meant I somehow had to learn how to ride a bike between now and then or just sprain a muscle—any muscle—and bow out.

What should have been a simple practical joke spiraled out of control because, how amazing was it that I was a successful surgeon and also doing bike races? At least, that's what the nurses kept saying every so often when I left the safety of my office. It didn't matter that Troy had been racing for the past fifteen years. *Troy* wasn't known as the Dr. McSteamy of the group. So help me God, if one more nurse asked me if I could stitch myself up like they saw on *Grey's Anatomy*, I was going to lose my fucking mind.

My mouth still felt swollen. The only Benadryl in the office was in liquid form, and I chugged half the bottle. My allergic reaction was so severe that if I didn't, I'd end up in the hospital.

I was able to collapse against the couch in my office before I face-planted against the door—my dreams were filled with a certain woman, only she tasted like Benadryl, and when I told her I was sorry, she told me to go die.

And then she started yelling at me in Chinese.

The next thing I knew, I was eating chicken fried rice and ordered extra soy sauce, only to yell at myself, "Don't eat it! Don't eat it! You'll die!"

And that's when it occurred to me.

She knew about my allergy.

I jolted awake.

Just like she knew about my inability to ride a bike.

And my irrational fear of frogs after being chased by one when I was seven.

"Holy shit!" I pounded my fist against the leather couch as streams of late-afternoon sunlight filtered into my office. "She tried to kill me!"

When I was actually able to form a more coherent sentence that didn't include every curse word I knew, I called Lucas.

But the bastard son of a bitch didn't answer.

Of course he didn't answer! Because he'd probably already talked to Avery, who had clearly given all the shit she had on me to Austin.

A sense of dread washed over me. Just how drunk did he get to confess all my secrets—at least the ones that he knew about—to Avery? The bastard was on a friendship time-out—that was for damn sure!

"Dead," I said to myself. "He's *dead*."

A knock sounded at my door.

I rubbed my eyes. "Yes?"

The door opened, revealing the man of the hour himself. Lucas winced when he looked at my face and then he pointed. "Are those hives?"

I hastily searched the area for a sharp or heavy object to throw at his mocking face and came up empty. "No," I hissed, my voice dripping with sarcasm. "Adult acne."

"I heard Proactiv's what the kids use these days. It may help," he said with a smirk before taking the seat farthest from the couch.

"I'm probably going to kill you," I said cheerfully. "When I'm not high on Benadryl, and I can piss without passing out in the toilet."

Lucas made a disgusted face.

"Are you here to apologize for helping Austin nearly commit homicide?"

His guilty look said it all. "It's a soy allergy. It's not like you sucked off a soybean!"

"No!" I stood. "You don't get to be defensive! I almost died! And who the hell sucks off a soybean?"

"People who like soy?" Lucas shrugged. "How the hell do I know? And what do you mean you almost died?"

I took a deep breath and explained. "She kissed me—"

"She kissed you?"

I held up my hand. "Stay with me. She kissed me, and then my lips started swelling right along with my throat."

"Son of a bitch," Lucas muttered. "The kiss of death." He shuddered. "Kind of has a whole new meaning now, yeah?"

The urge to slap him was strong.

My hand twitched.

He eyed my hand and then me. "Surgeon's hands. You have surgeon's hands, Thatch. You don't want to punch me and be rendered incapable of performing. Besides, what would all those beautiful breasts do without you?" He stood. "They'd stay flat, and the world would cease to exist." He made an exploding sound effect and threw his hands into the air in chaotic fashion.

"No." I shook my head. "Just . . ." I sat back down, still dizzy from the damn Benadryl. "The breasts will survive. I, however, would lose my damn mind. You know I need to work to keep myself sane."

It slipped.

I hated admitting weakness. And that was one of them. I was a certifiable workaholic. Yes, I loved my job, but it was more than that. I felt like I had to prove myself to my father. To the man who basically threatened to disown me for going into plastics. I worked my ass off for a reason. And money wasn't it.

"One man's work, another man's play," Lucas said in a speculative tone. I knew he was joking, but it still grated my nerves that his impression of my job was standing over a woman while I motorboated her new breasts.

"Alright." I clapped my hands together and ignored the lingering anger at him, my father, the situation, myself. "Lay it on me, what did you tell her? Because as of right now, my mind is going into some really dark places. Scary places. Places where people with soy allergies go to die."

"Your mind's in China?"

"I'm too drugged for this." I squeezed my eyes shut, then opened them. "So?"

"Why did you break up with her?" His eyes narrowed, all traces of humor gone from his ugly mug. "The real reason. You know you can tell me, right?"

My mind went back there.

To that night.

To what happened that day.

To the opportunity Brooke had given me.

The out she gave me.

And the relief mixed with sadness I felt at Austin's horror-struck expression.

The absolute torture it was, to end things, when all I wanted to do was hold her in my arms and apologize and tell her the truth.

All of it.

But my dad's words haunted me.

And so I did the unthinkable.

"I was done with her. Besides, aren't you calling the kettle black? You literally had your hand in every honey pot imaginable, dated multiple women at the same time, got away with it because of that damn cleft in your chin, and made no apologies. So I kissed another girl while dating Austin. It's not like I slept with her!" By the time I was done talking, my chest was heaving, and Lucas was giving me an unreadable expression. And then his lips curled into a smile. "What? What's that look? I don't like that look." I got up and paced.

"Everything," he said in a smooth, confident voice. "Avery said I basically told her everything, but she did manage to write a few things down." He pulled a folded piece of paper from his pocket and dangled it in front of me. "I almost didn't give this to you . . ." His smile vanished. "But you just changed my mind."

"Thank God." I breathed out a sigh of relief and snatched the paper out of his hand, careful not to rip it as I unfolded it and straightened it against my desk, rolling out the heavy creases.

Lucas stood and looked over my shoulder. "It could be worse."

I clenched my jaw as my anxiety tripled. "It. Could. Be. Worse." I clenched the edge of my desk so hard, my knuckles turned white. "This list goes to thirty."

"Right." Lucas drew out the word slowly, then pointed. "But frogs are on there twice, so it's really only twenty-nine, you know?"

"I'm going to kill you."

"In your Benadryl-induced state?" He snorted. "Hardly. It would be like a turtle chasing a sprinter." He slapped me on the back. "Just in case you weren't aware, you're the turtle in this scenario."

"Thanks," I snapped.

"Turtle power." He threw his fist in the air. "Alright then, my work here is done. You can finish nap time while I keep myself far away from tequila lest I tell Avery you accidently kissed your grandma on the lips once—and still can't stand cherry ChapStick."

"Lucas!" I yelled. "Damn it, man, you aren't even drunk! You can't just run around saying shit like that! Austin hates me, like literally hates me so much, she slit my tires. To my car."

Lucas whistled. "Of course it was your car—it's not like you have a bike." He grinned and then laughed while I flipped him off. "Sorry, too soon?"

"You're dead to me."

"Drinks later?" He put on his sunglasses, completely ignoring my nervous breakdown, and opened the door. "Say, seven?" Right, because that was smart, drinks after Benadryl.

"Fine," I grumbled. "But you're paying."

"Okay."

He turned around.

"And this doesn't mean I'm not still pissed."

"It's Austin," he said plainly. "Do you really think she's capable of destroying your life?"

Too late, I wanted to say.

She destroyed my life the minute she walked into it.

Because I knew we were on borrowed time.

And the idea of that—left me without the ability to breathe.

"Yes. I do," I managed to croak out.

"She's a woman scorned—she'll get over it. Besides, I'm setting her up with one of my colleagues. It may help her get over you."

I saw red.

Blood red.

"The hell?" I roared, gaining attention from people in the hall.

Lucas shut the door behind him, blanketing me in a tense silence where the only sound was my heart as it slammed against my chest.

Another guy?

A part of me recognized that if she wasn't with me, she was going to end up with someone else—but I'd completely rejected the idea that she'd actually date so soon after our breakup.

A rebound?

Austin?

And why the hell did it bother me so much that I'd successfully pushed her into another fucker's waiting arms?

Oh, right.

Because I loved her.

Life was cruel.

And one thing was certain.

My hate for the situation matched that love I had for her—pushing me into a territory where the only option was the desperate one.

I was going to have to just let her go.

I glanced back at the list.

Well, that, and try to survive the hurricane that was Austin Rogers.

Yeah. I definitely needed to invest in a cup.

And a helmet.

Chapter Five

Austin

"So?" I twisted my hands in my lap while Lucas took a painfully long time to pull off his sunglasses, shrug out of his jacket, and lift his coffee to his lips.

By the time he took a sip, I felt like I was at the sloth DMV from *Zootopia.* My eye was starting to twitch, and I'd bitten my tongue twice to keep from yelling at him or launching myself across the table and demanding answers.

"Easy." Lucas shrugged. "He's a coldhearted bastard, who's going to most likely die alone—or with a prescription of Viagra in his bedside table and a girl thirty years his junior telling him to go harder." He leaned forward, his eyes twinkling with amusement. "I gave him the list."

I exhaled while Avery busted out laughing. "Oh, this is classic, you've even managed to turn his best friend against him. Well done, Austin."

Had I not been focusing on Lucas, I wouldn't have seen the horrified look on his face. Was he really on our side? Or Thatch's?

"Whoa, whoa, whoa." Lucas held out his hands. "It's not like I wanted to undermine him." He coughed. "Again. But he was being so—"

"Thatch," we said in unison. There wasn't really a way to explain the guy. He wasn't arrogant, not necessarily, but he was the type of guy that once he let you in, you realized you never really knew him in the first place. He had layers, and he only showed as much as he wanted. Basically the guy had pretty severe trust issues, thus our remark.

"Right." Lucas breathed out. "Plus he lied to me and then tried to blame me for his own cheating behavior."

The table fell silent.

Lucas cursed. "Fine, so I wasn't exactly the best influence."

"You had a calendar," Avery pointed out.

"For women," I added. "Multiple women."

"Scores of women." Avery nodded. "Who you dated at the same time."

"And slept with." We shared a look.

"Whoa!" Lucas scooted his chair back and held his hands up. "I just joined Team Austin! I'm on your side! And yes," he said, shifting uncomfortably in his chair and tugging at his black tie, "I wasn't a good influence, but I'm happily living on the other side of that leaf, whereas Thatch set up camp on the dark side, alright?"

"Man has a point." Avery sighed happily and kissed Lucas on the cheek. "Thanks for handing him the list—it will make things so much easier for Austin."

Lucas shook his head. "It's cruel what you're doing—you know that, right?"

"But, Lucas"—I batted my eyelashes—"I'm not doing anything—that's the best part."

He snorted. "Exactly, you're just making him paranoid as hell until he goes insane. Trust me, he's going to lose sleep at night and give someone a third tit. The poor guy is already stressed enough as it is. Do you even realize how many breast augmentations he does in a day?"

"Malpractice lawsuit." Avery nodded, completely ignoring Lucas. "We could work with that."

"We aren't getting him fired," Lucas said in a steely voice. "He needs his job. He loves his job, he likes cracking bone on people's noses and injecting them with God knows what, plus he's good at it. Just . . ." He stood and reached for Avery's hand. "Torture him for a few weeks so he feels a bit of pain, then drop it."

I gulped. He was right.

And hurting him wasn't going to make me hurt any less.

But revenge—it did feel good.

But so did kissing him.

That meant his mouth was a very dangerous and addicting thing.

Like his hair.

His body.

His taste.

Ugh.

"Austin," Lucas called. "I may have also mentioned to him that I'm setting you up on a blind date. That seemed to make our friend Thatch want to rip the wallpaper from the wall and scream in caveman-like fashion." He lifted one shoulder in a half-assed shrug. "Thought you might want to know."

"Don't," I whispered. "That just gives a girl like me hope that he'll pull his head out of his ass and see what he lost, and I'm pretty sure my only chance of that is if Santa gives Thatch a soul for Christmas, or at least a heart."

"Ouch." Lucas winced. "Alright, whatever you say. I have to get back to work, so try not to get arrested." He paused and then shared a look with Avery. "But if you do? Try to keep the cuffs, yeah?"

With a laugh, she gave him a quick kiss before walking him to the door.

I lay back in my chair and sulked.

We were at the same coffee shop where Avery had told me she'd been confused over Lucas. I had been blissed out over my relationship with Thatch at the time and told her how real it was, how honest, how wonderful.

Now she and Lucas were in love.

And I was in hate.

It sucked.

I checked my phone for any texts from Thatch. See! I needed to nip that right in the bud!

"Crap." I stood and grabbed my bag. I was going to be late for class. Again.

"Avery!" I elbowed her and Lucas on my way out. "I lost track of time. Gotta go, my social media class starts in ten."

"Call me?"

"Yup!" I ran toward my waiting Mercedes. As I drove, I cranked the music.

At least I had something to distract me from heartache.

A professor who hated my guts.

I hit the accelerator harder—I couldn't be late. Not again.

Come on, come on!

I prayed for time to slow and for my car to gain speed as I finally made it to campus.

Only to see the old parking lot under construction.

"Shit!"

Yeah. I was going to be late.

So late.

Chapter Six

Thatch

"Alright, I know this seems strange, and I'm sorry my hands are cold." I winked, cupping her left breast in my right hand before cupping the other with my left. "But I need to mark you up a bit."

I loved my job. Loved my patients—for the most part.

But there were always those consults that you knew were going to go badly before you even stepped into the room.

This was one of them.

Or should I say she?

Most of the eighteen-year-olds I worked on were spoiled brats who either flirted way too much with the man who was about to touch their breasts, or argued with whatever professional opinion I might have about them.

It had already been a long day.

And judging by the bubble gum that had just popped in my face a few minutes before when I introduced myself—it was about to get a hell of a lot longer.

The teen jutted her chest out like she was God's gift.

She wasn't.

After all, wasn't that why she came to me? She wanted more?

There were three types of patients when it came to breast augmentations. First, you had the ones who had always had flat chests and wanted to feel feminine—they were my favorite. I loved the confidence a simple alteration could give them. Oftentimes they cried at the first consultation, and I did my damnedest to make sure they were happy with their body when I was done—just like I did my damnedest to make sure they realized they were already perfect before I even started.

Second, there were the patients who sought out perfection, even though nothing on their body was ever good enough and nothing would ever be good enough. But those weren't even as bad as the third category.

The ones who thought that a simple alteration would change their lives, the ones who thought beauty really was all about what was on the outside, not the inside.

Another pop of bubble gum in my face. Exhibit A.

These types always wanted their breasts bigger, bouncier, fluffier—yes, a girl had asked for "fluffy tits" once, and since I wanted to stay one of the best plastic surgeons in Seattle, I showed her the door.

The hell? Fluffy?

I was still groggy from all the Benadryl, but I needed to do this last consult before I met up with Lucas. Even I knew that drinking heavily with antihistamines was a bad call—but I hoped that if I ate enough food, the alcohol and the drugs would even out.

Besides.

Austin.

That was reason enough to risk it, right?

Shaking my head, I barked out measurements to my nurse and drew a line across the bottom of the breast. "Right is off by half a centimeter."

The patient looked down. "I think it looks fine."

"Do you now," I said in a bored voice. God save me from eighteen-year-old girls who ask for breast augmentations instead of cars and the parents who are rich enough to gift the surgery. What the hell had society come to?

"Can you make them bounce more?"

If I had a penny . . .

"Sure," I huffed out, irritated that I was irritated. Normally I loved my job, but normally I wasn't nursing a Benadryl hangover, or the sad obsession with licking my lips in hopes her taste would still be there.

Damn it.

It was all her fault.

Everything.

The drinking.

The late nights staring at the pillow she used to sleep on.

While drinking.

The drunken and then deleted texts I didn't have the balls to send.

Technically, it wasn't her fault; logic told me this, just like logic also pointed across the hall of my apartment building. Logic also said I got myself into this situation—even though it wasn't a fault of my own making.

Hell, someone really needed to take away my phone or at least invent an app that kept drunk, stupid ex-boyfriends from making complete jackasses out of themselves every single time they drank whiskey.

"Almost done." I cleared my throat and called out a few more measurements, then pulled the white paper garment back across the girl's pert breasts. "You're a perfect candidate for breast augmentation." Hell, I could say it in my sleep. In fact, I'd been notorious for grabbing Austin's breasts in my sleep and shouting out numbers like she was my nurse.

Yeah, I was screwed in the head.

Austin.

Damn it.

It always came back to her.

Then again, that's how life worked. Choices always came back to bite you in the ass. My first poor choice was taking her home that night.

My second?

Cheating on her.

On purpose.

"Doctor?" my nurse prompted.

"Sorry." I forced a smile. "As I was saying, you're a perfect candidate. Now, why don't you change back into your clothes, and I'll have Dawn talk to you about surgery and financing."

I was bored.

I was angry.

I was hurt.

And I only had myself to blame.

Because it's bullshit when people say they cheat by accident. You don't accidently fall on someone else's face. You don't accidently drop your clothes to the floor.

I knew exactly what I was doing.

I could still taste the air of the bedroom.

Smell the girl's shampoo before I touched her lips.

And I still felt the searing pain once the kiss finished—because I had totally ruined the best thing that ever happened to me.

Not all cheaters are created equal.

I did exactly what I swore I would never do—after seeing my parents suffer—but I did it for the right reasons.

So yeah, some cheaters suck.

But some . . . Sometimes, it's okay to cheat.

I would do it again.

If it meant saving her.

I would do it every damn day.

"Dr. Holloway?" Mia knocked on the door.

I stood and excused myself.

Typically, the appointments lasted a lot longer, but whenever I had teen patients, they didn't want to discuss sizes or use medical terminology.

They wanted bigger.

They always wanted a high-profile implant.

And they wanted to know if they would still feel sensations in their nipples. Beyond that, they didn't ask questions, because most of them didn't think of it as surgery.

So I walked out the door.

A headache blaring between my temples, I quickly grabbed my shit so I could meet Lucas.

◆ ◆ ◆

"You're late." Lucas took a long sip of his beer and peered at me over the glass. "Thirty-one minutes and ten seconds late, but really, who's counting? I thought I was going to get stood up."

"Sorry," I rasped, waving down the waitress. "Traffic was hell and I was—" Embarrassment washed over me. What? Checking the backseat just in case someone was hiding in my car? Irrational fear number two. Or making sure that nothing fell from my visor? Irrational fear number three. Or—and this is the best part—double-checking because I still didn't trust that I really didn't see anything lingering on the leather of my backseat.

I was going to kill Austin.

The list Avery wrote was long.

Extensive.

I'd studied it for a good hour and come to the conclusion that I was doomed to live in a constant state of paranoia until she was satisfied.

So basically, I was just waiting for Jack to pop out of his box.

For the rest of my miserable life.

While having to perform surgery a few times a week.

"I was"—I cleared my throat—"just checking a few things out with the car."

"Oh, is it having trouble again?" Lucas asked in a curious voice.

"You could say that," I said quickly, then changed the subject. "So, how's Avery?"

"She's amazing!" a feminine voice said from behind me. "And she's also bombing guys' night. Sorry, Lucas thought you were going to be a no-show."

"It's fine," I said with a tight smile because, lo and behold, who was with Avery but her other half?

Her best friend.

Her very sexy best friend.

In half a dress.

I quickly looked away. "Austin."

"Hitler," she said sweetly. "Tell me, how is the KKK these days?"

"Too far." Avery coughed into her hand and made a "cut it out" motion. "So, what's everyone drinking?"

I made a mental note to keep my hand over my drink just in case Austin had arsenic and decided to see how fast it could kill a man when mixed with rum and Coke.

"Beer." Lucas lifted his glass.

Avery scrunched up her nose. "I hate beer. I think I'll just order some wine." She pressed her lips together and looked at the drink menu anyway while Austin glared at me from the corner of her eye and slowly reached for my drink.

I pretended not to notice, then jerked it away from her and downed the entire thing in one giant gulp. The minute I was done, she grinned like she'd just won.

And I realized, just sitting near her was causing paranoia. I didn't want her to have my drink or put anything in it, so I decided to what? Get drunk off my ass?

"I see what you did there," I whispered. "Clever."

"Just wait." She bit down on her bottom lip in a way that drove me insane—and she knew it. My blood heated as my hands balled into fists. The waitress came and went, and I was thankful I wasn't sporting spandex shorts anymore.

Because it would be impossible to hide how much Austin affected me—how much she always would.

Suddenly she glanced at her phone and then at the door; her smile grew and I didn't like it. It gave me that funny feeling in my gut again—like all hell was about to break loose, and I was going to be the unlucky target of whatever scheme she'd thought up in that gorgeous head of hers.

"Dad!" she shouted.

"Oh, freaking hell." I closed my eyes briefly before opening them and standing.

Her dad was a pompous ass.

A protective, pompous ass.

So the fact that I had broken his baby girl's heart? Well . . . let's just say I was suddenly really thankful he was a Democrat and voted for gun control.

"Bradley." I held out my hand.

He stared at it, then slowly gripped my hand viciously hard, pumping it a bit too hard for my liking before releasing it. "So, I hear you're going to race with us?"

"Us?" I repeated.

"Daddy!" Austin giggled. "I told you it was a surprise, but oh well, I guess the cat's out of the bag!"

I forced a smile.

"Team Rogers!" Bradley nodded and slapped me hard on the shoulder. "Why, we've taken first place every year."

Well. Shit.

"First, you say?" I struggled to find my breath. I couldn't even ride a bike let alone beat someone else on it! Maybe they'd still count me if I carried a ten-speed over the finish line? No? "That's really impressive."

"We don't lose." His eyes narrowed as he jabbed a finger against my collarbone. "But one of the guys is out, and when Austin mentioned how much you enjoyed cycling, I figured what the hell, you know? Bury the hatchet and all."

There was a hatchet?

Just how big was this hatchet?

"That's very big of you, Daddy." Austin stood up on her toes and kissed him on the cheek. "You here meeting someone?"

His eyes darted between the two of us. "A work friend." His easy smile was back. "Thatch, we ride this Friday at six a.m.! We'll meet at Gas Works Park."

He shook my hand again and walked off.

Six. Freaking. A.m.

Austin turned to me with a triumphant grin. "Do you want me to tell him? Or should you?"

Thankfully, the waitress had returned with another drink. I downed half of it and sat in the hard wooden chair while Lucas and Avery both stared at me with laughter written all over their amused faces.

"Laugh all you want." I shook my head and grabbed my glass again. "But I don't back down from a challenge!" Why the hell was I shouting?

"Dude." Lucas cleared his throat and wiped a tear from under his eye. "Last time you tried—"

"Not now!" I roared. "Damn it, man, do you keep any secrets?"

"No," Avery piped up.

"Do any of you have any idea how traumatizing it is to just get back on the bike after—"

"Stop overreacting." Lucas waved his hand in front of my face. "That ice cream truck missed you by a mile at least."

All heads turned toward him.

"Thanks, man. Thanks a lot," I grumbled, sipping the rest of my drink, well on my way to committing to a constant state of drunkenness.

Damn Austin.

"Ice cream truck?" Avery just had to point out as she whipped her head in my direction, humor gleaming in her green eyes. "How old were you?"

"Lucas, I swear to all that is holy, if you open your mouth, I will punch you in the face."

"I guess that explains number twenty, 'Hates ice cream.'" Austin sighed and twirled her two straws around in her drink. "I'm pretty sure hating ice cream is right up there with hating children."

"Which really explains so much, don't you think?" I countered in a condescending tone as I eyed her up and down. It was a low blow. It was mean. It was also necessary to get her the hell off my back.

God, I didn't want this.

Though a part of me knew I deserved it.

I should have never, ever, ever, allowed her in.

Because as much as I'd like to think I'd pushed her off the relationship cliff, she was pretty damn good at clawing her way back to the top just so she could be the one to shove me off it.

"Once an asshole, always an asshole," she sang, and then glanced at her phone. "Well, kids, it's been fun, but I have a professor who hates me and a final project I haven't even started." She stood and gave me a pitiful glance. "Which is too bad, since I'd love to teach you how to ride sometime."

I felt that look all the way down to my toes.

But mainly I felt that look where I sure as hell shouldn't have.

Between my legs.

It took every ounce of strength I had to level her with a glare and say, "I guess turnabout's fair play, since I taught you to ride first."

Lucas spit out his drink while Avery groaned into her hands.

Austin tilted her head. "Did you, though?"

"Okay!" Avery waved her hands between us. "So, this social media class and hateful professor? What's that all about?"

Austin seemed to deflate as she grabbed her keys out of her purse and snarled in Avery's direction. "My professor's just looking for a way to fail me—apparently, he hates any girl student who doesn't have giant boobs. He passes the girls with the big boobs and the guys who salivate over his ability to get his own students into bed. Disgusting, really."

I frowned at Austin's chest. She had a great rack, a gorgeous rack, I would know, I'd seen it. What the hell kind of professor wouldn't pass her?

"I'm late enough to gain his unwanted attention and probably the only student who doesn't fall all over herself for him. Anyways"—she grabbed her leather jacket and shrugged into it, pulling her pretty, dark brown hair with golden highlights over the soft black material—"for my final project, I have to start either a blog or a YouTube channel and gain a following of more than a hundred people to pass the class, which may sound easy, but I've been procrastinating, and it's due in three weeks." Her shoulders slumped forward. "I still don't have any ideas."

I snorted. "Shocking, since when it comes to payback, you're the Queen Bitch." Okay, yeah, I was more than buzzed. It slipped out. All of it. The nasty words and the hurtful way my voice echoed them, like she was really getting to me.

Maybe because she was.

"That's it!" Avery shouted, slamming her hand down on the table and scaring the shit out of Lucas enough for him to choke on a peanut and almost need the Heimlich.

"What?" Austin frowned. "What's it?"

"Thatch!" Avery shouted gleefully.

And I was waving down the waitress for a third time.

I was going to kick Lucas's ass if I ended up in AA.

"What about Thatch?" Lucas looked as confused as I felt.

"Austin." I hated the way Avery's eyes lit up like she'd just found a way to solve world hunger—and I was the answer. "Start a blog about hating your ex!"

My mouth dropped open. "I'm sorry, start a what blog?"

Avery was rubbing her hands together as Austin's smile grew wider and wider.

"So, document how to hate an ex?" Austin asked. "I think I've got that down."

I shifted uncomfortably in my seat.

Hate was a strong word, too strong. Did she really hate me? And wasn't that the plan all along? Use her hate, use her anger?

"Yes!" Avery held up her hand for a high five. "You can do weekly blog posts on how to break up with your cheating boyfriend, share your story." Avery glanced over at me. "Sorry, Thatch." And then she looked back at Austin. "It's perfect!"

"But what would I call it?"

"Cheated." This from Lucas.

"Thanks, man." I saluted him with my middle finger. "Oh also, you're dead to me."

"Ah, you said that a few hours ago, and look, still friends."

He lifted his beer in acknowledgment of our ended friendship and smirked.

"Don't be so dramatic." Austin narrowed her eyes at me. "It's not like I'm going to air all your dirty, skanky laundry. This will totally be from the scorned person's point of view! I can add in articles from different women's magazines and *BuzzFeed*, and post quizzes!"

"Yes!" Avery giggled. "Quizzes like 'Is Your Man Faithful?' 'Does He Have a Small Wiener?'"

All eyes fell to me.

"I'm a plastic surgeon," I said evenly. "If it started small, it sure as hell isn't that way now." I grinned tightly at Austin. "Right, sweetheart?"

She blinked slowly and then narrowed her gaze at my crotch. "You know? I can't really remember."

I smirked and leaned in close. "The hell you can't."

"Okay." Lucas stood and put a hand on my chest. "Maybe I should cut you off."

"Thanks for the idea, Avery!" Austin waved at us. "I'll think about it." She hugged Lucas and then gave me a chilly glare before turning on her heel and walking away.

Lucas whistled. "You couldn't just listen to your best friend when he first told you to leave her the hell alone. No, you had to go and show her your bedroom and then your cock. I warned you, man."

I didn't respond as my eyes followed Austin's body until the door to the bar slammed behind her.

I had nothing in my defense.

Because men like me, men like my father, we didn't understand commitment—something he reminded me of on a daily basis.

The minute he moved back to Seattle.

And into the same building as me.

Chapter Seven

Austin

It was going to be a late night.

Like really late.

Not only did I have an assignment to finish, but there was no chance in hell I could actually sleep after that run-in with Thatch. Why? Why did he have to be so cruel? And why was I like a dog with a bone? I wanted to let it go.

I wanted to let him go.

I wanted to be free from whatever emotional bondage he still used on me.

But every time I saw his face, I was torn between wanting to knock out his perfect teeth and wanting to kiss him with reckless abandon.

Maybe it was because no one had ever broken up with me before? Probably because I'd never had a serious relationship—until Thatch had given me a key.

A freaking key to his apartment!

"He doesn't want you, Austin," I mumbled to myself. I mean he made that clear the minute I walked in on him with his tongue down another girl's throat.

Taking a deep breath, I tossed my keys onto the kitchen table and pulled out a wineglass, filling it to the rim before opening my laptop and waiting for it to power up.

My mom wasn't home. Then again, she was rarely home at night—she was always out with her girlfriends doing wine dates and dinner parties. It was her thing—actually it was more my dad's thing, since all of the women she hung out with were capable voters.

And my dad was going to be out late—he had made that much clear earlier.

I shivered. The only light illuminating our massive house was from the computer and the TV in the family room.

Moments like these reminded me just how lonely I really was. Yes, my house was huge, yes, we had a ton of money.

But I'd have traded all of it for a chance to have a conversation longer than five minutes with either of my parents and not revolving around politics or my MBA.

They checked in once a day to make sure I was alive and breathing, and that was about it—unless I got a bad grade, which was probably why I was so stressed about my current class.

So when Thatch broke my heart and ran it over with his stupid car, I was left to sob alone in my room until Avery rescued me.

Loneliness sucked.

I gulped back the wine, clicked on a free website builder, and started to slowly pick out themes.

A minimum of one hundred followers.

I had to make my content interesting.

I drank more wine.

And three hours later, when I was well on my way to finishing the bottle, a smile spread across my face as my hands hovered over the keyboard.

"Eat shit, Thatch," I slurred, and began to type.

◆ ◆ ◆

My head felt like someone had run it over with a semitruck and then decided to beat me with my cell phone. "Ugh." My mouth tasted like bad decisions.

And a sense of panic had started to swell in the center of my chest.

The details of the night before were a bit fuzzy.

I slowly lifted my head from its spot facedown on the kitchen table right next to my computer, and blinked up at the black screen.

What happened last night?

I remembered Thatch in all his Thatchness.

The bar.

And my assignment—yeah, that's why I'd left early.

The panic in my chest grew until a jarring paranoia had me clicking the return key on my computer as if my life depended on it.

Two empty wine bottles stared me down.

Oh no.

Oh no, no, no.

My computer woke up a few seconds later to the website I'd started to build, but I couldn't remember the password.

I tried every single one I could think of.

And then ran into the bathroom to puke my guts out.

This, this was what it felt like when you finally hit rock bottom.

I washed my hands, then braced myself against the sink, slowly gaining enough courage to glance into the mirror and see the damage.

I let out a gasp and covered my mouth.

My forehead said "erohw."

And the letters were in marker.

What the hell?

Erohw?

Oh hell. My forehead spelled "whore" backward.

I scrubbed with my hands, only to probably push the ink farther into my skin.

With sloppy movements, I grabbed a washcloth and ran it vigorously over my forehead, only succeeding in making my skin angry and pink.

"Think!" I took deep breaths and closed my eyes. How had I written that on my forehead anyway? Furthermore. WHY?

Wine.

More wine.

Giggling.

"He's a whore." Yup, pretty sure I yelled that at my computer and then registered the account to my email and . . . I let out a little groan and slowly made my way over to my computer and typed in "erohw."

Bingo.

My password.

I'd written my password on my forehead. Well done, Austin. Well freaking done.

Well, at least I hadn't done anything worse, right? I mean, it could be worse—it could always be worse. Look at the bright side! I got my assignment done and—

"Holy shit," I gasped for the second time that morning, and hoped that I was hallucinating.

But every time I hit "Refresh" . . .

There it was.

In all its glory.

The Cheated website.

With the title of the first post: "A Single Girl's Guide to Getting Even."

It would have been fine.

Except for right underneath it, I'd uploaded a picture of Thatch, on which I'd drawn a mustache along with a pitchfork and red eyes—compliments of Photoshop.

And beneath that?

A video.

I was seriously afraid to press "Play."

What the hell had I been thinking?

I covered part of my face with one hand while clicking on the "Play" button with the other. Gulping, I turned the sound up.

"Are you filming me right now?" Thatch slurred drunkenly into the camera.

"No."

"Liar." His smile was easy, gorgeous, albeit extremely drunk. "Give me the phone, Austin."

"Nope."

"Austin!" He started chasing me around the bedroom, stumbling all over the furniture as if straight lines were foreign to him. It was his birthday, and I'd gotten him well and drunk so I could have my way with him, or at least that's what I'd said—because the truth of his birthday made me sad. According to him, his birthday had always been full of loads of gifts and empty promises. He wanted for nothing, but something told me that all he really wanted was attention. I knew that feeling well, so I figured it was better to help him forget.

His knee collided with the bed, and he went sailing to the ground and stayed on his knees. "Um, Thatch?"

"Baby." His eyes were so unfocused, it was comical. "There's something I gotta say." He swallowed, then pressed his hands to his chest and started to sing Enrique Iglesias's "Hero," completely and totally off-key, not to mention wrong. "I kiss tears of pain." Yeah, those so weren't even the words. He paused way longer than necessary. "Pain!" he said again, his large body swaying from left to right. The last part was more shouting than singing. "You always take breaths away." I waited as he leaned forward and then collapsed on the ground and whispered, "Away." Then he yawned and fell asleep.

Oh hell. He was going to kill me.

Why? Why did I get drunk?

See! Drunkenness leads to bad choices. His drunkenness made him sing Enrique Iglesias, and my drunkenness forced me to share it!

Maybe nobody had seen it yet?

Maybe I'd get lucky and could delete it before it got out of hand, or—my face fell—maybe, like a loser, I'd linked the web page to my Facebook, Twitter, and Instagram.

And already I had over two hundred comments on the post.

My phone buzzed.

I stared at the screen as Avery's name lit up.

The phone stopped buzzing.

Then started all over again.

She would keep calling until I answered.

Finally, I swiped and held it to my ear. "Yeah?"

Laughter, and then a snort, met my hello. "Thatch is going to kill you!"

"Tell me something I don't know," I said through clenched teeth, then frowned. "Hey! I promised him revenge, and he still refused to tell me why, so he can just—suck it!"

"That's the spirit." She giggled. "But a word of warning, Thatch isn't the type to take things of this magnitude lying down."

My stomach clenched. "Meaning?"

"Meaning, according to Lucas, he's an equal-opportunity revenge taker. In fact, Lucas said the last person he would ever want to start a war with would be Thatch."

"But, but—" I did a little circle in place and tried to calm my racing heart. "Lucas helped us! He helped me, the whole list thing and—"

"Right, the list was Lucas's idea, remember? His way of helping you get even without you actually engaging in a battle that you'd most likely lose! He was trying to help you NOT get in this situation!"

"You're telling me this now!" I shrieked.

A knock sounded at my door.

Eyes wide, I waited as my heart slammed against my chest.

Thump, thump, thump-freaking-thump.

He'd only been to my house once.

I was being paranoid.

"Austin?" Avery yelled. "Hello!"

"I, uh, someone's here," I whispered.

"You live with your parents. Of course someone's there." I could just see her rolling her eyes.

"But—"

"Look, all I'm saying is you've basically just dropped a red flag in front of a horny cheating bull—keep your guard up and your A game strong."

"Thanks," I said through clenched teeth. "Great advice, anything else?"

"Hiding out until this blows over wouldn't hurt either."

I huffed out a breath and grumbled my good-bye, then very slowly went over to the main entrance and peeked between the blinds.

There was something in front of the door, but I couldn't make it out. It looked like part of a yellow flower, but I couldn't tell if it was part of the potted arrangements by the door or something else.

I opened the door a crack and then wider.

A huge bouquet was sitting on my doorstep.

I rolled my eyes—I was ridiculous to even think he might have sent me flowers. My dad always bought my mom flowers, once a week. It was kind of their thing.

Head still pounding, I bent down to pick up the vase and screamed bloody murder when I turned the glass around and saw a giant tarantula inside, just waiting for me to pull out the flowers so it could pounce.

I almost dropped the vase.

Almost.

Shit!

I looked around. What the heck was I supposed to do? If I put it down, the tarantula could escape—if I put it in my house, the creature would most likely find its way into my bedroom and eat my face while I slept.

With shaking hands, I set the vase back down on the ground and went in search of a bucket I could put over it—surely, the pet store could use another giant flesh-eating spider, right?

It took me longer than it should have to find an old bucket in the garage that wasn't infested with dirt and more spiders—the last thing we needed was some sort of *Arachnophobia* situation where the spiders mated and created a superspider.

I shivered.

I hated spiders.

Thatch wouldn't go that far.

Would he?

There was a note tucked between the pretty roses, but the last thing I was going to do was pull it out and aggravate the hairy thing.

It was officially the morning from hell. I was sweating, most likely going to be late for class—again—and had had a run-in with one of my biggest fears.

The front door was open when I made it back to the front of the house. Frowning, I stepped over the threshold. Where had it gone?

"Hi, honey!" Mom held the temporary glass vase in her hands, her boobs so big and pressed up against the spider side. "How was your night?"

"Mom, no!" Bucket raised high in the air, I ran toward her, ready to slam it down on her hands if need be. But clearly, she was used to my dramatics, since she frowned and reached for the card, tugging one of the roses up.

"Thatch?" She turned the card around, and that's when the aggressive little monster crawled right out of its prison and landed on my mom's hand.

What happened next was like something out of a war movie.

She screamed, glass went everywhere, and I swore the spider made some sort of high-pitched noise while I charged at it with my blue bucket. I captured the furry beast just in time before it scurried into the living room.

But the spider had been drugged.

That was the only explanation for why the bucket moved across the wood floor like the spider was pumped full of 'roids and well on its way to eating through the plastic.

"I think . . ." I was breathing too heavily, and my mom was standing on the countertop. "That we need to call animal control."

"That"—she pointed down at the bucket—"is possessed!"

The bucket made a scraping noise against the floor. I jumped onto the couch and yelled.

And that, folks, is when I realized we had an audience in the form of a slow clap from the open door, and a cell phone held high in the air, the camera lens pointed at me.

"You!" I glared at Thatch, unable to move from my safety zone on the couch.

"What?" He tilted his head. "I was in the neighborhood." His cocky grin was menacing, aggravating.

"I'm going to murder you!" I yelled. "You KNOW how I feel about spiders!"

"Spiders?" He stared down at the bucket. "I'm not responsible for the shipments of flowers, I hope you realize that. I was just trying to send you flowers to apologize for last night—oh and . . ." He checked his watch and made a face. "You should probably go—don't want to be late for class."

He held up his phone, snapped a picture, and walked off; two seconds later, he retraced his steps and called over his shoulder, "I hope you know . . . this is war."

I fumed and screamed after him, "I thought you wanted to be my hero!"

He turned fully around and braced his hands in the door frame. His look said it all. He was pissed, not just a little, but a whole lot. "Consider this my warning. Post any more shit, and I'm going to make my way down my own little list. Bike shorts are one thing, but this? A viral video. War."

"You wouldn't dare!" I said, calling his bluff.

He nodded toward the bucket. "Funny, because I think I just did. Have a good day!" He winked at my mother. "Mrs. Rogers, sorry for the mess."

Chapter Eight

Thatch

"I'll be your hero." The first sentence that was texted to me by an unlisted number.

The hell?

The morning just kept getting weirder.

When I went to grab my coffee at my usual Starbucks, the barista stared up at me with wide blue eyes and said, "Enrique Iglesias is boss."

"Okay." I drew out the word slowly. "Thanks for the coffee, good talk."

As if that weren't weird enough, my Facebook feed was full of hero memes, one of them a picture of me wearing a cape.

"What the hell?" I scrolled through my phone.

And then a video started playing on my newsfeed.

From Austin's page.

I'd been meaning to unfriend her—it was too hard seeing pictures of her all the time.

Instead, like a masochist, I'd remained friends so I could stalk her and get angry all over again at my decision to push her away.

My drunken voice sang out not only the wrong key to the "Hero" song but also the wrong words.

"Holy shit," I whispered as I stared at my drunken self belting out a song in a pitch that probably only dogs could hear and understand.

It was already going viral.

With more than five hundred shares and two thousand comments.

The video had been shared from her new website.

And when I clicked on the website, lo and behold, there I was, in all my satanic-looking glory.

I was going to murder her.

MURDER.

This was my life she was messing with! I had a career—a reputation!

Damn it.

That's why they always warn you about scorned women.

I quickly sent out a text to Lucas to meet me at my office and then tilted my head as a sign in the pet store window proclaimed "Tarantulas."

A smile curved my lips.

Oh, she wanted to play?

I'd play alright.

◆ ◆ ◆

Her forehead had the word "whore" written on it backward. She'd been using a mirror. Enough said.

I took a picture because it had been so hilarious.

And then I posted it to my Facebook page but made it private, selecting her profile along with Lucas's and Avery's. At least she'd know I had my own version of blackmail hanging over her head. Above the picture, I typed, "Who cheated who?"

After all, she might blame me for our relationship being destroyed, but a part of me still blamed her.

Blamed her for asking too much too soon.

Blamed her for making me feel like it was what I needed to do in order to stay with her.

◆ ◆ ◆

"Austin." I breathed her name as she rocked her naked body against mine. I could never get enough of her. She wasn't the type of girl you slept with once and conveniently lost the number for the next day.

It had taken me one full week with her to realize that I didn't want something easy; I wanted her.

Lucas was going to lose his shit the minute I told him that rather than break up with her, I was going to ask her to be my girlfriend.

I grinned to myself like a complete loser.

"Harder." Her fingernails dug into my skin, and pain, mixed with the pleasure of being inside her, sliced through my body. "Thatch—"

I silenced her plea with a kiss.

Our fling was supposed to be quick.

Fun.

But nothing about her deserved to be rushed—her skin smelled like fresh rose water and tasted sweet, like she bathed in sugar. I was addicted to the way she tasted.

"You always feel so good." She hooked her arms around my neck. "How is that possible?"

"I'm a surgeon." I winked. "I'm good with my hands."

"Yeah, you are," she agreed, her eyes locking on mine. "I like you."

"I like you too." I swallowed my stupid nerves. I'd never done this. Never committed to anyone—my parents' failed marriage was one of the main reasons I never had more than a one-night stand and was thriving in a lucrative career where I had enough money to buy my own damn happiness. It was no use investing that happiness in another person—they'd just let you down.

"Be my girlfriend?" I asked in a quiet whisper.

Her eyes widened and then she was kissing me, pushing me onto my back and rubbing her hands up and down my chest.

I let out a moan. "Is that a yes?"

"It's a hell yes."

◆ ◆ ◆

I shook my head at the memory and made my way toward my office, ignoring the funny looks and whispered hero references all the way to my desk.

At least I wasn't paranoid about what she was going to do to me anymore—she'd already embarrassed the hell out of me. There was no way she could do worse.

No chance in hell.

Chapter Nine

Austin

"What do you mean it doesn't count?" I fought to keep my voice even as my evil professor looked at my website. "It went viral!"

"You posted an embarrassing video of an ex-boyfriend singing off tune." He rolled his eyes and closed his computer. I swear he had some sort of God complex, since he was in his forties and had women falling at his feet, mainly hot undergrads. "Of course it went viral, but that's not what this class is all about. What you posted is fine, but it's a flash in the pan. It took absolutely no effort."

Hah! I nearly died from a spider attack because of that video, but whatever. I bit my tongue and waited for him to fail me.

One of my classmates walked up to the desk and gave him a flirty wave. Her top was so tight, I could see nipple.

He grinned and waved back.

Bastard!

"What you need," he said, returning his attention to me like I was an epic disappointment, "is something that is actually interesting. Maybe you can document something important to you? Your father's campaign for reelection?"

Thanks, but I'd rather barbecue the trapped tarantula and eat it.

When I didn't say anything, he kept talking.

"This man broke up with you?" His eyebrow arched. "That happens every day, and as fun as it is to watch someone else's misery, people don't root for that sort of thing, they forget about it. Besides, it lacks importance in society."

Another girl walked by, another perfect girl winking at the dear old professor. I was half-tempted to snap my fingers in front of his face to gain his attention.

"Okay . . . ," I said slowly, trying not to cry. "So, you want me to stop posting embarrassing videos and do what? Makeup tutorials? That's the only other thing I'm noticing that goes viral fast and would get me followers. I'm not trying to be difficult here, I just don't know what you want from me."

His intense stare wasn't helping my nausea, and the last thing I needed to do was puke all over the man who held my MBA in the palm of his hateful hand.

"It's easy to lose a guy, it's easy to get even—do the hard thing and you'll figure it out. You're an MBA student. Use your brain." He shrugged. "You can go."

"But—"

"Three weeks, Austin. You have three weeks to figure out your niche in social media. All you need is one hundred followers invested in your story. Make them love you. You just have to decide what you want it to be. This"—he tapped his computer again—"isn't it."

I barely made it out of his office without crying angry tears. A part of me knew it was my fault. I'd gotten drunk and posted a stupid video, partially out of hurt, partially out of anger. The tears had more to do with Thatch than my class.

I found an empty bench and sat, miserable.

Hungover.

In a war with a man who was going to put spiders in my bed.

And all for nothing.

I'd worked my ass off for eighteen months to do the MBA fast-track program with UW, and now a stupid elective class was standing in my way of getting that degree! An elective class that most people didn't even have to take unless they were getting their MBA in marketing.

My story. He'd said I needed to make them love me. Love the story. The story, the story.

A couple holding hands walked by me. The girl looked like she'd been crying, and then the guy stopped walking and hugged her. When he pulled back, his eyes briefly fell to her mouth before he kissed her.

I tilted my head.

Their mouths met.

Jealousy slammed into me.

I had to look away.

Stupid heart.

Stupid invested heart.

Stupid boob-obsessed professor!

I jerked to my feet.

That was it.

He was right, anyone could post a video.

Anyone could exact revenge.

But a documentary on his favorite subject by way of Seattle's youngest and best-looking plastic surgeon?

I grinned.

And then stopped smiling when I realized what type of sacrifice this would require on my part.

It would be hell.

Epic.

Hell.

And I was going to have to beg on my hands and knees—oddly enough, one of Thatch's favorite positions—so maybe, just maybe, it would work.

Either that or he was going to laugh in my face and send me to one of his creepy partners who I had seen leering at me last time I was in the conference room.

I shuddered.

This was business.

Not personal.

I needed that grade—and if there was one thing I knew about Thatch, he'd buried his heart a long time ago. He'd be fine. After this, we'd go our separate ways.

It might even give me the closure I so desperately needed.

Chapter Ten

Thatch

"I have a proposition for you." Austin's raspy voice always did mess with my head. I quickly turned around.

She was dressed in a short black skirt with a black-and-white striped T-shirt that showed an inch of pale skin at her waist. Her black gladiator sandals wrapped all the way up her calves. Basically, she was trying to kill me by way of high-heeled sandals and a hell of a lot of thigh.

"Austin." Damn it, could my voice be any hoarser? "I'd say this was a pleasure, but I wouldn't want to give you the wrong idea."

She flinched before moving swiftly into my office, closing the door behind her, and grabbing a chair.

"Yes, please come in. It's not like I have a job where I have appointments," I grumbled, at my wit's end with whatever the hell kind of drama she was about to unleash on me.

"I'm going to fail my class," she blurted, eyes wide with worry. "And I can't fail, not after everything I've gone through to get to where I'm at. I'm living at home still, and I just—" She took a deep breath. "Failure isn't an option. Ever."

Which was probably why our failed relationship drove her insane, not that I was going to say that out loud.

"Why is this my problem? Didn't that little video of me go viral?"

Her lips twitched.

"It's not funny," I snapped.

"Admit it, it's sort of funny." She tilted her head in that adorable way that would make a weaker and lesser man fall to his knees and beg for forgiveness.

I clenched my hands into fists.

Yeah, not gonna happen.

"Tell you what, I'll admit it's funny when we can laugh about the spider chasing you onto a couch."

She jabbed a finger in my direction. "It had superpowers, and you know it!" In a flurry, both hands went into the air. "That bucket was at least five pounds! And he moved it with his head!"

"The bucket was five ounces at most, and I hardly think spiders move things with their heads." I rolled my eyes. "You were saying?"

She wrung her hands together and then hung her head, all traces of fear and humor gone. "My professor says the video's not good enough, that it has no staying power. The whole point of this class is to use social media for marketing and branding, and all I did was drunkenly post a video of you singing off-key."

"Wait, go back, you were drunk?" I hadn't ever really seen her out of control, which made me wonder what caused her to go to that place to begin with. Was it me? Was it the class? Maybe a mixture of both? And why did the idea that she was thinking about me and losing control turn me on so much?

"Not the point," she said through clenched teeth. "Let's focus on the dilemma—my dilemma."

A knock sounded at my door.

"Yes?"

Our office assistant, Mia, poked her head in. "Sorry, your eleven o'clock is here."

"Five minutes."

She nodded and closed the door.

"Get there faster, Austin."

Austin bit down on her plump lip. I'd been obsessed with her mouth from day one. It was far from perfect, which was probably why I liked it. My job was to fix the imperfections—and it almost always seemed like a travesty to fix something that made people so unique in the first place.

No amount of money or begging on her part would get me to perform any type of surgery on her.

Ever.

"I sort of came up with this new idea. You see, my professor—the one who hates me?—literally can't take his eyes off girls with big boobs, and I thought, 'Hey, why not do a project on his favorite subject?' I can document the process of getting a breast enhancement, pepper it with other surgeries you perform, and at the end of three weeks, when the project is due, I will livestream, with your permission and a patient's, a surgery. Not only would the blog be interesting because of the subject matter, but also because you and your office were just recognized by the city of Seattle. It would be great publicity all around, for you and myself. I'd also be helping brand you, which would most likely get my professor off my back. I know you'll need to clear it with legal, but . . ." She finally took a breath. "What do you think?"

"I don't know what to think." I sighed and leaned against my desk. "Other than, how desperate do you have to be to ask me for a favor?"

"So. Very. Desperate." Tears filled her eyes. "I have to pass this class, and you're the only surgeon I would actually trust with this."

"What do you mean?"

"Well . . ." She shifted in her seat. "I mean, I want to go through with the consults and any other appointments leading up to the surgery as if I were one of your patients. That's the only way to really document what it feels like, the emotions around a stigmatized elective surgery or the fear and excitement before going under the knife."

Hell.

Her breasts.

Her body.

My hands.

She wanted me to be professional when all I would want to do was suck her nipple rather than use a black marker on her skin.

"I just need your expertise and I'll get out of your hair," she said quickly.

"You do realize I'll be actually touching you, right?" I felt the need to point that out, hoping to God she'd realize how messed up this was. It brought a whole new meaning to looking, touching, but not claiming. Things were complicated enough between us without trying to clinically examine her during the day while I dreamed of her every night.

"Thatch, please." She leaned forward. "If you help me, no revenge list, and you won't be always looking over your shoulder, wondering when I'm going to pounce."

Okay, I did like the sound of that. I'd already had two sleepless nights and was about to change the locks—she still had one of my keys. Stupidity, thy name is Thatch.

I opened my mouth to say no.

To reject her—again.

"Take down the video and we'll talk."

"Remove the spider from my house and you have a deal." She stood and held out her hand.

Something told me not to shake it. The logical part of my brain. The part that said this would only end badly.

But really, what could go wrong? Her threats of revenge were going to disappear, and our war would end without any casualties.

I took her soft hand in mine and whispered, "One more thing, Austin."

"Hmm?" Her breathing was erratic.

"You're teaching me how to ride." I released her hand and stood.

Her mouth dropped open.

I closed it with my finger and winked. "A bike. Get your mind out of the gutter, Rogers."

"I knew that!" I didn't think it was possible, but her face grew redder as she smoothed out her skirt. "So, should we go over our schedule tonight while you remove the stupid spider from my house?"

"Oddly enough, I'm already regretting this," I said, more to myself than to her. "And yeah, how about we go to your house, I'll remove your pet spider, and you can tell me all about how you're going to use me to get an A."

"You're a whore, you're used to being used."

"Funny, since that word was written on your forehead this morning." I paused. "Literally. Written." I smirked. "Right there." I flicked her forehead and grinned.

"Hero!" she coughed into her hand and then thrust out her chest. "Besides, backward doesn't count."

"Backward always counts." I crossed my arms. "So, friends again?"

"Well, we aren't enemies." She forced a smile and then looked down at her feet. "Thanks, Thatch. I owe you."

Wow, thanking me must have been painful if the look on her face was any indicator.

"Oh, I know," I whispered. "I know."

Chapter Eleven

Austin

Thatch was supposed to be at my house any minute.

My palms were sweating.

And every time I thought about shaking his hand, all I kept thinking was, *Holy shit, you didn't just sell your soul to the devil; you willingly gave your heart, soul, sanity, and most likely your body*, all with one desperate thought.

Pass class.

Move on with life.

Away from the parents' house.

Away from politics.

Away from Thatch.

I was going away, but what exactly was I moving toward? I frowned at the thought. I hadn't really considered life beyond graduation because it had been my sole focus—get out from underneath my parents' thumbs, be independent. Then get a job, get married. I gulped.

Why? Why did I always have to associate Thatch with all of those future-goal words?

My chest burned right where my heart was located—bad sign, a really bad sign, that he still affected me in a physical and emotional way.

No matter how many times I repeated to myself in the mirror that he was a cheating jackass with gorgeous blond hair, my body reminded me of how rock hard he always was.

How caring.

Thoughtful.

The way he took his time when he kissed me, like it was almost more important than sex, and how he always, and I do mean always, laughed in bed at all of the funny and yet sexy situations we'd gotten ourselves into over the month we dated.

My body was a treacherous bitch.

And I kind of hated her.

"Down, girl." I placed my hands on the counter and gave myself another pep talk.

This was business.

Not personal.

He was only helping me because he knew the marketing would be good for his own brand, for his reputation.

He's doing it for his job.

Not for me.

Not for me.

Okay, all I had to do was repeat that like a billion more times and then I'd be good to go.

I eyed the bucket in the corner.

It had stopped moving a few hours ago. I was 99 percent sure the spider could actually sense my anxiety and was just playing me for a fool, like when armadillos play dead and then take off running.

Wait, that's the wrong animal . . . I warily eyed the blue bucket again. Regardless, that bastard was just biding his time until I lifted the bucket and gave him his freedom.

"Not gonna happen, Charlie."

"Please tell me you didn't name the spider?"

I jumped a foot, pressing my hand to my chest and nearly stumbling into the granite countertop. "Don't you knock?"

"The door was open." Thatch shoved his hands into his tight jeans, his biceps straining against a black vintage T-shirt. Why did he always have to look so perfect? Even his blond surfer hair was pulled back into a low knot at the back of his head, which usually meant he'd just gotten done with another surgery.

"Be honest." I needed a serious subject change. "How many body parts did you get to touch today?"

He let out a snort and walked down the three stairs in the entryway, his body swaying with way too much beauty and arrogance. The bastard.

"Six," he said, stopping right in front of me. I had to look up to meet his gaze. "And lucky me, I got an ass today."

"Wow, just changing the world one body part at a time, huh?"

"I like to think of it that way, yes." His cocky grin took my breath away and made me want in all the wrong places. Very wrong places.

I clenched my thighs together and narrowed my eyes at him. "Be honest, do you think it's possible for a plastic surgeon to stay true to someone if he sees that much tit and ass on a daily basis?"

"I'm pretty sure most obstetricians still like their own kids even after delivering tons of children." He crossed his arms. "And yes, it would be possible, if the person wasn't completely psychotic."

"Are you calling me a psycho?" My eyes widened—probably confirming his accusation.

"You put a bucket on a spider." He turned on his heel. "Then named it like you feel sorry for the fact that it's trapped. You tell me."

"Because!" I marched over to the bucket. "I do feel sorry it's trapped, it deserves to go to a nice home—just not my home—or any home within five miles."

"Austin," Thatch said, shaking his head, "it's not a puppy."

"It had fur!" I pointed at the bucket.

"This fur isn't friendly fur, it releases toxins on the skin and causes a rash."

I gasped.

"Calm down, it's not like you touched it, right?"

I shivered. "No, I'd like to think I'm a faster sprinter than that. My mom, on the other hand . . ."

He let out a low chuckle.

"It's not funny!" I slapped him on the chest.

"Your mom in the kitchen, flailing her arms and sending a giant spider careening into the air near your head while you sprint toward the couch. Very funny, some might even say downright hilarious." He placed his hand on the bucket. "And if you don't want a repeat, I'd at least get on the chair or find the couch again, it's gonna be pissed."

"Poor Charlie."

"Why Charlie?"

"Because I think it's a boy, and you can't name a boy Charlotte."

He rolled his eyes. "Sometimes I forget how young you are."

"Hey!"

"Sorry." He bit down on his perfect lower lip, his icy-blue eyes alert, as he slowly lifted the bucket, higher, higher, and then completely off the floor.

"Son of a bitch," he mumbled.

I covered my eyes. "I killed it, didn't I?"

"Um." He wasn't saying anything. Why wasn't he saying anything?

"Thatch?" I peeked between my fingers to see him scratching his head and doing a 360 in place. "Thatch, what's wrong? Is Charlie dead?"

"No?"

"It's either yes or no!" I snapped, jumping off the couch, ready to apologize to the poor spider I'd suffocated.

But there was no dead spider on the floor.

There was no spider at all.

Just a blue bucket.

And a clean floor.

"Thatch." My throat was suddenly dry as I whispered, "Where's Charlie?"

He grabbed my arm with his hand, his fingers warm as they dug into my skin, and then he whispered the words that no woman ever wants to hear.

"Don't. Move."

"Thatch," I said through clenched teeth, "if this is a joke, it's not funny."

"Do I look like I'm laughing?" His eyes were staring at my feet. I was afraid to look down. So afraid, but of course, when someone is staring that hard at something, you have no choice but to look, right?

Slowly, I lowered my gaze.

And wouldn't you know? There was Charlie, hovering near my big toe.

I was wearing sandals.

The gladiator sandals.

I was a gladiator without a weapon.

Completely screwed.

And as if Charlie sensed it, he lifted one of his hairy legs into the air, seemingly trying to taste the tension swirling around my pink toe.

"Stay calm," Thatch said evenly as he slowly knelt near the spider.

"I'm trying." My hands were shaking at my sides as the saucer-sized spider continued its weird mating thing with its legs in the air. "I think it's upset."

"It was in a bucket," Thatch hissed. "Of course it's upset! You can't even hide in a closet without freaking out."

"One time!" I whispered. "And it was really dark!"

"Translation—you're afraid of the dark."

"At least I can ride a bike."

"You want to do this right now?" He was still whispering as he slowly extended his large perfect surgeon's hands out to the spider, and suddenly, I realized how this would end.

The spider would bite him.

Thatch's bite would get infected.

And he wouldn't be able to do his job.

Or pay off his student loans.

Leaving him in debt.

On the street.

Naked.

Dead.

Thatch was going to die.

"Wait!" I slowly lowered my body to the floor. Fear pounded in my ears as I held out my hands and Charlie lumbered onto my palms. It tickled. It would be nice if I weren't so terrified of spiders.

Shaking, I walked over to the bucket and gently set him inside, this time right side up, so Thatch could transport him later. Just as I pulled my hands away, something sharp dug into my skin.

"Motherfu—"

Thatch grabbed me just before I collapsed against the floor, hands shaking and pain searing through my right thumb.

Before I knew what was happening, Thatch was carrying me over to the couch. Soft pillows met my back as he grabbed my thumb and held it close to his face.

"Am I going to die?" I whimpered. "Because the Discovery Channel said tarantula bites feel like bee stings—they're liars from the pit of hell!"

Thatch narrowed his eyes at the puffy red mark and then slowly dropped my hand to my side. "You'll live."

"Well, that's encouraging. Don't I at least get a sticker? A sucker? For saving your life?"

"You?" He chuckled and joined me on the couch. "Saved my life by getting bit by a tarantula?"

"Keep up!" Talking was at least distracting me from the throbbing pain. At least it had dulled a bit, though the fact that I had spider venom in my hand made me cringe. "If it bit you, you wouldn't be able to do your job."

He seemed thoughtful. "You mean I'd finally get a vacation where I'm allowed to sleep for longer than three hours?"

"Well, when you put it that way," I grumbled, and tried to cross my arm, then hissed as pain exploded down my hand.

He grabbed it again. "At least the venom is weak, it's really just the puncture wound from the spider's fangs that causes the swelling."

"Well, that's disappointing on so many levels. I save your life and I don't even get to turn into Spider-Man."

"Tough luck, maybe next time." He winked.

It was nice.

Sitting with him on the couch.

My legs on his lap.

My eyes focused on his mouth.

Abort! Abort!

I quickly looked away but not fast enough—he caught me staring where I shouldn't have been staring, and I felt like a complete loser for still lusting after him the way I was.

What was it about Thatch?

Other than everything?

He was brilliant. Hardworking. Gorgeous. And he fought spiders on behalf of a girl he'd dumped.

Damn it.

"This leads nowhere," he said in a hollow voice. "You understand that, right?"

It was like he'd just handed me the world's happiest balloon and then popped it with a giant needle.

I was utterly defeated and deflated.

Even though I knew going into this there was no hope of us getting back together, I'd officially turned into that sad, pathetic clinger.

I'd always made fun of "those girls."

And now "that girl" stared back at me in my own stupid mirror.

I let out a long sigh and nodded slowly. "This is strictly business, Thatch. You know how important this class is to me, how important getting my MBA is to me."

He looked away, his jaw clenched. "Parents still MIA for the most part?"

I nodded.

"And the reelection, I imagine your dad wants you to join his mayoral campaign again?"

A sick feeling grew in the pit of my stomach.

To my parents, I was a trophy. Something shiny and pretty they could trot out to gain votes from families who appreciated their having taken time out of their busy lives to sire a child.

Granted, I knew my parents loved me.

They just loved me in their own way—the only way they knew how.

"I have to graduate," I stressed again. "The job market's fierce out there, and an MBA will help with that. The sooner I graduate, the sooner I can start my own life away from all of this." I lifted my hands into the air.

This just happened to be a mansion.

A huge mansion.

With three interconnected swimming pools.

A tennis court.

Two movie rooms.

And a bowling alley.

I think I'd prefer anything but this. If I could choose to live in a dump with my parents and we'd be a family or I could have a mansion and scarcely see them.

I'd choose the dump every time.

"I'll do my best to help you." He lifted my legs off his lap. "But first, we ride."

I blushed. I couldn't help it.

"You can't do that anymore," he whispered, his blue eyes piercing. "You can't blush when I say things like that."

"Sorry."

He muttered a curse and walked away. I could have sworn he adjusted himself near the door, but I was too busy hiding behind the couch to fully commit to ogling him.

"Where's your bike?" he called over his shoulder before turning around.

"In the garage. It's kind of dark now, though, let's ride tomorrow after work." I totally said it without stuttering or blushing.

"Fine." He looked exhausted.

"Don't forget the spider." I pointed at the bucket. "And don't let it loose in nature. We can't have that bastard procreating with another, smaller spider and creating zombie spider babies that take over the world."

He just stared at me like I'd lost my mind.

And then shook his head as a smile played across his face. "You're entertaining, I'll give you that."

"I'll take that as a compliment, thank you."

"It was meant to be one."

We froze, both of us smiling at each other.

"Sleep," I whispered. "You've got a busy day tomorrow."

"Yup." He gripped the bucket in one hand; the muscles in his forearm flexed. "Take some ibuprofen and ice the spider bite. If you feel any muscle weakness or tightness in your chest, let me know and I'll prescribe you something."

"Ah, the power of the pen."

He rolled his eyes and waved with his free hand. "See you tomorrow morning at eight, Austin." He hesitated in the doorway. "Be sure to wear something work-appropriate."

"Oh, so you want me to wear a bike uniform?"

He flipped me off and quietly shut the door against my laughter.

Chapter Twelve

Thatch

I was more nervous for this workday than I'd been since I was out of residency and trying to prove myself. Our Wednesday morning staff meeting took longer than necessary, and by the time it was done, I was in need of coffee. Though for the first time in three days, I'd managed to actually get a good night's sleep—since I didn't have to worry about Austin releasing frogs or something else in my apartment.

Really, everything worked out in my favor, since I got a good night's sleep.

Even though Austin wasn't a real patient, I still needed to treat her like one. I just hated that every time I thought about examining her, I got so hard, I couldn't think straight.

Mia, our office assistant, waved me down with her hand, then covered the phone. "Austin Rogers is in your office."

And so it begins. "Thanks, Mia."

I only had one augmentation that day, and if the patient didn't mind Austin watching, I was going to let her scrub in and observe. She'd probably pass out five minutes in, but at least she would get some good material for her blog.

God, was I really doing this?

And if I was being honest, was it really about the fact that I was going to get more sleep at night because I wouldn't be living in a constant state of paranoia? Or was it just my sick way to be close to Austin without having to commit?

Austin was sitting cross-legged on my couch, wearing black stiletto heels and black on black—it looked hot as hell with her golden-highlighted dark brown hair and pale skin.

"I thought I said work-appropriate," I admonished, unable to keep the lust out of my voice. I willed my eyes to look at anything but her long perfect legs, the same legs that I used to wrap around my body during sex.

Austin stood. "Hah-hah, very funny, my dress isn't short or tight, it's perfect."

I'll say.

My eyes greedily drank her in.

I cleared my throat. "Right, so why don't I give you some paperwork to fill out, the typical patient forms we ask everyone to go through. Once you're finished, we'll start on the initial consult."

"Consult?" she repeated.

"Think of it as an interview that you get to guide." I started to relax as I went over to the Keurig.

"I brought you coffee," she interrupted, and thrust a large cup around my body and into my waiting hand. "Hazelnut latte, right? No whipped cream? No calories? No fun?"

Her voice was shaking. This was going to be harder than I'd thought.

"Thanks." I kept my voice cold, detached. "We both get to feel each other out, you decide if my bedside manner is what you are looking for in a plastic surgeon." I really should not have said the word "bed" . . . or "feel." Already I was rising to the occasion. "And"—I turned around to keep myself hidden—"I decide if you're a good candidate. We'll start with a simple breast-augmentation consult since, according to you, your professor will eat that right up, but if we have time, we can go over a few more elective surgeries before your three weeks are up. Sound good?"

She was quiet. Too quiet.

I glanced over my shoulder.

To find Austin staring at my ass.

When I cleared my throat, she jerked her head up and blushed. "I'm so sorry, I just . . . sorry." She partially covered her face with her hand and let out an embarrassed moan. "Breast augmentation first and then other things, got it."

"Great." I forced a smile I didn't feel—after all, I was officially getting no action from a girl I actually loved. No chance in hell my body was going to be cheered by it. "Why don't you go ask Mia for a new-patient form and a clipboard, and I'll have one of my nurses call you into an exam room in, say, a half hour?"

"Perfect." She stood and turned on her heel, marching out of my office like she owned the place.

A small smile formed across my face as I caught a glimpse of her thumb and the Little Mermaid Band-Aid wrapped around it.

I refused to find that adorable.

And that, mixed with her incredibly sexy body—one I was going to touch in about thirty minutes—was slowly driving me insane.

Damn me to hell.

I pulled my long hair into a bun at the nape of my neck and stared up at the clock.

Hell on Earth in twenty-nine minutes.

◆ ◆ ◆

I grabbed Austin's clipboard and went into the exam room, making sure to read through every single item as if she were a real patient.

"Austin," I said warmly, "how are you feeling?"

She blinked up at me with wide eyes. "Like I just gave you way too much medical information for a silly little slit that goes in here"—she pointed at her breast—"while you stuff whatever the hell you stuff up in here"—she pulled her hand away—"and sew me up."

"I can't decide if I'm offended at your lack of knowledge about a breast augmentation or just surprised you even know where they are at all."

She sucked in a breath. "Professional, remember?"

"Right." Yeah, this was going to be a hell of a lot harder than I'd thought. "Let's get started with your sheet here, feel free to take notes for your blog, and when it's time to examine you, I'll have one of my nurses pop in."

"Wait, what?" She went white as a ghost. "A nurse watches?"

I stopped reading her chart and glanced up. "A nurse always watches, so I don't get sued for touching you inappropriately."

"But," she said, her look frantic as she lowered her voice, "it's all inappropriate if we aren't together, isn't it?"

I let out a long sigh. "Austin, it's my job. Besides, you don't think these things when you're at the gyno, do you?"

"My gyno doesn't look like Brad Pitt and James Franco's love child!"

I laughed. "Wow, and it's funny because I so often get told I look like Orlando Bloom with blond hair."

She slumped in her chair. "I don't feel comfortable with your nurse seeing my breasts."

"So, she can't see them, but the ex-boyfriend you hate can?"

"I don't hate you." It was the second time she'd admitted it in the last twenty-four hours. That had to mean something.

"But you don't exactly like me, do you?" I just had to ask.

Austin was quiet and quickly averted her eyes to her hands on her lap. "So, did I fill out the chart right?"

"Yes, you're very good at checking boxes. Well done."

"Hah-hah, sarcasm."

"You know you don't actually have to fill in the boxes, right? A simple check mark will do."

"When I get nervous, I color!" she snapped. "You know this. Lay off."

"Well, it looks like in order to keep your design intact," I said as I showed her the clipboard, "you had to gain a stroke and heart palpitations."

"Hey, the heart palpitations can be real—I'm freaking out about passing this class, and I got bit by a spider last night!"

I glanced down at her swollen thumb. "Does it still hurt?"

"No. Ariel made it all better," she said in a sarcastic tone.

The day was getting longer by the minute.

"Alright." I scanned the rest of the sheet. "So basically, at this point I'd ask you if you have any blood-clot issues, since you also filled that in when you were trying to create a smiley face with the boxes."

"Nope."

I leaned back and let my training take control. "And why a breast augmentation? What's your end goal here?"

She was silent.

I glanced up. "Austin?"

"I guess, for the only reason any woman wants plastic surgery. I want to be noticed?"

Funny how she wrongly assumed that only insecure women stepped into my office, when really it was only about 10 percent trophy wife–types and 90 percent women who'd had a mastectomy and wanted to feel feminine again, or women who birthed beautiful children and because of nursing, lost a part of themselves they wanted back. I bit my tongue and looked her up and down. *Noticed?*

"A guy would have to be dead not to notice you," I said out loud.

Our eyes locked.

Shit.

I cleared my throat. "Alright, so you want to be *noticed.* Do you have any idea how large you'd like to go? For example, a high-profile implant is going to look fuller and give you the lift that a push-up bra would give you. A moderate implant may look more natural, depending on your body type, but . . ." Shit, I had to keep it professional, but I couldn't help picturing her perfect pert breasts and the way they'd always filled my hands, overflowed across my thumbs, and . . . There I was clearing my throat again. "Having seen your body," my voice rasped, "I wouldn't suggest a moderate because it could add weight to your small frame."

She stared at me like I'd just lost my mind and then asked in a small voice, "So, you would perform surgery on me?"

"That is what you're here for, right?"

"No, I mean, for real," she explained. "You would . . . make me better?"

"Damn it, Austin." I placed the clipboard on the table and wanted to follow after it with my head. "Listen when I say, there is absolutely nothing I would change about your body, not now, not ever."

And there we were again, eyes locked, bodies a mere foot away from each other.

All I had to do was lean in.

All she had to do was follow.

I reached out to touch her just as a knock sounded and our head nurse poked her head in. "Dr. Holloway, are you ready for me?"

"Yup." I shot to my feet and pointed to the gown on the table. "You can keep your skirt on, but take your top off and try to drape this the way that Nancy instructs. I'll be back in five minutes."

I couldn't leave that room fast enough.

I walked down the hall into my office and slammed the door behind me, taking a few soothing breaths as I leaned against my desk.

The fact that she would even question the way I had always felt about her body, considering the way I worshipped it with my mouth and hands, completely floored me.

It never once occurred to me that she would be insecure after our relationship ended. Of course, it made sense, I was in the business of fixing flaws, so it was my job to find them.

Only, whenever I was with Austin, the only flaw I saw—was me.

Chapter Thirteen

Austin

Nancy was nice.

If you liked women who should be aging naturally, but instead looked like they had had their faces frozen one too many times and had their eyebrows nailed to the top of their head.

She was beautiful in a really harsh, she-could-either-be-eighty-or-forty way.

I wasn't against plastic surgery—I was just more a fan of its looking natural—and nothing on Nancy looked natural.

When she left to let me change, I peeled off my shirt so fast, I nearly caught my head inside the neck hole—not because I was eager to get Thatch's hands on me, but because I wanted this whole embarrassing situation to be over.

I was uncomfortable, and I knew Thatch. I'd had sex with him, he'd seen me naked, and my teeth were still chattering.

I made a mental note to include that in my post.

That no matter who it was.

You were still topless in a doctor's office while bright fluorescent lights peered down on you, revealing every single flaw hidden in the dark.

A loud knock had me jumping out of my skin.

"I'm r-ready," I said, trying to sound confident.

Thatch strolled in along with Nancy right behind him.

He washed his hands.

Wait, why was he washing his hands?

"I don't want you to be cold," he whispered so only I could hear. "And who knows where my hands have been."

He was making a joke.

Trying to make me feel better.

But it only made me feel worse—because my body knew exactly where his hands had been not so long ago.

All over me.

"Alright," Thatch said, snapping me out of my pathetic trip down sexual-fantasy lane where Thatch wore an eye patch and slapped my booty. "I'm going to jot down a ton of stuff that won't make any sense to you, basically to see if one breast is bigger than the other, measure distance from the nipple to the breastbone, so just hold still and try not to slump, alright?"

I gave him a jerky nod while he pulled out a marker.

It was like sorority hazing where they would use markers to circle every imperfection and write horrible names like "slut," "whore," and "bitch" on the pledges.

Only it was five thousand times worse.

Because I wasn't drunk.

And nobody joined me in my shame.

It was just the sexiest man alive, with a marker in his hand, hell-bent on pointing out what was wrong so he could fix it.

Oh, this had been a really stupid idea.

Thatch smiled warmly at me. "Relax, this is what I do, you even gave me a shiny award for it."

I nodded my head. "You're right. Okay." I straightened my shoulders and stood tall. "I'm ready."

He pulled back the fabric, revealing both of my breasts, and sucked in a breath as his eyes dilated, the marker frozen midair.

"Dr. Holloway?" Nancy coughed. "Everything alright?"

"God, yes," he whispered under his breath. "Sure, Nancy, I just forgot I left the garage door open."

I gave him a funny look because he didn't have a garage.

And he gave me one back that said, *Shut your mouth before I doodle on your face with my marker.*

So I did.

He cupped my breasts briefly, lifting the right, then the left. I really tried not to respond. I did. Swear. But when his knuckle grazed my right nipple, my body reacted. He noticed, because, duh, how could he not? My breasts were basically begging for his attention like the little sluts they were.

Meanwhile Dr. Thatch was just doing his job.

I was in hell.

He fired off measurements while his nurse wrote them down, and as he predicted, none of them made sense to me.

"Your left is larger than your right," he said in a detached voice.

"Great," I said in a "please kill me" voice.

"Just slightly, though, you wouldn't notice it."

No, but he would.

He *did.*

I had to wonder if that's what he'd done after sex, mentally gone down a checklist of all the things he'd fix on my body if only I'd let him.

"Almost done." He looked up at me for the first time since the examination started. "Nancy," he said without looking back at her, "grab one of the sports bras from the cupboard, please."

"Right away." Her back was to us.

And then Thatch's hands were on me.

On both breasts, massaging with his fingers as he leaned in and whispered in my ear. "You. Are. Perfect."

He pulled back before I could say anything.

Tears welled in my eyes.

How did he even know what I was thinking?

And why? Why did he have to be so nice? It was hard to be angry at him for hurting me when he was nice.

And beautiful.

Don't forget beautiful.

Nancy handed him the bra, which he handed to me. "Go ahead and put this on."

I slipped off the hospital robe and pulled on the sports bra.

"Alright." He grabbed a clear implant that had rough edges and another that had smooth edges. "The rougher implant is a cohesive gel. It holds its shape better, but it feels harder." He held it out to me.

Did that mean I had to touch it?

"Go ahead, grab it," he encouraged with a small smile.

I weighed it in the palm of my hand. "Hmm, it does feel . . . kind of hard."

His head jerked up so fast I nearly dropped the implant. His eyes blazing, he quickly took the implant away and replaced it with a smoother-looking one.

"This one is . . . softer, it feels more real," I said.

"This is a saline implant, and because you really don't need to go larger than one cup size, I'd suggest this." He grabbed another. "Now, go ahead and stuff them in your bra like you used to when you were twelve while dancing to Britney Spears."

I laughed. "I never had to stuff my bra."

The smile froze on his face.

Nancy cleared her throat.

"So just"—he scratched his head—"shove it in."

"Like this?" I scrunched up my nose. "I just shove this in here."

Was it my imagination, or was he sweating?

"Yup." His voice was hoarse. "Just right . . . inside."

"Okeydokey." I put both implants in front of my breasts and looked down. "Huh, imagine that, I look awesome!"

Nancy laughed and nodded her head. "It makes you look so much thinner."

How cute, she's passive-aggressive too. I didn't even want to know how many times she probably dreamed of being in Thatch's pants.

Or how good it would feel to let her know her dreams would never measure up to how amazing it really was.

Then again.

That pesky little emotion called rejection slammed into my heart.

We weren't together.

He was free to screw whomever he wanted—even his forty-something-to-eighty-something nurse.

Thatch grabbed me by the shoulders and turned me toward a large mirror. "So, what do you think?"

"I think . . ." I eyed my body. The implants did add more of a curvy feel to my tall and lanky shape, but they felt fake. In fact, just wearing them in this sports bra made me feel like a poser. Like I was one step away from turning into Nancy over there. "I think I'll have to think about it?"

He exhaled like he was glad that I wasn't so impressed with my new breast size that I'd actually contemplate going under the knife.

"Alright then." He moved away from me. "I'll just let you get changed and I'll be right back."

He left with Nancy.

I stared at myself again in the mirror, then slowly pulled out the fake implants.

My chest deflated.

And I had to wonder—why would he want me?

No surprise he'd broken up with me.

Because in the end, how could he not cheat? How could he stay in a relationship when he didn't have to?

When he did this every day?

When he was around so much perfection each day of his life?

Well, at last, I did have my answer.

I just wished it didn't suck as bad as it did.

Chapter Fourteen

Thatch

She was waiting for me.

She had been waiting for me for the last five minutes.

But I literally couldn't get my own body under control. I'd been staring at the door, thinking about the same horrible things for what felt like an hour.

Puppies being murdered.

Whiskey shortage.

Riding a bike.

Frogs.

Death.

And still, still, I was hard as a rock and ready to make sure everyone in the hallway knew it.

"Damn it." I shut my door and turned toward the closed window, then grabbed myself as visions of Austin's perfect body surged to the surface, making it almost painful to touch myself.

"What are you doing?" a voice said from behind me. A familiar voice. Her voice. Swear my dick all but leaped out of my hand in search of that voice and the body it belonged to.

"Nothing," I lied. My body straight up hated me for that one, while my brain screamed, *Turn around, bend her over the table, lift the skirt, just lift the skirt!*

The sound of a door shutting should not at all be erotic. Or the buzzing of a computer.

The tense silence.

But all of it—was killing me.

Austin made her way around to face me, hands on hips. "Nancy said since I wasn't a real patient and just doing this for research, that I could come find you."

"Did she?" My hand was out of my pants, thank God.

But I had guilt written all over my face, and I knew it.

Austin's eyes lowered.

While I prayed for control that would keep my cock from meeting her halfway.

"Someone can't keep things professional, hmm?"

"It's been a while." Good, Thatch, that really sounds professional, that you hadn't had sex in a while, and you suddenly got a boner the size of Texas when you touched a woman's boobs—at your workplace.

Good thing Austin had never been a real patient.

My ass would have been fired so fast.

"So." I stepped away from her; it was uncomfortable as hell trying to move in my black slacks. "The next appointment is a pre-op appointment. Our finance people talk to our patients about options, and once you pay the deposit, we schedule the surgery."

"Wow." Her eyes darted from my cock back up to me. "That's really fast."

"Yeah."

Her eyes narrowed. "How many times? Be honest."

"How many times, what?"

"How many times have you jacked off to a patient?"

The question cooled my lust immediately as I locked eyes with her and said, "Zero. I don't count this time, since I was caught quite literally with my pants almost down."

Her expression couldn't be any more stunned. "Seriously?"

"Yes. Seriously," I grumbled, and my body finally went back to normal, though it screamed at me to stop being an idiot and just screw her into next week.

"So, right now, had I not walked in . . ."

"Can we just drop it? Please?" I sat in my chair.

She leaned over my desk. "What happens when I leave?"

"Nothing." Liar.

"Uh-huh." She plopped on a chair across from me and then very slowly leaned over so I could see her cleavage through the V of her shirt, and just like that, my body was back on board. She continued to lean forward, until I was worried her breasts were in danger of spilling out of her top, and then she stood, grabbed her purse, and started walking toward the door. "Do you need me for anything else?"

Well, if that wasn't a loaded question.

"Actually"—I glanced at my computer to keep myself from staring at her breasts—"I have one augmentation this afternoon. If it's okay with you, I'm going to talk to the patient and see if she'd be willing to let you scrub in."

Austin's face lit up. "Seriously?"

"Of course. She's really sweet, and now that her husband has passed, she's been hell-bent on starting over—she has an incredible attitude and is probably one of only a few patients I've worked on who would probably vote to stay awake so she could watch her own surgery."

Austin made a face and paled. "I think that would be traumatic."

"She used to be a nurse," I said, then added, "She finds the human body fascinating."

"I just bet she does," Austin said in a huff.

Frowning, I stood and checked my watch. "Why don't you go grab some lunch and meet me back here at three. I'll double-check to see if she's comfortable with you standing in. If she says no, I'll text you."

"I'm a bit shocked." Austin tilted her head, pressing her lips together like she was trying to keep herself from smiling.

"About?"

"You still have my number."

Sighing, I tucked my hair behind my ears and shrugged. "We broke up. That doesn't mean I'm going to completely cut you from my life."

"Huh." She grabbed her purse from the chair and didn't say anything else. "I'll see you in a few hours."

What the hell did that "huh" mean?

And why did I care?

Mia was at my door again, ready to knock, when Austin walked out and waved good-bye.

"Dr. Holloway, your next appointment is in exam room three."

"Right." I had a job to do. And now that Austin was gone, hopefully I would be less distracted and horny and able to get through the rest of the afternoon without wanting to blow my head off.

"I'll be right in," I mumbled, glancing back at my computer.

The computer that still held the screen saver of me and Austin at dinner.

The dinner when I had asked her to move in with me.

She was wearing a red dress.

It was one of the best nights of my life—when I decided to take a leap, and she leaped with me.

It didn't last long.

Not with the Ghost of Christmas Past staying in my same building—not with his inability to keep his head out of my life, or his demands to himself.

Sometimes I hated my own family.

And the fact that when I needed my father the most, he was drunk.

And when I wanted him to stay the hell away from my personal life, he refused to leave—and ruined the best thing I'd ever had.

Chapter Fifteen

Austin

I'd never seen a surgery before—and I refused to count that one time in sixth grade when we were forced to watch a knee scope and I almost puked.

I had only been twelve!

I was an adult now.

I could totally handle watching someone get cut up.

Shivering, I downed the rest of my fruit smoothie and walked toward the elevators. I really shouldn't have worn such high heels, my feet were starting to burn where my skin rubbed the soft leather, I knew I was going to get blisters when I put the suckers on, but I wanted to be tall—I hated how big Thatch was in the first place because he'd always made me feel small, safe. And I was a tall girl, all legs.

So high heels were my armor.

And I needed armor around him.

Since the armor around my heart had a tendency to just fall to the ground whenever he smiled at me. Ugh.

Why was it so hard for me to get the hint?

He didn't want me.

Though he did seem to be having trouble giving his body that memo if what I walked in on was any indication. It had looked like he was literally seconds away from pleasing himself by the potted plant. Then again, I wasn't vain enough to assume he was even thinking about me.

With my luck, he was envisioning Nancy's fake pout.

Or another girl's boobs.

Ugh, everywhere I looked, I saw perfection in that stupid office building.

I thought I was over my body-image insecurities that had been triggered by my ex from high school—until I started dating a plastic surgeon and was actually exposed to a small dose of what he did on a daily basis. While I was dating Thatch, I hadn't given my flaws a ton of thought, or maybe I just pushed all of those dangerous thoughts away. And now? Now it was all I could think about.

Maybe I was being judgmental, but why not go into emergency medicine? Why encourage people to spend thousands of dollars on fixing flaws? On gaining perfection at the expense of their health?

"Austin." Mia winked at me. "Dr. Holloway's in his office, waiting."

"Thanks." Heat rushed into my cheeks.

She had knowing eyes, that office assistant.

My heels screamed in outrage by the time I walked to Thatch's office. The door was open, and he was pulling his blond hair back into the hottest, messiest man bun I'd ever seen in my entire life.

It was impossible not to physically react to how beautiful the man was. I sucked in a breath and pressed a hand to my chest while I waited for my heartbeat to slow back to its normal rhythm.

Thatch in jeans. Hot.

Thatch naked. Hot.

Thatch in scrubs?

Holy Teenage Mutant Ninja Turtles. It wasn't fair.

Blue scrubs shouldn't be sexy.

And they sure as hell shouldn't fit him the way they did, making his biceps somehow look bigger, or his face that much more sculpted.

He glanced up and smiled. "Hey, you ready for your first surgery?"

My body cheered while my brain told all my lady parts to calm the heck down. That smile wasn't for us.

Not by a long shot.

Professional. Be professional.

Passing the class.

That's all that mattered.

"Sure!" I chirped in a cheerleader-like fashion. Oh man. I was so dead when it came to this guy. "Do I need to change?" I tugged at my blouse.

He nodded and walked around his desk, pointing to a chair. "Those should fit. I'll wait outside."

For some reason, that deflated me.

The fact that he was going to wait outside and not watch my strip-tease. I inwardly groaned. We weren't dating! What did I expect!

Besides! This was his workplace, after all!

I quickly went to work taking off all my clothes and said a prayer of thanks when I noticed a pair of Nike tennis shoes in my size. They looked new, so I wasn't sure if he had someone grab me a pair so I wouldn't have to wear my heels with scrubs, or if he just kept women's shoes size nine lying around.

Well, that was a depressing thought.

I pulled my hair back into a low bun and opened the door to announce I was ready.

Thatch started at my feet and slowly raked his eyes up my body, stopping at my hair. "We match."

"Man buns for the win?" I teased.

His lips twitched. "I think I pull it off better."

Damn right he did. Bastard. "Just admit they're extensions already."

"Hah." His gleaming white smile was almost too much, as in, I almost stumbled against his rock-hard body and had a near heart attack. "Let's go."

His pace was fast, I tried to keep up as we weaved through the office and then took the elevator up one level.

My heart was hammering inside my chest so hard, I felt like I was going to puke. Why was I nervous? It wasn't like I had to perform the surgery!

"This way." He marched through the halls like he owned them. People stared, they whispered, and it was like he didn't notice how freaking hot it was when he took charge.

He stopped and typed in a passcode, and a glass door made a whooshing sound as it unlocked.

"You're not touching anyone or anything, but if you want the full experience, you can wash up," he said as he started lathering his hands, suds going clear to his elbows as he washed and washed and washed.

"I think you're clean," I pointed out when it had been at least two minutes.

With a laugh, he started rinsing off just as Nancy walked in, a mask covering her mouth. "Ready?"

"Of course." His answer seemed so easy and carefree. Meanwhile, I was freaking out—still freaking out.

She held open gloves for him, helped him into his surgical attire or whatever the heck they called the thing she just put over his clothes and his feet.

It was like watching a live version of *The Night Shift.*

Only this wasn't emergency surgery.

Elective—it was elective.

And yet, he still had to take these kinds of precautions.

I could feel my adrenaline spike when Nancy walked over to me, covered my mouth and nose with a mask, handed me a scrub cap, and basically shoved me in the right direction with a pat on the back.

The operating room was really bright; that was the first thing I noticed. And the second?

There was a team of at least four people.

Not including the patient who was looking up at Thatch with complete adoration.

A pang of jealousy sliced through me as I waited in the spot I'd claimed by the wall.

"How are you feeling?" Thatch asked in a soothing yet commanding voice.

"Oh, I'm just ready," she said with tears in her eyes. "Very ready for this. Have been for a long time."

I held my snort in.

Why was she so emotional over breast implants?

A guy—I'm assuming the anesthesiologist—inserted something in her IV, and then Thatch asked her what her weekend plans were, like he wasn't pulling down her sheet and getting ready to cut her up.

There were Sharpie marks on her body, and a section of her skin was a bright orange.

"Oh, I plan on watching some Netflix and . . ." Her speech slurred and her eyes closed.

"Austin." Thatch said my name loudly. "You can get closer. She's sedated, and you know I don't bite."

Hah, false, he did bite.

And often.

Typically my neck.

And sometimes the inside of my right thigh.

I shivered.

And then I took a step forward, and another, until I was close enough to see both of her exposed breasts, or what should have been breasts.

I saw scars.

And a flat chest.

I couldn't help my gasp as the room stilled around me. Before I knew what was happening, a tear slipped down my cheek and then another followed.

I was a complete bitch.

That was all there was to it.

Because while I'd been on my high horse, judging anyone and everyone who had walked into Thatch's office to fix their imperfections, it had never occurred to me—that he would be giving implants to a breast-cancer survivor.

"Scalpel." Thatch leaned over her and made an incision near her armpit. The incision seemed a little too small to stuff the implant into. There was a lot of blood, and then he shoved it in and I nearly puked.

Her chest inflated—and even with the blood and weird colors, I could tell it was going to look amazing.

He moved the implant with his fingers, then leaned down, measuring, watching, waiting. Everyone was silent.

He repeated the process for the right breast, and when Dr. Perfectionist was finished, he sewed her up with angry black stitches that I assumed would dissolve over time.

I was assuming a lot.

But I was afraid to ask questions.

Because the whole situation felt—oddly holy.

Like he'd just done more than give her breasts—like he'd just given her back her femininity.

Tears welled in my eyes for a second time as Nancy and another nurse rolled the bed out of the OR.

When Thatch turned around, his eyes narrowed. "Austin? Are you sick? What's wrong?" He tugged off his apron thing and gloves, then his mask. "Austin?"

I shook my head. "I need to go."

"But—"

"I'll see you later. I just . . ."

I didn't finish.

I had to get out of there.

I had to find my hate for that man somewhere.

And it wasn't going to be in an OR where he gave women something precious back.

And it wouldn't be where I watched his magical hands perform a surgery that he could most likely do in his sleep.

"Austin." His voice had me paralyzed. I froze, but didn't turn around. "You owe me a bike ride, remember? I'm supposed to ride with your dad and one of my partners on Friday morning."

"Tell them you're sick."

"Austin."

"Fine," I barked. "My house, seven."

And then, like a loser, I ran out of the room, away from the man who still held my heart and refused to give it back.

Away from the only man I'd ever wanted.

Chapter Sixteen

Thatch

I'd been on edge ever since Austin ran away from me like zombies were chasing her and threatening to eat her brains if she stopped.

So I said the only thing I knew I could say in order to see her again, because I was a sick man, or maybe because I knew that my addiction for her was getting worse, and like a true addict, I told myself, just one more taste and I'd quit.

One more look at her body and I'd leave her for good.

One more taste of her lips and I'd really delete her phone number.

Just one more.

By the time I made it back to my apartment to shower and get dressed, I was in a really shitty mood. What the hell had caused her to panic like that?

She survived a tarantula bite without passing out—so why was she so pale after watching a breast augmentation? There were literally fewer stitches for that than most surgeries, it wasn't like I was chipping away on someone's nose and doing some reshaping or a tummy tuck.

I shoved my key in the door lock and froze. "Dad."

"Son." He came out of his apartment and crossed his arms. "We should get something to eat like old times, maybe have a few beers."

I wasn't in the mood for his shit.

Besides, he already sounded drunk.

"I'm busy." I pushed my door open.

Naturally, he followed.

"With that little whore?" He chuckled darkly. "Thought you broke up with her?"

I clenched my teeth and made a fist. I would not hit him.

Again.

"I did." I exhaled through my teeth. "Remember, you basically witnessed the whole thing since you live across the hall and don't understand the meaning of the word 'privacy'?"

"She was sexy, I'll give you that."

I closed my eyes and leaned against the countertop. "What do you want?"

His smile was cold. "What I always want, to hang out with my only son!"

"You're thirty-two years too late. Now, leave. I had a long day."

He threw his head back and laughed. "Oh, a long day, huh? What? Touching women's tits? I bet it was hard, still can't believe you'd go into plastics when you could have been a real surgeon, like me! Like your grandfather, well, he was up for the Nobel Prize in Medicine—"

"Yes, I know. You've told me about a million times." At least I was bigger than he, able to use my weight to get him toward the door. I put my hands on his shoulders and shoved him in the direction of the open hallway. "Leave. I think you've done enough parenting to last a lifetime, don't you?"

"Get your hands off me!" He jerked away from me and sneered. "She's no good, just like your mother! You hear me? She's a slut and a whore and a—"

I punched him in the nose hard enough to both feel and hear a crack the minute my knuckles made contact.

"Damn it! You broke my nose!"

"And you're probably going to have to find another silly plastic surgeon to fix it." I slammed the door in his bloody face and leaned my head against it.

Anger surged to the surface.

God, how was it possible to be raised by such an asshole?

Then again, it wasn't like he or my mother did much raising. More like I'd spent time with my grandparents and the housekeeper.

It was getting harder and harder to keep the anger away. Especially when I looked into Austin's eyes and saw someone who truly wanted to help.

Someone who'd so often asked me if I was okay, if I wanted to talk about my childhood. She'd single-handedly shown me in less than a month what it would be like to share pain with someone right along with love.

And I'd rejected her.

Rejected all of it.

Because sometimes, you reach a point where you know your pain is too ugly to share and that sharing it destroys what you love the most.

And yet, I had wanted to share that part of myself with her more than anything—until it was no longer in my power to do so.

It was better she not know the truth.

For everyone.

A chill washed over me at the thought of her finding out.

No. He'd promised.

And as much as I hated my father, I knew he would at least keep his promise when it came to that.

Otherwise, he wouldn't get any more money.

And since a drunken retired surgeon wasn't fit for work, I was his only meal ticket until the divorce went through and he was given his half of the fortune my mother had inherited from my grandparents.

All of my father's problems could have been erased had he not lived like a celebrity billionaire and screwed everyone other than my mom.

With a curse, I jerked away from the closed door and made my way into my bedroom. I needed a fresh change of clothes and a shower.

And a giant swig of beer, if I was going to make it through the evening with Austin.

Alone.

I needed my body under control—especially since my heart was already dangerously close to just bursting whenever she looked at me with tears in her eyes.

God, what had set her off today?

Well, I was going to find out.

Even if it was a horrible idea.

The last thing I needed was her tears.

I'd rather have her anger.

Anger you got over.

Sadness?

Lingered.

I would know.

I'd been sad a very long time.

◆ ◆ ◆

"I don't think so." I crossed my arms. "Hell. No."

Austin laughed and grabbed my arm, which was a bad idea, because it caused a tingling sensation that spread through my chest and made a beeline south. "You said you needed to learn!"

"On a bike!" I jerked away from her and pointed. "Not on whatever the hell that is!"

"Dora the Explorer." She nodded triumphantly. "With pink streamers and a badass basket that you can put all your cool toys in!"

"Austin." I ground my teeth together.

"Thatch." She moved her eyebrows so she was making a grumpy face like I was being a poor sport or something. "Come on, if you can rock a man bun, you can rock a Dora bike! Just find your inner explorer!" She just had to honk the horn.

Of course, because what child's bike would be complete without a horn.

"Or"—Austin shrugged—"you can teach yourself and just admit to Daddy and your partner that you lied . . ."

"I hate you so much right now," I grumbled. "Okay, so how do I get on it?"

Austin gave me a blank stare and then pulled the bike out in front of her. "Well, Thatch, it's a lot like putting on pants, one foot goes over and, voilà, you're riding a bike."

"It has training wheels!"

"So you don't get a boo-boo." She winked. "Now, your turn. Just put one leg over the side, become one with the pedals, and fly!"

It was stupid.

My fear of riding bikes.

And sure, I'd told Lucas it came from almost getting hit by an ice cream truck, but that was a half-truth.

The whole truth?

I'd just learned how to ride my bike without training wheels—and was on my way back home to tell my parents.

Only to find my dad making out in his car with a woman who wasn't my mom.

The musical sound of the ice cream truck still made me sick to my stomach, just like ice cream, just like bikes.

"I can't," I whispered once I was settled on the tiny, uncomfortable, not to mention offensive little bike. "It looks like you're going to have to push me down the stairs so I'll be too injured to ride." I got off the bike and shuddered.

Austin put her hands on her hips. "I'm not shoving you down the stairs."

"A week ago you would have been all over that."

"A week ago I was still angry."

Her admission shocked me. "You're not angry anymore?"

"It's hard to be angry now that I've seen you operate on a breast-cancer survivor and give her back her identity," she said in a defeated voice, suddenly staring at her sandaled feet.

I moved closer to her, taking one tentative step. "Is that why you ran?"

She nodded.

"You know," I said, letting out a sigh. The sun was setting, causing pink streaks to stream through the clouds. Her house was twenty minutes away from my apartment on a good day—the view was beautiful, though, overlooking most of Seattle. "The stigma behind plastic surgery still pisses me off."

Behind thick black lashes, Austin glanced up at me. "What do you mean?"

"That it's bored housewives with too much money and not enough confidence who pay me to make them perfect, when really most of my cases are people who just want to feel better about themselves. Burn victims, cancer survivors, moms who have put their bodies through hell after childbirth, or even just people who want to slow the aging process a bit. It's not what people assume. It used to make me angry, but I know what I do. Granted, there will always be the outlier, the person who suffers from body dysmorphia and tries to get surgery after surgery until his appearance borders on monstrous—but those cases are rare."

Why was I telling her all of this?

"Why are you telling me this?" She'd always been a bit of a mind reader.

"No idea." I shook my head. "So, where are we on the whole accident thing? A broken leg should do it."

Austin smirked. "I'm not going to break your leg, it looks like you're going to have to come clean and tell them you're afraid of bikes, even the ones with streamers."

"It's not the bike," I whispered under my breath. It was what it represented, just another thing stolen from me—compliments of my dad. "Maybe I'll just fake an illness."

"Hmm." Austin leaned the bike against her garage door and crossed her arms, causing her lush breasts to strain against her thin white tank top. Would I never be able to have a normal reaction to her body? Ever? Already my body strained to touch hers. "We could always give you food poisoning?"

"Food poisoning would mean I'd need to take the whole day off."

"Followed by a miraculous recovery?"

"Maybe." I kicked the ground with my shoe.

If I wasn't learning how to ride a bike, my time with her was over. Which meant I needed to go.

But I didn't want to go.

Ask me to stay.

"Well . . ." She threw up her hands. "We aren't going to solve your problems outside, getting eaten alive by mosquitoes. You want wine or something?"

We locked eyes.

Being friends with her would be impossible.

I'd always want her.

I'd always crave her.

But wine was wine, right?

"Sure." I found myself agreeing, just like I found myself stupidly following her back into her massive house and sitting at the bar while she poured me a healthy glass of red and then one for herself.

Chapter Seventeen

Austin

Wine with Thatch. Everything between us had started with wine. Wine and then pizza and then a silly little line where he asked if I wanted to see his comic-book collection. I knew he'd been full of shit, but his personality had been magnetic. I was helpless, caught in his delicious web of sex.

And I'd been a willing victim.

But the guy I'd stumbled into bed with—and the guy I was currently having a nice adult glass of wine with?

Two totally different people.

Gone was the heart-stopping smile he usually chose to hide behind, and in its place, he looked stripped bare. As if he were finally about to lay all the joking aside and reveal some sort of truth.

"So, you wanna talk about it?" I asked, swirling the wine in my glass a few times before taking a slow sip.

"About?" He didn't make eye contact.

"Tits."

He spit out his wine in his glass and glared at me.

"Sorry, I couldn't help it."

"Try." His eyes narrowed.

With a laugh, I nodded my head toward the door. "All boobs aside . . ."

He snorted.

"What's up with this whole bike thing? You looked ready to shit yourself out there, and the Thatch I know is more badass than that, so what gives?"

"I wouldn't say badass," he grumbled.

"You've swum with sharks—twice—and somehow managed to find a nice loving home for Charlie."

He burst out laughing. I missed his laugh. It was deep, infectious, just like his smile and the crinkles by his icy-blue eyes. "What makes you think I didn't just kill him?"

"You save lives, you don't take them." I jabbed a finger at him. "Surgeon."

"Hah." He set down his wine, and a piece of hair fell out of his sexy-as-hell man bun, kissing his cheek. I was jealous of that strand, actually wanted to rip it from his head and stash it under my pillow and have a good cry.

Okay, no more wine for me.

I scooted my glass far, far away from my body so I wouldn't give in to temptation.

"Let's just say bike riding is attached to some really shitty memories, and every time I touch a bike, Dora or not, the memories come back, and I'd really like to keep them locked down, you know?"

Well, that was more information than I had expected.

"That makes sense," I finally said.

He was quiet.

"So . . ." I just had to fill the silence with my voice, didn't I? "What's on the agenda for tomorrow? Ass implants? Penile enlargement? More boobs?"

"How is it that you make my job sound so exciting?" A smile tugged the corners of his mouth. "And sorry to disappoint, but the last penile enlargement I did was a good month ago—we don't get those often. Most of the guys who come in don't fully understand the potential side effects."

"Like ED?"

"How about total impotence? Infection? Losing all sensation and the inability to get a full erection?" He shook his head. "Yeah, not worth it."

"Well, that just ruins my day," I said jokingly.

"Tomorrow I have a rhinoplasty," he said cheerfully. "And the office does pro bono work for kids with cleft palates. I'm seeing a potential patient tomorrow."

There went my heart again, thudding to the rhythm of Thatch's name.

I reached for my wine. Bad Austin.

"That's really nice of you."

"It's not their fault, you know?" he said, talking mainly to himself. He'd already finished his wine and was standing up.

I panicked.

I wanted him to stay.

But I didn't know what else to do to get him to stay other than take off my top and flash him boobs and hope he'd jump at the chance to touch them again.

Sighing, I stood right along with him, grabbed the wineglasses, and managed to somehow trip over my own feet and land facedown on the ground, broken glass sticking out of my cheek.

"Austin!" Thatch was on his knees in front of me, while I was attempting to not freak the hell out over the blood gushing down my cheek.

I reached for the glass.

"Stop." He shoved my hand away from the wound and proceeded to slowly pull out a piece of glass that was about an inch thick.

"That hurt!" I yelled, holding my hand to my face.

"Shit." He jumped to his feet, I heard water running, and I was already feeling woozy over the chunk of glass that had just been joined with my skin.

When Thatch came back, he had a wet paper towel and was dabbing my face. It stung like crazy.

"You won't need stitches." His face was so close, I could almost taste him.

Tears filled my eyes as I nodded.

Tears of embarrassment.

Tears of rejection.

Great, I was just full of tears where he was concerned.

His soft hands brushed across my cheek again, and then he was back on his feet.

I stayed put on the floor, not trusting myself to get up.

He returned a few minutes later and knelt in front of me. Something cold hit my cheek, stinging a bit, and then he spread a small Band-Aid across my cheek.

"Ariel?" I asked.

"I figured Iron Man would look more badass."

I smiled, then groaned. It hurt to even smile.

His clear blue eyes professionally examined my face again, and then he turned away—like he was afraid to look at me directly in the eyes. "It's just a cut. Take some ibuprofen tonight, and if you have any trouble, call me tonight, alright?"

"Trouble?" I repeated. My cheek stung, and the Band-Aid tugged the skin near my mouth, making my face feel tight.

"Just call me if it hurts." He stood and held out his hand.

Call him if it hurt.

It always hurt.

Always.

But what to do when the man offering his help was the one who caused the hurt in the first place? I refused to tell him yet again how he broke my heart—that he'd broken us. That I was still upset and dealt with my tumultuous feelings on a nightly basis when I slept alone in my childhood bed.

"Thanks for this," I said lamely, pointing to my cheek. "I guess I should get working on my assignment, right?"

"Yeah." He rocked back on his heels. Silence stretched between us. "What time are you coming tomorrow?"

I licked my lips as he finally stared me down, his face emotionless.

"After class," I finally said. "Possibly in time to take some really interesting notes on a rhinoplasty."

The corners of his mouth tugged into a playful smile. "Sounds exciting."

"I'm sure it is."

"Tomorrow." He leaned in like he was going to kiss me and then froze. I was afraid to move.

Finally, he leaned over and kissed my forehead, then walked out of my house basically the same way he walked into my life, with a slow, confident swagger that left me aching in all the wrong places.

Mainly. My heart.

Chapter Eighteen

Austin

The cursor kept blinking at me. My new blogger site mocked me.

Because the only stupid words I could think to type were things like, *His hands were smooth as they cupped my breasts, his thumb an inch from my nipple as he measured. He was warm.* I gulped. *Large.*

And every time I typed those words, I had to delete, you know, because I wasn't writing an erotic novel.

I leaned my head down against the computer and sighed. After the trauma of feeling a piece of glass stick out of my cheek, I decided to go to bed and wake up early to write my first post before class.

And there I was, an hour before I had to leave.

Still staring at the blank screen where no words were present, and wondering how I was going to sound professional when every single touch had me nearly jumping out of my skin and ready to maul the good doctor.

The difficult part—I knew what his mouth tasted like.

I knew what his touch felt like.

So, my body couldn't help itself—it craved him.

"Be professional," I repeated to myself as I started to drily document what happened at a breast-augmentation consult and with my emotions during the appointment.

I replaced the word "erotic" with "gentle."

Made sure to include that the experience was a bit jarring but that because there was a nurse present, it didn't feel that awkward.

The blog post wasn't all that spicy—but it talked about boobs, made Thatch sound like a good doctor, and I knew that if someone was interested in legitimate content via a firsthand experience, they would find it in my post.

I hit "Publish" and grabbed my things.

The minute I stood, I had one of those flashbacks, the really aggravating ones where your mind goes, *Wait, we didn't get to overanalyze this moment last night, quick, do it now.*

I groaned.

And closed my eyes.

I could almost feel the brush of his lips across my forehead.

What the hell did that even mean?

And why!

Why would he do it?

A forehead kiss was almost worse than a mouth kiss—because it conveyed a degree of tenderness.

And sadness.

Love.

He just had to go and ruin a good night's sleep and a productive day by kissing me on my stupid forehead.

Whatever. Thatch had his chance and he rejected me—he even had his chance to explain—he chose not to.

So, forehead kiss or not—I wasn't for him.

I just wished my body and mind found it easier to align with that simple fact.

Besides, after I passed this stupid class, I'd have absolutely zero reason to hang out with him.

The thought was a bit depressing.

So, I focused on happier ones.

Like the fact that at least for today, I was going to see him.

Yeah, I was screwed.

◆ ◆ ◆

"So, how's it going?" Avery asked with concern as she handed me a MoonPie and winked. "You know, other than the weird Band-Aid on your face and that dreamy look in your eyes."

She'd texted me with all caps that if I didn't give her an update on the Thatch situation, we'd be on a friendship time-out, and last time that had happened, I'd had to buy her a week's worth of Starbucks to get back into her good graces. Besides, maybe she'd have some Thatch wisdom. God knew, I needed to be fully armored every time I walked into that man's office.

Especially after the day I'd had with him.

He'd held a child's hand and told him he was going to fix his cleft palate. I'd literally had to leave the room so he wouldn't see me cry. The blog post was going to be killer. In fact, I couldn't wait to write it and include research on cleft palates as well as up-to-date nonprofits that worked with children. Before I'd left, Thatch had given me a bunch of awesome resources, damn him.

"Chocolate?" I pleaded.

"Please." She rolled her eyes.

I dug into the MoonPie. Yes. That was what I needed. Sugar.

Avery smirked and then pulled out a can of Mountain Dew. My eyes got so blurry, it was hard to see her. "You love me."

"This stuff will eventually kill you, you know that, right?"

I snatched the can out of her hands, my fingers going numb from the cold, and popped the tab, chugging at least half before putting it down on the table. "How did you know?"

With a sigh, Avery placed her arms on the table and leaned forward. "You do realize that when you get sad, you start sending me random emojis, right? A toaster. A high five. A chicken. Today you sent me ten shrimp." I winced. "In a row."

"Sorry. It's my cry for help."

"Yes, kind of like your bat signal." She grinned. "So here I am, on a Thursday night, at your yet-again-empty mansion, cheering you up."

"You're a good friend."

"Lucas says he's going to run you over with his car and bury the body if you keep me longer than an hour."

"Geez, possessive much?"

"He also said if I don't show up, he's coming here."

I groaned. "Is it really so hard to share?"

"Funny. You'd think he'd be all over sharing, being the whore he is, but now that he's in a committed relationship, it's like he forgot all the rules of kindergarten."

I bit off another piece of chocolate goodness and sighed. "Honestly, I'm fine."

"And there it is, the 'honestly.'"

"Huh?"

"Truthfully. Honestly." Her eyebrows arched. "Those are your tells, basically you're not fine, and I bet you ten dollars that if I checked under your bed, I'd find a half-eaten Snickers."

My cheeks heated.

"Uh-huh." She tapped her fingernails against the table. "So, are we watching a movie and ignoring the giant Thatch in the room, or are we going to talk about how much of a struggle it is for you to see him every day and not hump him?"

I scowled. "I would never hump him at work!"

She was silent.

"I mean . . ." I shrugged, picking off another piece of MoonPie. "He does have this really sturdy desk that I'm pretty sure could hold both of us, and I'd probably be lying if I said I haven't thought about it at least one time."

She coughed.

"Or a dozen."

"There we go."

"But . . ." I banged my forehead against the table a few times before glancing up again. "It's like he's immune to everything! When he did the breast exam, he was all horny, I saw it, and he was sweet last night, and now, ever since that day, he's been super distant."

"It's been three days."

"Exactly!" I threw my hands in the air. "Three days of him being so professional that I want to flash him!"

"Yeah, maybe not the best life choice." Avery scrunched up her nose. "Have you been wearing sexy clothes? Perfume? Makeup?"

My mouth dropped open. "Do you know me at all?"

She was silent and then pointed at my outfit. "Did you wear that today?"

"No, I came home and changed for our date!"

"Whoa!" She held up her hands. "I'm just trying to help."

"What's wrong with what I'm wearing?"

"You're in black skinny jeans, a tank top, and black heels. You look . . . sad."

I frowned. "I thought black was professional."

"It is, but you look like you're in mourning."

Tears filled my eyes.

"Oh, honey." Avery got up and quickly pulled me in for a hug. "You're still sad, aren't you? About Thatch?"

"I just don't understand," I sniffed. "And I hate that I'm this hung up on him, I've never been this girl!"

"Maybe it's because he's your first love."

I nodded.

"Okay, so you know how we came up with this revenge plan, and it totally backfired and people still call him hero on the street?"

I burst out laughing through my tears. "Yeah."

"So that wasn't the best idea, but I think this one may cheer you up even more."

I blinked and wiped another tear from my cheek. "Okay, hit me with it."

"Dresses."

"Sorry?"

"Short dresses."

"Short dresses," I said dumbly. "That's your plan?"

"No." She grinned. "Keep up!" She jerked me to my feet. "It's yours!"

Chapter Nineteen

Thatch

"I'm in fucking hell."

"Cheer up." Lucas slapped me on the back. "It can't be that bad."

"That. Bad," I growled. "Did you not hear what I just said? How the hell did you do this? Work with Avery without using whatever power you had as her boss to make her—"

Lucas grinned. "No, keep going. I'll just beat the shit out of you rather than offer you whatever wisdom I was going to bestow."

Groaning, I finished my burger and wiped my hands. "I've worked with her four days. It's Thursday, Lucas, and I'm ready to lose my mind."

"Don't forget you still have to fake an injury or sickness so you don't have to go riding with her dad tomorrow."

"Helpful," I said through clenched teeth. "I'm not sleeping, I'm constantly hard as a rock around her—yesterday, a middle-aged grandmother came in for Botox, Austin watched and kept sucking on her lower lip, and I literally had to excuse myself like I was ready to shit my pants—and go take care of business."

Lucas burst out laughing and then stopped when I glared. "Sorry, it's not funny."

"She is shadowing me for two more weeks." I groaned into my hands. "It's a nightmare, a complete and total nightmare."

"What if she shadows another doctor?"

"I sent her to Turner's office, and that jackass checked her out so long that he's lucky to still have all of his teeth, no chance in hell am I dangling her in front of the single partners."

"Hmm." Lucas grabbed his sunglasses and twirled them around in his hand. "So, let me get this straight. You're going crazy because you want her, but you don't want her, yet you don't want anyone else to want her? Do I have that right?"

I opened my mouth, then shut it.

"Still feel like keeping silent on why you broke up with her after she was willing to forgive you for tonguing another woman?"

The silence was going to eat me alive.

Right along with the guilt.

And shame at why I did what I did.

But I'd prefer to have all of it and protect her rather than leave her exposed in the way her family already was.

Just thinking about it made me sick to my stomach.

"You look pale," Lucas whispered.

"I gotta go." I tossed my napkin down on my plate. "I guess I'll just count down the days until she's gone."

"You could always make one of those Christmas chains," Lucas said helpfully. "Or . . ."

I paused, my sunglasses halfway up to my face. "Or?"

"You could always just kiss her."

My body leaped at the thought, my heart hammering so hard against my chest, I thought it was going to beat right out and go running down the street. "Yeah." I laughed. "And hell could freeze over."

I heard a sharp gasp.

Austin was standing right behind me with Avery.

Well, hell.

I wasn't sure how much they'd heard, but by the tears welling in Austin's eyes, it had to be most of the last minute.

"Austin." I swallowed back the lump in my throat.

"Uh, hi." She waved at me even though she was a foot away. She was wearing a short black T-shirt dress, slouchy boots, and carrying her ever-present giant-ass purse.

"Sweetheart." Lucas stood and kissed Avery on the mouth. "You're twenty minutes early."

"We went shopping, and I wanted to get your approval on Austin's new wardrobe. I mean, we needed a guy's opinion from someone who wouldn't eye-screw her." Her voice was strained.

I was such an idiot.

A few minutes earlier and Austin would have known that I didn't mean it the way it sounded. A few minutes earlier and she'd have known just what type of pull she had on me, and how damn difficult it was to keep her at arm's length.

Instead, I'd hurt her.

Her normally cheerful face was pale, her lower lip trembling as she stepped completely around me and stood in front of Lucas. "So, will you help?"

Rejection hit me hard and fast.

Right along with irritation.

What the hell?

"I'm a man." I felt the need to point this out as the entire group turned to look at me. Yeah, I was a total idiot.

"A man who's late for his one thirty," Austin said in a low voice.

Damn her for knowing my schedule.

"Aren't you coming?" I challenged in a haughty voice I didn't recognize. "You know, I am doing you the favor, right? If you're not going to shadow me when I have the interesting cases, you won't have enough information for your posts, and you'll fail your class." God, stop talking!

Lucas shot me a "really, man?" look while Avery's eyes narrowed.

Austin glared at me. "Well, I would hate to fail, or upset you by taking advantage of your . . ." She tilted her head. "Kindness."

I was so turned on by the way her long legs looked in that dress that I was having a hard time seeing straight.

Yeah, I was being kind.

Or just an out-of-control idiot who had no choice but to keep it in his pants until she was out of my life forever.

"Let's go," I barked.

"Lead the way, boss," Austin said under her breath. I knew she meant it as an insult; she was mocking me, whatever. It still made it painful to walk. I really needed to go out on a date or something—completely push her out of my system by way of another woman, but my body totally rejected the idea.

Kissing someone else had about as much appeal as buying a frog as a pet.

My office was two blocks from where Lucas and I had met for lunch.

It might as well have been miles.

A tense silence stood between us, making me feel so far from her that I wanted to scream.

I opened my mouth to apologize about a million times, only to close it and keep silent. Maybe that was my problem—I was too good at not saying anything, because sometimes, it was silence that saved people, not words. I knew that better than anyone.

The elevator dinged.

We walked side by side down the hall.

"Dr. Holloway." Mia nodded at me and winked at Austin. "Your one thirty is in exam room number four."

"Thanks." I grabbed the outstretched clipboard and motioned for Austin to follow me into the room.

"Justin." I opened the door. "Hi, I'm Dr. Holloway, I have a"—I glanced at Austin—"student researching plastic surgery. She's just going to sit in on our consult, if that's alright with you? She's signed a confidentiality agreement, so rest assured everything about your patient profile will be kept private."

"Fine with me." He peered around me at Austin and smiled. "So, a student, are you studying to be a doctor?"

"No, I'm getting an MBA," Austin's happy voice responded, and I don't know why, but I hated that she was talking to him. "I'm just here doing some research for one of my final projects."

He was younger than me.

Good-looking.

Why the hell was he here again?

I glanced down at the sheet and almost groaned out loud. "So, let's talk about the calf-implant procedure, shall we?"

Justin nodded. "Man, I've been working on my calves for years." Impossible, he was a child. "And no matter what I do, they never get bigger, so I thought, 'Hell, why not, I have the money. I mean, women get breast implants, why not get calf implants?'" He winked at Austin.

It was tempting—the idea of plucking those eyelashes out one by one.

Clearing my throat, I began asking him all the usual medical questions as I quickly went through his paperwork.

"Well, you're the perfect candidate, why don't I take a look?"

He was wearing shorts, which made it easy. "You have lean calf muscles." I touched his calf and pressed the skin in. "Why don't we go over a few pictures of implants I've done on men your size and shape and go from there?"

When he didn't answer, I looked up.

Of course he didn't answer, he was currently checking out Austin like she was available—and poor Austin was taking down notes like she usually did.

"Hey." I snapped my fingers. "If you're serious about this, I need your full attention, alright? Elective surgery is still surgery."

"Sorry." His cheeks went pink as he lowered his voice. "But she's hot, I mean, how can you work around that and not get distracted?"

How indeed.

"I'd bone her."

"Get out." I stood, stomped over to the door, and jerked it open.

"Huh?" He blinked in confusion. "What do you mean, 'Get out'?"

"Get the hell out of my office," I said coldly. "And don't come back."

I towered over him.

Speaking of calf muscles, mine were just twitching to get a good kick in. As it was, my hands were shaking with the intense need to knock the guy's teeth in.

"Are you serious?" Justin rolled his eyes. "I'm a paying patient!"

"Not anymore you're not. If you don't leave now, I'll be forced to call security."

"Jackass." He shoved past me and then Austin, slamming the door behind him.

Austin whistled. "Good bedside manner? I think I may uncheck that box."

"He was being disrespectful," I said in a huff.

Austin's eyes widened and then she burst out laughing. "Oh wow, he was being disrespectful? Interesting, so the only person who can say anything disrespectful about me is you? But if anyone else does it, you're ready to kick his ass?"

"Yes," I said through clenched teeth. "No." Hell. "Austin . . ." I licked my lips. "Can we not do this right now?"

"Fine." She walked over to where Justin had been sitting and plopped into the chair. "Then let's get on with the exam."

"I'm sorry, what?"

"I didn't get any notes other than your going through the patient's forms with him—what else do you do during a consult for a calf implant, Doc?" She crossed her legs, and I could see a generous amount of thigh the way she was sitting.

Yup. I was in hell.

And it was scorching hot.

"Fine." I feigned indifference when really, my left hand was shaking so badly, I had to shove it into my pocket. "Typically, I'll show them pictures of different implants, and then we'd discuss . . . size."

"Big," she blurted. "I want huge."

It hurt to breathe. Why did everything have to be a sexual innuendo with her?

"How big?" My voice was strained.

She tilted her head to the side, then pointed at my legs. "Well, how big are yours?"

"Mine are real."

"Yeah, but how big?"

I was going to burn in hell, because the only thing I really wanted to do was take off my damn pants and say something stupid like, *You tell me.* Then she'd point at my cock and I'd say, *Wrong leg*, and then we'd screw against the nearest wall.

Yeah, there went that whole malpractice-suit business resurfacing.

Only when Austin was in the room with me.

The fact that I didn't have a nurse with me was a mistake.

Right along with the door being closed.

"Why don't I just show you pictures?" I cleared my throat.

"Aw, Thatch, you afraid to flash me a bit of leg?" She winked and moved in her chair, causing her dress to ride up higher—damn it, I could almost see ass cheek.

"I, uh." My eyes begged me to look down, so I fought like hell to keep them focused on her eyes. "It's just a leg."

"Right, so you shouldn't have any problem showing me yours."

"You're being ridiculous," I snapped, then tugged up my pant leg. "This is from squats, running, actual exercise. He had leaner muscles, most likely from long-distance running or cycling."

"Hmm." She touched my calf with her finger, trailing it down to my ankle. "So where does the implant go in?"

"Go in," I repeated.

She nodded, still not removing her hand.

"At the . . . Achilles." I blew out a curse, then braced both of my hands on her thighs, slowly running them down past her knees until I grabbed each calf with a hand and squeezed. "I'd put it in here." I gripped harder. "And sew you up here." I squeezed again. "You'd recover in a few painful weeks—the end. Though I'd kill any doctor who'd dare mess with your legs."

"They are kind of lanky."

I don't know how it happened, but one minute I was gripping her legs in my hands, the next, my hands were inching back up her thigh, my fingers eagerly dipping into her luscious skin until her dress was up past her waist. Her half-lidded eyes told me all I needed to know as I hooked her legs around my waist and lifted her into the air. "I've always loved your legs."

She gulped, her lips parted.

I leaned in.

My pulse hammered between my ears in anticipation of her taste. The exam room's phone rang.

I sighed, then slowly slid her back down to the floor. My body cried out.

I answered on the fourth ring. "Yeah?"

"Your father's in the hospital . . . ," Mia said in a low whisper. "Again."

"Hell." I pinched the bridge of my nose. "I'll be right there."

I hung up, ready to punch the wall. "I gotta go."

Austin's eyes narrowed. "You look like you're going to be sick."

"I'm fine," I snapped.

"Thatch—"

"You're not my girlfriend anymore. I don't have to tell you shit. Go write your silly little blog so whatever this is"—my voice cracked as I waved a hand between us—"can finally be over."

She sucked in a breath. "I swear, it's like one minute you're the guy I fell for, and the next, I don't even recognize you."

"Maybe because the guy you fell for just wanted to get laid, ever thought of that?"

She gasped and slapped me across the cheek, then stomped out of the room, slamming the door behind her.

Chapter Twenty

Austin

"He's turned me into a stalker," I whispered into the phone while I slumped down behind the wheel of my car and waited.

"Why are you whispering?" Avery said on the other end of the phone. "And who are you stalking?"

"Because stalkers whisper, and I'm stalking Thatch."

"Okay, that's it, intervention time, you can't keep just hoping he'll come back, sweetheart. Ugh, I knew it was a bad idea for you to hang out with him for your final project—you're going to get attached, then get hopeful, and then, boom, I'm going to find you buried under a pile of MoonPies."

"What a good way to go, though, you know?"

"No, Austin!" she yelled. "Not a good way, not even a normal way! You need to get over him, and you can't get over him if you're still pining for him. This is my fault. I told you to dress sexier in hopes that he'd snap out of it, but when we walked in on their conversation . . ."

Pain sliced through my chest. "Yeah, I don't think that conversation bears repeating, it was rough."

In fact, he'd been nothing but hot and cold to me since our little heart-to-heart at my house a few nights ago. It was like a switch was constantly being flipped.

And he hated me.

Then didn't hate me.

Almost kissed me? Maybe?

Damn it!

"He doesn't get to hate me!" I yelled into the phone, my eyes searching for Thatch's car. "I'm the woman scorned! How dare he take that away from me! It's like ever since I promised I wasn't going to get even, he's been . . . mean and distant, hot, cold—like the other night he kissed me on the forehead, and today he picked me up and nearly had his way with me!"

Avery gasped. "What? Why didn't you tell me this?"

"Because I was too busy stalking. Sorry."

"Why are you stalking again?"

"Well, after he picked me up and nearly pulled my dress off—"

Avery gave a little cheer.

"Yeah, I wouldn't celebrate just yet," I said, then continued. "So he was leaning in, I met him halfway, he got a phone call and suddenly he shut down, like completely shut down."

"So you followed him out of the office?"

"Right."

"And then tailed him with your red car?"

"I didn't say it was the smartest plan, Avery!" I snapped.

"Sorry!" She yelled right back. "Okay, so where are you?"

"The hospital," I said lamely. What was I doing with my life? I couldn't even take a hint, could I? He was helping me because he felt bad, he rejected me, and I still couldn't leave it alone—I had to go and trail him with my freaking car!

I was "that girl" again.

I hated that girl.

I needed to go out on a date and forget about Thatch once and for all.

So when Thatch walked out of the hospital looking like absolute hell, when he slammed his hands against his steering wheel and screamed at the top of his lungs?

I ignored the need to go make it all better.

Because that's what I wanted to do. I wanted to support him. I wanted to pull him close and ask what he was doing at the hospital. I wanted to be the person he went to when he was stressed.

But I needed to get a clue. If he wanted me there, he would have told me to come, or at least shared why. I wasn't in his life anymore. The sooner I realized that, the better.

"Austin? You still there?"

Sighing, I closed my eyes and whispered, "Lucas still got that friend?"

◆ ◆ ◆

I had tears streaming down my face from laughter. Matt, my blind date, was hilarious, his gestures so big and over-the-top that I hadn't stopped laughing since we sat down. He immediately put me at ease.

He was dressed a bit too nice for my taste, in a full pin-striped suit with a purple tie that he kept adjusting. According to Lucas, Matt was a higher-up at a bank, though I didn't ask what he did, and since he didn't offer, I figured it was too much info for a first date. I imagined if we hadn't met right after work, he would have been wearing something more casual—just like his personality.

From his dimples to his big brown eyes, he reminded me of a cute puppy—unfortunately not one that I wanted to take home and invite into my bed.

"So, what do you do?" he asked, popping a peanut into his mouth and chewing a few times before dabbing the corners of his lips with a napkin. The guy had good manners on lockdown. It should be attractive. The suit, the smile, the easy banter, he was the whole package. But for some reason, all I wanted to do was reach across the table, muss his hair, and ask if he'd ever been tempted to sport a man bun.

"School." I jolted myself out of my weird Thatch daydream. "I'm getting my MBA at UW's fast-track program." He popped more peanuts into his mouth and smiled with it closed. He reminded me a lot of my dad. Impeccable manners, nice suit, chewed with mouth closed, smiled with his lips, but the smile never quite reached his eyes. Was that what this whole Thatch thing had done to me? Pushed me into the arms of someone who could be my father? I shivered. "I'm a few credits shy of graduating, so hopefully once I'm done, I can get a good-paying job." In the real world. With real people like Matt, whose starting salary was probably more than I would make in five years.

"It's tough out there." He nodded seriously as he leaned in, no doubt to give me some amazing life advice, since he's been in the field for more than three years. Holy shit. I was on a blind date with my father. How did this happen? "But Lucas says you're wicked smart, I'm sure you'll be just fine."

Wicked. Smart.

Hah.

I regarded him with what I hoped was a "gee, you're really great" look and slowly started to grab my phone from the table; all I needed was to make up an excuse.

My dog died.

My father needed me.

Avery's in the hospital.

Or maybe just the truth: my dad has that exact same suit, and I'm pretty sure if I married you, it would be like incest.

He blinked at me.

I smiled back.

Insert a few beats of silence.

Because we'd officially run out of things to talk about.

It was awkward.

Gone was the teasing, easy banter; ah, I was wondering when the awkward blind date would arrive. There was no warning; instead, tension settled around our tiny little table at my favorite bar like a cloud of stink, and all I could do was pray for an interruption from the universe.

"So . . ." I glanced at my phone and then back up at Matt. "You must work really long hours, huh?"

"Yeah." Fake smile was back. Great. "I mean, I love my job, so it's worth it, but I hardly have any time for dates." He checked his watch. "In fact, I have to be up early tomorrow, but I'd love to see your place."

It took a minute for what he said to sink in. "My place?"

"Yeah." This time his grin reached his eyes. Of course it did—the bastard thought he was getting laid. Sorry, I hadn't had enough alcohol, and I'm pretty sure even with my rose glasses on, I would have still scrunched up my nose at his offer.

"I live with my parents," I said sweetly. Take that!

"I know," he countered. "Your dad's the mayor."

A prickly sensation washed over me. "Lucas told you?"

"I researched you online."

Well, that's . . . nice. "Um, why?" asked the stalker. Great, Austin. It's not like you wouldn't have done the same thing if you weren't so sad all the time about Thatch!

"I don't date nobodies."

That was his answer.

I don't date nobodies. He slid his hand across the table and placed it on mine.

I was just getting ready to jerk my hand away and toss my drink in his face movie star–style when a gruff voice sounded from behind me. "Get your fucking hands off her."

"Thatch." I leaped out of my seat—two more feet and I would have been in his arms. "Thank God."

"Who the hell are you?" Matt stood and puffed out his chest.

Thatch straight up growled and then said in a low voice, "A surgeon. Her boyfriend. Great in bed. Rich. And right now? Leaving. With Austin."

Matt's eyes bugged out of his head. "You need to go, *without* my date."

"The hell I will!" Thatch and Matt were chest to chest.

And then Thatch made a really poor life decision—he shoved Matt in the chest, causing Matt to flail backward. When Matt regained his footing, his right arm surged through the air, hitting Thatch square in the nose.

"Son of a bitch!" Thatch held his nose as blood gushed down his lips.

"Better hope you're a good surgeon, asshole." Matt straightened his jacket. "Sorry you had to see that, Austin. Should we go?" He held out his hand.

I wasn't sure if I wanted to laugh or cry.

"No." I shook my head. "I think this date is over."

He frowned. "You're choosing this guy?"

Thatch glowered at Matt.

What can I say? I'm a glutton for punishment. "Yup, I guess I am."

Thatch's taut muscled shoulders visibly relaxed while Matt shoved by us both and said, "I'm too good for this shit."

Sighing, I grabbed my phone and purse, shook my head at Thatch, and said, "Let's get you home, Rocky."

Chapter Twenty-One

Thatch

My only goal had been to apologize to Austin for treating her like shit and being distant; anything beyond that, I wasn't sure I could stomach.

But now that my dad was in the hospital, I figured the truth was getting closer to being exposed, and I'd rather she hear it from me first.

God, my parents were so good at ruining my life, weren't they?

And now they were going to ruin hers.

Fantastic.

My nose throbbed. Luckily, I didn't think the bastard broke anything, though it hurt like hell to the touch. When I'd texted Lucas for Austin's location, he hadn't said jack shit about her being on a date.

So I wasn't prepared to see another man touching her hand—my hand.

I still felt those hands slide down my skin at night when I fought back the anxiety over our breakup. I still dreamed of the woman attached to those hands.

My nose pulsed—yeah, life wasn't fair, not by a long shot.

"We'll pick up your car tomorrow." Austin finally stopped the silent treatment as we pulled in front of my apartment complex and she got out of her car, slamming the door behind her.

I followed suit, and hated that she was making me feel small, like I was the one who had done something wrong—I did just defend her honor, right?

The bastard was touching her!

The worst part? He was allowed to.

She wasn't mine.

My fault.

I'd done this.

And I was finished.

I couldn't even handle him breathing near her and touching? No. Just no.

Thinking about it was almost as bad as reliving it. His hands looked manicured. What the hell type of man goes and gets manicures?

His suit made me want to puke.

And I could have sworn I saw a ring on one of his fingers, and not a wedding ring, no, a gaudy gold thing that looked like he was one step away from becoming a pimp.

I followed her up to my apartment, dug my keys out of my pocket, and quickly ushered her inside. Dad was supposed to still be at the hospital, but I didn't want to take any chances of a run-in—not before I got a chance to talk to her about everything.

"Um, were you robbed?" Austin asked once we made it inside and I flicked on a few lights in the kitchen and living room.

I searched for a towel and some ice, and muttered, "No."

"You sure about that?" She pointed to all the magazines lying on the floor in front of the couch, the clothes thrown all over my floor, and the dirty dishes in the sink.

Yeah, I was normally a complete clean freak. I liked to be organized in both my personal and professional life—and Austin knew this.

So my apartment looking like shit? Out of character.

"I may have lost my temper." I glowered at her.

"And you took out your temper on the clothes? What about the dirty dishes?" She walked around the breakfast bar and shook her head at the sink. "What's going on?"

"Nothing," I said quickly.

"Bullshit." Her blue eyes searched mine. "Thatch, you punched a complete stranger tonight, and your apartment looks like the police broke in to search for crack."

I snorted. "What if I told you I wanted you to leave it alone, just for tonight?"

She licked her lips, her gaze traveling across the counter as she no doubt took in the mess. "I'd say you've probably left it alone too long, but it's not my place, not anymore." She turned toward the sink and flipped the faucet; water started pouring out.

I frowned, the motion hurting like hell. "What are you doing?"

"Dishes."

"Austin—"

"You should go lie down."

"Austin, you don't have to do my dishes." Austin in my apartment was a bad idea, a horrible idea. It made me want things that I knew weren't within my reach, not anymore.

"I want to do your dishes." She started washing off plates and putting them in the dishwasher. "Now, talk dirty to me."

I nearly tripped over my feet on the way to the couch. "What?"

She glanced over her right shoulder and smirked. "Tell me all the dirty details about liposuction. Ready. Go!"

I smiled, a real smile, and lay back against my leather couch. "That's what you want to talk about? Fat sucking?"

"Can you really die from it, like Cher's mom in *Clueless*?"

"Huh?" The hell was she talking about?

"Pop-culture reference, I'm disappointed in your lack of knowledge."

I shrugged even though she couldn't see me. "I didn't really watch a lot of TV when I was little." I was too busy trying to stay away from my parents, so I basically enrolled in every after-school program you could think of. Besides, when they weren't home, it felt too lonely and empty in that big house.

A familiar pressure settled on my shoulders, spreading across my chest like a vise.

"Thatch?"

"Sorry, did you say something?"

"Yeah, but I like talking to myself. I do it all the time at my house. I swear I haven't seen my parents in days."

Yeah, I bet.

"Oh?" My skin prickled with both awareness and knowledge.

"Eh, it's normal."

I closed my eyes as the throbbing in my nose lessened.

"Hey." Austin was suddenly next to me—I smelled her before I even opened my eyes. "Other than a good old nose job where you get to chip away at someone's bone with a freaking hammer . . ."

I smirked.

"What's your favorite surgery to perform?"

I frowned. "Nobody's ever really asked me that."

"Well, now that you have exactly"—she held up her fingers and checked her phone—"ten fans." Austin shrugged. "You gotta give them what they want, and one of my commentators wants to know what type of surgery you prefer. I figure I can use that as my third blog post this week."

I tilted my head and then patted the spot next to me on the couch. I had no idea why she was being so nice after I kept treating her like shit, but I'd take it.

She bounced onto the couch next to me and tugged her knees underneath her body, exposing a lot of leg.

Too much leg.

Yeah, being friends with Austin very well might kill me dead.

"Alright." I cleared my throat. "So, I don't know if I would call it my favorite, but I love a good tummy tuck."

Austin's wide-eyed expression was classic. "You like tucking people's stomachs into their bodies and cutting out fat?"

"It's a bit more complex than that, but I get a lot of middle-aged women who get tummy tucks after popping out multiple kids, and I always think to myself, 'That's the least I can do,' you know? Help them get their pre-baby bodies back. Women come in after severe weight loss, and it's just, I don't know, I sound like an idiot probably, but it's an honor to work on them."

Austin's smile couldn't get any bigger. "Well, I'll be damned, Thatch Holloway has a heart."

"Hah-hah." I shook my head. "Yeah, well, don't tell anyone. Wouldn't want to ruin my jackass reputation."

She rolled her eyes. "Please, you just got one of the most prestigious awards a plastic surgeon can get, and at what? Thirty-two? I'd say you have a good reputation, Doctor."

My entire body came alive when she called me that. She'd never in all the weeks I'd known her—even the entire month we'd dated—called me "Doctor."

I think my dick liked it a little too much.

My body was literally straining in her direction. And the throbbing I had been feeling in my nose very conveniently went somewhere else.

Hell.

"Okay." Austin cracked her knuckles. "So, show me. I'm your patient, where do you cut?"

"Cut?"

"Slice." She made a quick motion with the side of her hand. "You know, where do you cut the person open? How many incisions? How deep? Are you really tucking?"

"Whoa, that's a lot of questions."

"Give the readers what they want."

"So," I said, then licked my lips and leaned forward. We were inches apart as my pointer finger grazed her hipbone and moved inward. "Typically," I said, my hands shaking, "I ask a patient where they wear their swimsuit bottoms or underwear, as most incisions are made too high."

She gulped, "Oh."

"So"—yeah, I was going to do it—"since you wear a lot of bikini-style underwear with the occasional boyshorts—"

"You remember my underwear?"

I didn't dare look at her. "How could I not? One pair said 'Slap me' on the ass."

She grinned at me, and I tried to fight the smile, but I couldn't, not when it was Austin, not when I was touching her, when we were that close.

"What's next?" Was it just me, or was her voice a bit breathless?

"Next"—I cleared my throat, keeping my hands pressed to her stomach—"I make the incision based on what I think garments will cover up." I noticed her breathing pick up. "The central point of the incision has to be at least seven to nine centimeters above the top point of the . . . vulva."

Her breath hitched as my hand moved from her stomach lower toward the juncture of her thighs.

"That's very . . ." She gave me a once-over. "Technical."

"Surgery usually is," I answered. My hand hadn't moved, but I wanted it to; I wanted to dip lower, to feel her heat, to kiss her senseless and forget about all the shit that was keeping us apart and just love her.

"I should go." She didn't move.

"You probably should, but . . ."

We were both silent; her eyes searched mine. "But?"

"You don't have to."

"I think I know what happens when I stay, and I don't think I can stand your telling me that you only want to get laid when you meet me. So"—she put her feet on the ground—"I think I will go."

My heart sank.

"Look on the bright side, you won't have to ride with my dad tomorrow, since you have an injury." She pointed at my nose, and I stood to walk her to the door, every step heavy with dread.

It was my fault.

And there was no way out of it.

"Honestly, I'd forgotten all about the bike ride," I admitted. I'd been too focused on all things Austin and seeing my dad in the hospital.

She reached up and kissed me on the cheek and backed away, but not before I pressed my lips to her forehead.

"Bastard," she grumbled.

"What?" Confused, I watched her grimace and then make a face of complete disgust.

"You!" Austin rammed her finger into my chest. Hard. "You aren't allowed to do that anymore! It means something to me, the forehead kiss, okay? So don't do it! Don't, because it's mean, and you're mean, and it makes me forget that you broke my heart and stomped all over it and for some sick reason think that it's super fun to repeat the process on a daily basis, and I really need to pass this class and get through these next few weeks without waking up in the middle of the night with a stupid ache in my chest that refuses to go away whenever I think about what happened between us—what broke, and why I wasn't able to fix it."

Completely stunned, I reached behind her, locked the door to my apartment, grabbed her hand, and led her away from the one and only exit.

"Thatch, what are you doing?"

I didn't answer.

I was too angry at myself to answer, angry at the situation—pissed at my parents, and ridiculously enraged with hers.

When we reached my room, I shut that door too and drank her in. "If I told you I wanted to make love to you today and forget about it tomorrow, what would you say?"

"I'd say you were an asshole."

I smiled at that. "But?"

"There's always a 'but' with you," she grumbled. "The small part of my heart that you still refuse to give back would probably jump with joy and make my life a living hell if I didn't at least think about it."

"Small part?"

"You choose to focus on that part rather than the thinking-about-sex part?"

"The heart matters more than sex."

"Says the guy who said he just wanted to get laid."

"I lied," I admitted. "You know me better than that."

"Words hurt regardless of whether you mean them, Thatch."

"Stay." I reached for her.

She jerked away. "And tomorrow?"

"Tomorrow, you can try to teach me how to ride a bike again."

"I sense another 'but.'"

"Don't ask me why we broke up. I won't tell you. And you'll just get pissed. Trust that I'm protecting you in the only way that I know how."

"And the cheating?" She just had to ask. "The reason you kissed Brooke?"

I shrugged. "I like kissing."

"You're an unbelievably horrible human being."

"And yet you're still thinking about it . . ." I smirked and started walking toward her. "About how good it was between us, about how good it could be tonight if you just say yes."

Austin narrowed her eyes. "My hand is literally itching to slap you."

"May make you feel better." I shrugged.

I shouldn't have given her the opportunity. Her hand went sailing through the air and met my cheek with such a loud slap that I stumbled to the side.

And then her little fists were beating at my back, shoving me against the nearest wall.

I let her.

And when she slowed down.

I swept in for the kill.

And kissed her.

Chapter Twenty-Two

Austin

Thatch kissed a woman as if he knew her body better than she did. It was like his lips could sense the perfect amount of pressure to apply in any given kissing scenario. Moaning, gasping, begging for more weren't just options; they were necessary.

It was survival.

I'd been a victim of his kisses.

Just like I'd been a victim of every inch of his sexual prowess, and I knew, if I didn't stop the kiss, I would be a victim again.

But my body begged me to just linger a bit longer. It told me to wait until I felt his tongue sliding across mine, until he tugged my lower lip and did that thing where he sucked it between his teeth just long enough to get me to gasp and open my mouth wider, where he'd slip in and take advantage, plundering my mouth until his air was mine.

My body trembled beneath his heated touch; he knew exactly where I needed him, where I always craved him, and he took advantage of it, stealing any sort of no that I wanted to speak, and turning it into a yes, yes, yes, holy crap yes!

Finally, his long, passionate kisses stopped, replaced with slow, heated pecks across my lips. I pulled back; his gaze darted between my eyes and my mouth.

"Thatch—"

He placed a finger across my mouth. "I need you."

Anything but that.

Any words but those.

My kryptonite.

Because until Thatch, I'd never really felt needed or even wanted. My parents barely acknowledged my existence.

I'd only ever had Avery.

Her parents were more like parents to me than my own.

And then Thatch had come along, and he was fun, and different, and confident, and suddenly I found myself getting lost in everything he represented, but what hooked me was the day I found out it was all a front.

What hooked me—was his damage.

The glimpses he gave me when he thought I wasn't really paying attention, the brief spouts of anger, the restless nights, the moments when I'd find him ending a phone call and gripping the phone so hard, I was afraid it was going to break in his hand.

He never talked about his past.

And because of that, I just assumed he wanted to focus on his future—our future.

My biggest mistake in our relationship wasn't falling for Thatch; it was thinking that he needed me as much as I needed him.

Because when I touched him—my world felt full.

So how could it not feel that way for him?

How could he not feel the same?

"I need you," he repeated, his eyes wild.

So, like an idiot, I kissed him again—and sealed my fate against his mouth, knowing that his track record proved he was a cheater and that I didn't have any part of him—even though he still held every part of me.

I was that stupid girl.

The one I'd judged.

And I fully embraced it.

Because when it's you in that situation, you imagine yourself as the game changer—you imagine you're different.

Thatch nipped my lips over and over again, his hungry moans making me dizzy as I fought to catch up with his hands as they tugged my clothes away from my body in record time.

Thatch didn't do slow.

Not with sex.

He took his time with kissing.

But sex had always been aggressive—not quick, but he definitely didn't wait to get to the point.

So when he slowed down, and leaned his forehead against mine, then pulled me away from the wall and pressed me down against his bed—I knew I was suddenly in over my head.

He peeled his T-shirt from his body, revealing a six-pack cut from stone right along with pecs that I teased him couldn't be real.

Men like Thatch shouldn't exist in the real world—they belonged in vampire novels and paranormal movies.

His biceps flexed as he slowly crawled over me, kicking off his jeans in the process. Our lips met in a frenzy while his hands moved behind my neck, tugging my body upward toward his.

"I missed this," he said between kisses.

"Me too," I admitted, trying to keep the tears at bay. Sex, I could totally just do sex.

With the man I loved.

With the man who had broken my heart.

With the man who was going to walk away.

"Me too," I repeated out loud, needing to convince myself more than anything.

With a sigh he kissed down my neck and then stopped, his eyes flashing as he stared at my bare chest. "Never."

"Never?"

"Ever." He shook his head.

"Never ever?" My eyes blurred with unshed tears while he continued to suck me in with his laser-like focus.

"I would never cut you here"—he slid his hand down the side of my breast—"and shove anything here." He smiled. "Because this"—he closed his eyes and cupped my breast, his thumb grazing over my nipple—"is perfection."

"But what if I begged you?"

"Then I'd silence you with my mouth and keep you so preoccupied, you'd forget your own damn name." His answers always were a little too wonderful, damn him.

"Touché," I whispered.

"Seriously, Austin." He bent over and sucked so hard, I nearly came off the bed. "Never let anyone tell you any different."

"I guess," I panted, "since you're a plastic surgeon, you know your stuff."

He made a little sound at the back of his throat as he moved to my other breast, taking his sweet time—giving my body way more attention than it had experienced since our breakup.

"You taste the same." He licked the spot he'd just sucked. "How is it possible that I'm addicted to the way your skin tastes?"

"I think what you're saying is, you're addicted to my sweat."

"You're not sweating yet." He winked at me. "But you will be."

"Really? Because I really don't want a workout," I teased.

His injured nostrils flared, and then Thatch did what he did best—he found my weakness and pounced.

He hooked his arms beneath my legs and tugged me down the bed, my back slid against his cool sheets as my feet met the floor, he tugged me to a standing position and then, completely naked, walked over to the door and flipped on the switch.

My initial instinct was to cover my body.

But Thatch saw women's bodies all the time.

And suddenly he was in front of me again, kissing me, confusing me, digging his fingers into me, sliding his hands down my hips and then lowering himself to the floor, wrapping one arm around the inside of my thigh so his hand pressed against my ass as he kissed and sucked up that same leg.

I shivered.

What was he doing?

My body went hot and cold all at once when his tongue flicked my core and with a moan he pulled me forward, rocking my hips against his mouth. I tried to pull back, first because it felt too good and I was pretty confident I was going to just collapse on his head any minute, and second, because he could see everything.

Everything.

"I want to taste you forever." His words buzzed against my skin as I dug my hands into his long mop of hair and held on for dear life. "Love this."

This.

Not you.

I tensed.

"You're so warm." His tongue did something that I was pretty sure should be outlawed in the bedroom if girls were supposed to stay sane, and then I was coming apart, trying to hold on to all the reasons why this had to stay physical and not take a detour into emotional territory.

I had no time to recover.

No time to process the best orgasm of my life.

Because Thatch was too busy kissing me again, pressing me against the dresser, then lifting me against the wall. My back met the wall with so much force that I let out a grunt.

"Sorry." His mouth twitched.

"No you aren't." I was breathing too heavy, and yes, damn him, I was sweating; he'd made me sweat.

His eyes were still locked on mine. "Has there been anyone since . . ."

He gulped.

I wanted to lie.

Instead, I shook my head. "You?"

He licked my lower lip and whispered. "What do you think?"

"I think I may go to prison for murder if the answer's yes."

With a warm chuckle near my ear, he whispered, "I wouldn't be doing this . . ." He thrust inside me so deep, I almost couldn't breathe. "Or this . . ." He pulled almost completely out before slamming into me again; the picture next to my face crashed to the floor with a thud. "Or even this . . ." He gritted his teeth as pleasure exploded around me on his next thrust and my body convulsed around him. "If that were the case, Austin."

In a haze of lust, I noted the desperation in his eyes. I hated it. Because I didn't know the reason behind it.

So when he thrust harder, deeper, when I felt like I was going to either die or go insane, I held on to his hot, sweaty body and allowed myself to get lost in the pleasure of the moment, knowing it would be over too soon.

"God, I missed you," he gasped in my ear. "So close."

"I missed you too," I whimpered, my head falling back against the wall as I found my release. "Thatch!"

"Needed you," he said one last time before I felt him fill me. "So bad."

We didn't break apart right away.

Instead, panting, we stared at each other. I was afraid to move.

I didn't know if he wanted me to leave.

If I should leave.

If he was going to pretend like he didn't just rock my world.

I was in awkward territory. My heart was still hammering like I'd decided to sprint for the last thirty minutes, and my muscles felt weak. I wasn't so sure I would actually make it to my car.

"Come on." He pulled away, I immediately shivered, and then, he led me to his bed.

A bed I knew well.

He gently tucked me in on my side, kissed me on the forehead—damn it!—and then he whispered, "Sleep."

"Where are you going?"

His jaw tightened before he ran his hands over his mussed-up hair and then planted them on either side of his head. "I can't sleep, not after that. I have enough adrenaline to fuel an entire pack of Red Bull." He grinned easily. "I may watch TV or something."

I nodded and then said, "Maybe I can join you?"

Without saying anything, he walked back over to the bed, picked me up, comforter and all, and stalked out of the room.

We fell asleep to Jimmy Fallon.

And when I woke up a few hours later.

I was back in the bed—without Thatch by my side.

Chapter Twenty-Three

Thatch

"The hell you are!" I spit. "You can't come in!" I was seriously minutes away from calling the police on my own father. He'd been out of the hospital for three hours—and was already completely wasted.

"I'm your father!" Amazing that he wasn't even slurring his words, although his body swayed a bit. Damn it!

I had Austin.

Austin in my bed.

My Austin.

And I had to deal with this shit!

"Give me your keys." I held out my hand.

Dad shrugged. "I left 'em."

"You left them," I repeated. "Where?"

"No idea." He burst out laughing.

"Stay here," I said through clenched teeth while I ran back into my apartment, grabbed the spare key, and tried not to break it in half while I stomped back to my dad and then across the hall.

When I opened his door to let him in, he, naturally, tripped over his own feet and stumbled against one of his entry tables.

Swearing, I slammed the door and began doing the usual. Make a pot of coffee, search his house for bottles of whiskey, put a glass of water by his bedside along with a bucket to puke in, and an extra set of clothes.

By the time I was done, it was already six a.m., and I hadn't slept since the loud knocking this morning. Thank God Austin slept like the dead.

My dad was snoring on his bed by the time I made it back to my apartment.

Smiling for the first time in a while, I made my way into my bedroom.

My bed was empty.

Austin was gone.

And I could only imagine what she assumed.

That I'd somehow abandoned her in my own apartment.

After sex.

Noncommittal sex.

I hated my life.

And my dad.

In reverse order.

Chapter Twenty-Four

Austin

My morning was not starting well. I had three missed calls from Avery that I ignored because I still smelled like sweaty Thatch and was in the process of gathering my clothes so I could run home and shower before class, when my father decided, "Hey, let's make sure my daughter is alive and breathing."

Lunch.

He wanted me to go to lunch with him and my mom.

And of course he just had to text me that early to ask!

So basically, he had something to tell me—that was the only reason for his lunches, and of course he couldn't be a normal parent and have those types of talks at the house, because nobody would see!

I texted him back yes only so I'd stop getting messages from him with a question mark, and went in search of my underwear.

I found it in the living room, which was odd since I was pretty sure I was stripped naked in his room.

I quickly put on all of my clothes and grabbed my purse. Luckily it was still early, so nobody would see me sneaking out.

I made it as far as the door before it hit me.

Not the guilt.

Not even regret.

Just utter sadness.

I'd let him in.

I'd trusted him even though I had known I shouldn't.

And he'd bailed.

He'd actually left me in his apartment alone—that was how desperately he'd wanted to get away from me. I had literally driven him away from his place of residence!

Ugh. I pressed my fingers to my temples and eyed the ever-present notepad and pen near the entry. I itched to write a cute note that would sound super nonchalant, like, *Oh hey, thanks for the bang, my lady parts really needed that, hah-hah, know what I mean?*

I groaned out loud.

No.

Because all Thatch had to do was crook his finger and he could have any woman he wanted. Why did he have to be so good with the words?

Why?

Stupid, stupid Austin.

I wasn't going to leave a note.

He didn't deserve a note.

I didn't care how many orgasms he gave me! Or that he told me I was perfect. Tears stung the back of my eyes. Stupid tears. Why were girls so stupid?

Why was I so stupid?

I stomped all the way to my car and allowed myself a few tears once I was safely inside.

And just like Seattle.

It started to rain, pelting my windshield with angry drop after drop, totally matching my mood as I drove to what I knew would be an empty house.

Mom was probably already at hot yoga.

And Dad was clearly already at the office.

I opened the fridge and fished out a Mountain Dew, then closed the door. My own reflection in the shiny stainless steel mocked me.

"Shhh, nobody has to know," I whispered to myself.

Good, so Thatch had officially broken me and now I was talking to myself, and most likely going to go crazy. Thanks, man, really.

I made it to my bedroom, fished out a MoonPie from my nightstand, and went to wash the sex off my skin.

◆ ◆ ◆

"Austin!" Dad opened his arms wide, fake smile in place. He kissed me on both cheeks and then pulled out my chair.

My dad had impeccable manners.

Mom grinned over at us and then ordered everyone iced tea.

What a great, awesome family get-together.

"So, how are classes?" Dad asked once we'd looked at our menus.

"Great," I lied. My one class may just kill me, I ended up in my ex's bed, and I would probably still do it again if given the chance, oh and I have a broken heart. "Totally awesome."

"Glad to hear it." He winked and then did the usual glance around the restaurant. He lived off the looks he got when out in public; you'd think being the mayor meant he was a local celebrity. "So, I kind of have a job for you."

"A job?" Great, the last time he had a job for me, I was manning the hot dog stand during his last run for office. "What kind of job?"

He and Mom shared a look before my mom placed a hand on mine. "You remember Bill Sipher's son?"

"No." I shook my head. I purposefully forgot him because he gave me the creeps and transported me back to a time when I was so insecure, I was willing to do anything just because a cute boy said he liked me.

"Yes you do!" Mom laughed and waved at me like I was the most hilarious thing she'd heard all day. "The one with the braces?"

"Mom, when I was a teenager, we all had braces."

"About this tall." Dad held up his hand above the table. Four feet. He had braces and was four feet tall—no, guys, don't remember, can we get some bread? "He was your first kiss!"

My mouth went dry.

My first kiss.

I had a lot of firsts with him. Just talking about him gave me the creeps.

"Braden!" I yelled. I hadn't meant to yell.

Heads turned and then my dad, swear I do love him most days, stood and said, "Well I'll be damned, look who just walked in!"

Setup! It was a setup. Red alert. Abort! Must. Find. Exit. Oh no, he was walking toward us, escape route, escape route. "BRADEN!" I grinned like a maniac. "How long has it been? A year? Two?"

"Five," he said in a really pissed-off tone. "Give or take a few weeks when you refused to answer my phone calls, texts, and emails. But really, who's keeping track, right?" He flashed a smile.

I tried to match everyone else's enthusiasm—tried and failed. "I was busy . . . school, you know."

He eyed me up and down. "Still eating MoonPies like they're going to stop making them, Austin?"

Oh hell no.

No body shaming.

If he said one more thing about my body the way he used to, I was going to rip his face off and feed it to him intravenously through his asshole.

"Charming. As always," I said through clenched teeth. "So, what are you doing in town?" At this restaurant, at my table.

Of course, Dad had to pull out a chair for him.

I was in hell.

"I just graduated from Stanford Law and moved back into the area, and I caught up with your dad a few weeks back when we saw each other at the Everett Country Club." God, save me from that place. All of my bad family memories included that place, and it was also where Braden and I first hooked up. "And well, one thing led to another, and he mentioned you were still single."

I was going to kill my dad.

After.

After the horrible lunch.

Because my dad was all about appearances, and if I didn't grin and bear it, I would hear about it later, and the last thing I wanted was to get yelled at for not being the proper mayor's daughter.

Even if the guy he invited to lunch was a complete psychopath.

"So, law, that sounds fun. You always were really good at talking *at* people." I smiled and reached for my water, wishing a miracle from heaven would occur and the water would turn into wine, very strong, endless wine from God.

"Thank you, how sweet." His eyes narrowed. Shit, he knew something I didn't. What did he know?

"Austin . . ." Dad grinned wide. Oh no, here it comes. "You know the annual fund-raising dinner. It's coming up, and Braden here has agreed to be your date!"

"Has he," I said through clenched teeth. "How wonderful, but, Dad, remember, I told you I may not be able to go?"

He laughed. "But of course you'll go. How would it look if my one and only daughter didn't show up?"

"But—"

"You'll go," he said tersely.

"I'll go." I felt my entire body slouch into the chair, like my skin wanted to melt into the cloth so I could camouflage myself. Maybe then Braden would stop giving me the eye.

Braden and I had dated at the insistence of both of our parents. It was a good match.

Really.

That's what both my parents had said.

Like we lived in a historical novel and it was my one and only duty to marry into a family of money so that we could have even more money and take over the world.

A sickness started to spread from my stomach down my limbs; just sitting across from Braden brought back all the painful memories of our time together.

His constant remarks about my body.

And my junk food habits.

I used to cry myself to sleep because of that boy.

And the worst part? When I broke up with him, I got in trouble.

My dad actually grounded me.

At sixteen.

And later on, when it seemed like Braden had actually grown up into a nice young man—my mom's words—we saw each other at the club and started dating again.

He had complimented me—I hadn't realized how starved I was for positive attention, but soon after trying again, he turned on me.

And each compliment was backhanded, or followed by a negative remark, from my hair to the fact that I'd gained weight.

I was afraid to eat bread around him.

That's how bad it got.

Thank God for Avery. She finally helped me see that it wasn't normal or natural to be in a relationship where you're afraid to eat carbs or wear the wrong color on a date.

And ever since then—I told myself I would never get into a committed relationship again.

Sex.

One-night stands.

I was doomed to be single.

And I was okay with it.

Until Thatch.

I held in the tears.

I would not cry over him.

Or over the fact that I was in his arms last night and abandoned this morning and then thrown into a den of wolves.

Daddy reached across the table and held my hand briefly. "So, what do you think?"

Crap. They'd been talking about something important while I was taking a trip down memory lane.

Great.

"Uh, good." I nodded and smiled. That was really all I needed to do around my dad, since my opinion wasn't one he wanted or needed—I was there to agree with him. My mom knew her part well. She winked.

I loved them.

I did.

I just had days where I wished it were more about us as a family than about my father's job or his dreams of going to the White House—no joke, he actually told me when I was six that he wanted to run for president.

He'd been running for an office of some sort my entire life.

"Great." Dad dropped his napkin on the empty plate and checked his watch. "I'll see you two later." He kissed me on the top of the head before my mom stood, gathered her things, and trailed after him.

"Classic setup," I grumbled, crossing my arms.

Braden eyed me up and down and then reached for his water. "So—"

"No." I interrupted him. "We aren't doing this. Not now, not ever."

"But it's what your dad wants, and don't you want him to be happy? How would it look if you abandoned me, after agreeing to keep me company during lunch?"

Shoot. That's what I'd agreed to?

"Besides, your dad wanted us to talk about the benefit."

"No." I shook my head again and stared at my reflection in my spoon. My lips looked slightly swollen from last night, and my skin was flushed. It was like even my body couldn't get rid of Thatch, no matter how many times my brain told it to stop responding.

Stop caring.

My heart thumped wildly in my chest. "You know," I said, standing and pushing my chair back, "we'll catch up later."

"Austin." Braden's jaw clenched. "Sit. Down."

It was horrible, how my body immediately responded, because it was so ingrained in me to listen, to be a good girl.

The minute my butt hit the chair, I popped right back up, grabbed my purse, and left.

I ran.

Away from him.

Away from the man who'd emotionally abused me.

And away from the memories that always made me feel like less of a person.

The really sad part?

I'd replaced Braden with someone just as bad.

Thatch was no better.

Braden wanted me, but he was like a poison to my heart and soul; I would be miserable with him.

Thatch wanted sex—not me—and yet I was drawn to him, to all of him. He wanted me probably about as much as he wanted to catch a cold—he proved that much this morning.

Shoulders slumping, I walked slowly to my car, got in, and banged my head against the steering wheel.

The only positive in my day came later when I discovered a few more people following my blog.

I needed to finish my assignment and get the hell away from Thatch before our relationship turned into a situation where I lost myself again.

Chapter Twenty-Five

Thatch

I didn't text.

I didn't call.

I didn't chase.

Not because I didn't want to do all of those things—but because I knew that it wouldn't be enough. Austin had woken up to an empty apartment and assumed the worst—who wouldn't? But it wasn't like I wanted to tell her about my alcoholic father.

Because she'd ask questions.

And I'd tell her, because I'd been carrying all of the stress for so long; I knew it was only a matter of time before I blurted everything out.

I eyed the clock in the corner. She was supposed to come in today by two.

It was two thirty.

I closed my eyes and waited for my office door to open, and when it didn't, I went over to it and jerked it open myself, looking up and down the hall for any sign of her dark-brown hair or long legs.

Hanging my head, I was just getting ready to turn back around when I saw a flash of dark hair down the hall and then, she was walking toward me. Her face in a tight smile, her body hugged by a beautiful black wrap dress, and her chin held high.

So she was going to play it that way, huh?

Angry Austin was a thing to behold.

Fucking gorgeous.

Wild.

I had to bite my tongue to keep from charging toward her and tugging her into the closest exam room.

When she finally stopped in front of me, I pointed to my office and said, "We need to talk."

She stiffened. Hell.

"Dr. Holloway?" Mia's soft voice sounded behind me. "Your two thirty is ready for you."

I gritted my teeth together. "Be right there."

Austin's eyebrows shot up. She crossed her arms. "Well, don't keep the world waiting, Dr. Holloway." I hated that the way she said my name affected me so much, physically and emotionally.

"Come on." I didn't give her a chance to argue. Besides, she needed stuff for her blog? She was in for a wild ride with this client.

Miranda had been a patient at the practice for about ten years, and every year, there was just one more thing she thought she needed done, no matter how many times any of us told her she didn't.

I opened the door and swept in. "Miranda, this is Austin Rogers. She's a local grad student shadowing me. Will it be alright for her to listen in on our appointment?"

Miranda smiled. Her face was shot to hell with fillers—ones that Troy had no doubt given her and charged an arm and a leg for since I refused to give her any more. "Of course, that's lovely."

Miranda was a gorgeous woman, but few of her parts were still natural, and with her pushing seventy, it worried me to put her under the knife again. Surgery became riskier and riskier the older the patient.

"So, what did you want to discuss?" I pulled out a seat.

Miranda wasn't a typical appointment. She didn't come in for a regular consult. Rather, she came in and asked me to basically look at her from head to toe and tell her where I thought adjustments should be made, and ever since I had first seen her two years ago and got the lowdown from Troy on her past, I would tell her, *You're perfect, go eat a cookie.*

"A breast augmentation, maybe some Botox?" She actually blushed. "Remember a few weeks ago when I came in for a consult and . . ." She glanced at Austin, then back at me, her jet-black curly hair bouncing on her shoulders with the movements. "Troy said that I could benefit from a few things, and I just . . . I wanted a second opinion."

I sighed. "You don't need to worry about me telling him that you used me as a second opinion, and since I have Austin in here, there's no need to grab one of my nurses. Why don't you show me what you're talking about, hmm?"

What followed was a painfully long hour filled by me convincing her she didn't need anything done, and her arguing with me over what my partner had said.

"Listen." I rubbed my tired eyes with the back of my hand. "All I'm saying is that surgically, your breasts don't need the lift. If you need it emotionally in order to feel better, that's an entirely different thing, alright?"

She left.

Thank God.

But that meant the next two appointments were going to run into each other.

Austin didn't say anything as I breezed by her; she just followed, damn it. I was itching to talk to her, to explain myself, to do anything, and the worst part? Every time I made eye contact with her, her stare back was so hollow, I wanted to punch something.

Mia walked by us, handed Austin two granola bars and me a folder, and winked.

She deserved a raise.

I devoured the bar, knocked on the door, and introduced myself, and in that moment, knew I was absolutely, completely screwed.

Austin's mom stared back at us wide-eyed and then blushed bright red. "Austin?"

"Mom?"

Oh look! Hell!

Chapter Twenty-Six

Austin

My mom.

In Thatch's office.

Why was my mom in Thatch's office? Why was this happening? Had I just walked into an alternate universe, one where my mom used words like "nipple"?

I loved my mom, don't get me wrong, but, this?

Did Dad know?

As far as I was concerned, she'd never even discussed a boob job or anything like it. Besides, her boobs, unlike mine, were basically perfect, like every part of her!

I closed my mouth and shared a horrified look with Thatch, who looked like he was ready to puke, though I wasn't sure why. It was his job! And it wasn't like he was touching his own mom's boobs.

Too far, Austin. Too far.

"What are you doing here?" Mom and I said at the same time.

"Austin's shadowing me for one of her classes," Thatch answered, saving me from having to explain myself. I would not be thankful for the save. I would not let his kindness in this moment minimize his rejection this morning.

Spine straightening, I faced my mom. "So? Why are you here?"

"I um—" She looked panicked. "A—" The look she shared with Thatch wasn't normal. "A breast implant."

"Implants, you mean?" I corrected. "Not that Thatch can't just stuff one for you, but I'm pretty sure Dad would have something to say about you being lopsided in pictures."

Mom's strained laugh wasn't normal, not at all.

What the heck was going on?

Thatch grabbed her clipboard and then shielded it from my face, before pulling the top sheet off and shoving it into his front pocket. "So, from what I've read, you want to get small implants with a lift?"

Mom nodded.

"And this lift . . . is for . . . yourself? Your husband?"

Mom was silent and then said, "Of course. Both!"

"Right." Thatch clenched his teeth. "Well, let's see what we're working with."

Yeah, that wasn't normally how he did things.

I frowned. Why was he being so unprofessional? Maybe because he knew my mom, or at least had met her a few times when we dated? Regardless, she swallowed and then nodded to me. "Do I just—take off my shirt?"

I smiled. "Mom, relax, Thatch is really good at what he does." Thatch didn't look at me. "I mean, you know, when he goes to work sober and decides not to fondle your breasts for a little too long because he forgets he's supposed to be measuring things, or like that one time when he accidently gave someone a thripple."

My mom knew I was kidding. She laughed.

Meanwhile Thatch looked like he was ready to strangle me. "Amazing you even know what a thripple is, since you can't even say the word 'nipple' without blushing."

"Nipple," I blurted. "What's so hard about that?" I emphasized the word "hard" and glanced down at his crotch, my eyebrows lifting a bit as if to say, *Aw, poor baby can't even get it up?*

Mom let out a little squeak. "You know, I think I've changed my mind."

"Stay." I was still staring at Thatch. "Maybe he'll give it to you for free. After all, he did technically sleep with one of his patients, right Thatch? Wouldn't want that getting out." I was bluffing, but I was pissed and probably didn't realize how pissed I was until that moment.

"Bullshit!" he roared. "You aren't even a real patient!"

"I signed papers!" I fired back.

"You know." Mom grabbed her purse. "I think I'll just wait until later. Austin, I'll see you at home. Thatch." She waved and then closed the door behind her.

"What the hell is wrong with you?" Thatch yelled. "Do you realize that I can get fired for what you said?"

"Please!" I rolled my eyes. "It was my mom, and she wants a boob job about just as bad as she wants a third leg!"

"You'd be surprised why your mom wants what she wants."

"Oh well, that's cryptic, and you suddenly know so much about my family?"

His face paled again.

"Whatever, I'm leaving." I stomped out of the exam room and nearly lost an arm as Thatch jerked me toward his office and slammed the door behind us.

Chapter Twenty-Seven

Thatch

"I didn't leave you," I said hoarsely. "So stop taking your anger out on everyone else! I wouldn't do that to you."

"But you did," she argued. "I woke up alone!"

I ran my hands through my hair and tried to think of a way to explain without giving her all the details. "This morning, I didn't leave the building. I wasn't abandoning you or trying to get out of the awkward morning-after part where you wonder if you're going to get more sex or if the person's going to make a run for it."

She sighed and looked down at the ground. "Well, aren't you curious which it would have been?"

"Yes." My body ached for hers.

"Too bad." She marched over toward the door and placed her hand on the knob. "If you didn't leave the building, where were you?"

"Does it really matter? I didn't leave you."

"It matters to the girl you slept with and then abandoned most of the night, yes."

"I was with you until five o'clock this morning."

"Did you want a prize for cuddling?" she countered.

"Are you handing them out?" I tried joking.

She glared.

I held up my hands. "If you must know, I was across the hall."

Confusion marred her angry features. "Okay," she said, drawing out the word. "Doing what? Borrowing a cup of sugar? Pancake mix? What?"

I scratched my head. "My neighbor came home drunk, he was banging on all the doors, and he'd given me a spare key for emergencies, because sometimes . . ." Think, Thatch, think. "Sometimes I water his plants and feed his dog."

Her eyes narrowed. "And both the plants and dog are still alive?"

"Very funny."

"So you helped him into his apartment." She put her hands on her hips. I could tell she was mulling over the information to see if I was being honest or just trying to get out of trouble.

"I swear." I took a step toward her. "The last thing I wanted to do at five in the morning was leave my bed, with you sleeping in it."

She nodded, exhaling a breath that she must have been holding in. Austin leaned her body against the door and broke off all eye contact. "If I ask you a question, will you be completely honest with me?"

"Yes." Depends on the question. Please don't ask about my family, and don't tell me about yours.

"Have I gained weight?"

Yeah, so not what I was expecting. "What?"

"Weight." Her eyes locked on mine. "Have I gained weight?"

"Where is this coming from?" I had a sneaking suspicion I knew—her father valued the illusion of perfection above all else. How ironic that the world around him was crumbling, and he had no freaking clue.

"Nothing, never mind, you answered already." She reached for the door again, getting it only about an inch open before I slammed it closed and turned the lock.

"Hell no." I placed my hands on her hips and turned her toward me. "Look at me."

Slowly she tilted her chin up.

"I wouldn't change a thing about you."

Her lower lip wobbled.

"No, you haven't gained weight, Austin, but if you had? Who the hell cares? Life is about living, it's about being happy, and if you want extra dessert, eat the extra fucking dessert, alright? It's not like I don't know about your MoonPie stash or the fact that your drink of choice is Mountain Dew over wine. In fact, I bet you even had some this morning—it's your thing when you get stressed, and it's okay." A tear slid down her cheek; I wiped it away with my thumb. "Do you hear what I'm saying to you? It's okay. You're beautiful because you're you. Don't let a size define perfection, when it's your heart that I love the most."

Love.

Hell.

I just said love.

I didn't mean to.

I meant it.

I didn't mean to say it.

Out loud.

Her eyes widened just a fraction before she crushed her mouth against mine—and I just.

Lost.

It.

I was overcome with a swell of rightness when her mouth moved over mine, and—as much as logic told me I needed to push her the hell away—my body refused to listen, just like my brain, and my heart, the useless vessel she'd owned the minute she weaseled her way into my life and refused to back down even when I was a complete jackass to her.

An electric current of lust pulsed between us as I tugged at her knit dress, exposing her breasts; my tongue dipped and swirled inside her mouth, welcoming a deeper kiss—needing more of her as I wrestled off the rest of her dress and left it as a pool on the floor.

Chest heaving, I pulled away from her briefly to catch my breath, to see if this was still okay—what we were doing.

But she clawed at my back and kept thrusting her tongue inside my mouth like she was going to die if I stopped kissing her.

So I didn't.

It wasn't really an option for us anymore.

Quitting.

Walking away.

God knew it was the best option—it just meant I finally had to come clean, and I was so damn afraid that if I told her the truth, she really would walk away on her own accord and destroy me in the process.

I sucked in a greedy inhale of her skin like a complete lunatic; I could have sworn my testosterone was kicking into such high gear that I was ready to explode on the spot from a simple make-out session. It had always been that way with Austin, though—complete sexual madness.

"I've always wanted you naked in my office," I confessed, walking her back toward my desk.

"Interesting." She gave me a coy smile. "Since I've always wanted to do this!" She pushed off a stapler and my phone.

"Wow, don't go too wild," I teased.

"Well, I knew you'd have to clean it up, so . . ." She shrugged and then grabbed me by the neck and skimmed my lips with her tongue before opening her mouth up to me.

I took full advantage of her vulnerability, straddling her against the desk and slowly turning her around. I bent her forward and tugged her ear with my teeth. "Is this okay?"

"No, it's horrible, please stop," she panted in a raspy voice. "It's more than okay."

I slid her palms forward, pressing them flat against the surface of my desk before I quickly unbuttoned my jeans and freed myself.

My body throbbed as I strained toward her. The view of her ass was out of this world, her skin pulsing beneath my hands as I jerked her against my body and thrust deep inside.

Austin slammed her hands against the desk, arching her body back as I pulled almost completely out, then pumped into her again, unable to control the possessive urge to claim her—in my office—to mark her and show her that I wasn't ever letting her go—no matter the cost.

"Thatch—"

I silenced her with another thrust and cupped her breasts, my blood pounding in my ears as I felt her body respond.

"Dr. Holloway?" It was Mia on the other side of the door.

I ignored her.

"Dr. Holloway?"

"Son of a bitch," I muttered, and then yelled, "One minute."

"I'd say at least three," came Austin's response.

I nuzzled her neck and slowed my thrusts, our bodies moving in sync with each other, her eyes closed as her head fell back against my chest. "Just like that."

"Like this?" I swiveled my hips and kissed her below her ear, then peppered kisses down her jaw as I continued to move inside her—I would never get enough of her, of this feeling.

I was in too deep.

Figuratively.

Literally.

"Dr. Holloway?"

"Fire her," Austin moaned. "I'm so close."

"Well, in that case . . ." I started to pull away.

"Don't you dare!" she hissed. "I'll slit your tires again and get you a pet frog."

"Oh look, my erection's gone," I joked, my tongue teasing her ear as I pulled completely out and flipped her around, pulling her leg around my waist and entering her again, our gazes locked.

There was still so much fear in her eyes.

Fear I'd put there.

"You're beautiful." I kissed her forehead and felt her body come apart around mine.

"Dr. Holloway!"

"Coming," I said through clenched teeth while Austin burst out laughing.

"This is a business establishment, Doctor." Austin cupped my face with her hands and pressed a tender kiss to my lips. "I love you."

"What?" All the air left the room. "What did you just say?"

Tears filled her eyes. "I love you."

Tell her.

Tell her, damn it!

"I love you too." I shoved the guilty voice away.

Later.

I'd tell her later.

Because the last thing I wanted was to ruin the moment.

The moment I did the one thing I'd sworn I'd never do.

Fall in love.

And allow myself to be vulnerable to heartache. But quitting her? It was impossible, I'd learned that in a few short weeks.

And now, the thought of her walking away felt like a crack in the chest.

"Say it again." I kissed her deeply, tasted her.

"I love you," she whispered against my lips.

Chapter Twenty-Eight

Austin

"So I'm just going to come out and ask." Avery's eyes narrowed in on me and Thatch as we sat across from her and Lucas, holding hands and basically groping each other under the table. "Are you guys together?"

"Clearly they're sleeping together. Austin's neck has ten hickies. Who gives hickies anymore?" Lucas frowned into his glass. "Sucking on someone's skin, not natural; now, sucking on a woman's—"

Avery shoved a piece of bread into his mouth. "Hungry?"

With narrowed eyes, he pulled half of it out and chewed. "Starving."

"That's what I thought." Her deep blush said more than I'd like to know about my best friend and the guy sharing her bed, but whatever. Lucas Thorn wasn't a cheater anymore, and I was happy for them, especially now that I had Thatch back.

I shivered in response.

I'd spent the last week in his bed.

A full week of bliss where we argued over who made the coffee in the morning and which late-night TV show to watch. It was bliss.

It was exactly as it should be.

And I should be happy.

I was happy.

Except.

I still didn't know why he'd cheated and why he'd dumped me, and I felt like a dog with a bone, just chewing and chewing and chewing away at the stupid thing, hoping that once I finished it, I'd have the answers I needed.

But did I really need the answers?

He said he loved me.

Thatch's magical hand slid up my thigh, his fingers dipping beneath the edge of my skirt.

My lips parted as the warmth of his hand met with my skin in a way that probably should have been illegal.

"You're flushed," Avery pointed out. "It's not even hot in here." She tapped her chin. "Hands where I can see them."

"Move your hand, I kill you," I said out of the corner of my mouth.

Thatch smirked while Lucas gave him a nod of approval.

"What have you done to my best friend?" Avery threw her hands into the air. "She's two bad choices away from getting arrested for public indecency!"

"Nothing wrong with that," Thatch grumbled.

"There is everything wrong with prison time, my friend," Avery said seriously. "So, now that we've lured you guys out of your sex dungeon long enough to have a normal human conversation—how did this happen?"

I opened my mouth to say something, when Thatch interrupted. "It just did, why do you need all the gory details?"

Avery blinked at him, then at me. "Is this one for real?" She shook her head. "I'm a woman. It's what we do, we want the details."

Thatch groaned. "I'm going to grab another drink." He kissed the top of my head. "You need anything?"

"Nope." I smiled up at him and then stared at his amazing ass as he walked away.

"He's not a piece of meat, Austin," Lucas ground out.

"He forehead kisses." Avery sighed into her drink.

Lucas looked between us. "That's a thing?"

We both nodded.

Lucas's frown deepened. "Unbelievable, and yet another urban legend is proven correct. I always thought women assumed the forehead kiss meant friendship."

"It means"—Avery rolled her eyes—"that he cares. It's a tender kiss rather than a possessive alpha kiss of passion." She coughed out his name into her hand and then smiled sweetly.

"You love my kisses of passion." And like he needed to prove he was a legend, Lucas kissed her across the mouth, leaving Avery all flushed and dewy skinned.

I made a gagging sound.

They ignored me as they always did.

There must have been a long line at the bar. I glanced over at Thatch and nearly passed out when I saw my dad standing next to him.

"Mayday!" I jumped out of my chair and made a beeline for Thatch. He was pale, so pale. Shoot, my dad was probably talking all about the race again.

The race I basically told the entire city of Seattle that Thatch was competing in—with the mayor, and a doctor at his office.

Whoops?

I had been angry!

It was revenge!

And now it was time to save him. "Thatch!" I wrapped an arm around his waist. "Daddy, how are you?"

Dad pointed to his cheek. I went over and kissed his scruff and pulled back, frowning. He smelled . . . different.

Not like himself.

Then again, he was always with lots of people.

I shrugged and waited for him to answer.

"I'm good." Dad looked between us. "I'm surprised to see you two back together after . . . everything." His eyes narrowed.

"Dad." I patted his shoulder. "We're adults."

"That you are." His expression changed. "Thatch, I'll see you later, think about what I said."

"I will, sir." Thatch looked ready to commit murder.

"Hey?" I cupped his face with my hands and forced him to look down at me. "Is everything okay?"

"No." He swallowed slowly. "But it will be."

He kissed me, pressing my body against the bar top so roughly that a sharp pain hit me in the back from the barstool.

When I pulled away for a breath, I asked, "What did you guys talk about?"

"Riding," Thatch blurted, and then his eyes did that sexy smolder thing that had the entire world fading away around me.

"What kind of riding?" I licked his taste from my lips.

"The kind you're really good at." His body pressed me against the bar top again, his hips driving into mine.

"Oh?" I felt myself get hot and bothered. How was it possible that all it took was a look from this man, and I was ready to melt into a puddle on the floor?

"Yeah." He pulled back and winked. "Though I think this time you'll need a helmet."

"Wait, huh?" My mouth dropped open. "What kind of kinky crap are you talking about?"

"Spandex." He shivered. "At any rate, I really do need to learn how to ride a bike, I promised your dad I'd go on a ride with him sometime, and since I'm dating his daughter and don't want him to think I'm a dirty little liar, or worse, just trying to get into his good graces, I figure I'd better man up and get down to business."

"Well"—I took his hand in mine—"at least you have someone to help."

"One condition." He tugged me into his body. "No Dora."

"But she's an explorer!" I argued. "And the bike comes with a fanny pack."

His eyes narrowed.

I grinned. "Admit it, the flashlight inside the fanny pack was cool, and how nice that she's helping you learn Spanish at the exact same time!"

"You're impossible."

"You love me," I fired back, still breathless at his admission. "So it's Dora with the training wheels, and then when you don't run into a mailbox, we'll talk."

"Fine," he grumbled. "But no pictures."

"Deal." I held out my hand; he shook it. "You never said video."

With a groan, he tugged my hand hard enough to press me tightly against his chest, and our mouths fused.

And I just knew—this was forever, me and Thatch, and nothing would ever stand in the way of a future with him. Nothing.

Chapter Twenty-Nine

Thatch

The paper from my office was burning a hole in my pocket.

The paper on which Austin's mom had written her cell number and circled it a few hundred times.

I suspected that she wanted to know what I knew.

Which was a hell of a lot.

But I wasn't going to say anything.

Maybe I had it wrong; maybe she was seeing how it was possible that I wasn't saying anything to Austin or going to the press. Then again, I could be wrong about every damn thing and her mother didn't even know.

Hell.

Cheating.

You don't cheat by accident; your dick doesn't just slip into another woman, the same way a woman doesn't trip over her own feet and lock lips with another man.

Damn it.

I didn't call the number.

Austin was snoring lightly next to me. She was the only good part of all of this, and I had to trust that she loved me enough to weather any kind of storm.

I lay awake, staring up at the ceiling, my thoughts going back to that night when I realized my parents weren't who I thought they were.

◆ ◆ ◆

"Hello?" I tossed my keys onto the kitchen counter and frowned. My dad was supposed to meet Mom at the house and take her out for their anniversary, but shocker, he couldn't make it, so as a nice surprise, I decided to take her out for a meal. It was the least I could do. "Mom?"

I moved through the dark house.

Toward the back bedroom.

The light crept underneath the door. There was soft music playing and then, a noise that sounded a hell of a lot like sex.

I almost didn't open the door.

I wish I hadn't.

But I was young, and stupid.

Only nineteen, I'd just moved out of the house; the world was my oyster and life was good—my family was rich, my parents were paying for my undergrad, and I was going to change the world by following in my father's footsteps.

Seriously.

I wanted for nothing.

And I had no idea what the real world was like—had no idea that the reality of human existence meant pain.

I pushed the door open.

And saw my mom riding our lawn guy.

Reverse cowboy.

"Mom." I was too numb to walk out, to run away.

"Thatcher!" she yelled, and tried to cover up her body. "Where . . . ? I thought . . . ?" Her eyes clouded with tears. "Your father, he was supposed to be here . . ."

"But he'd see!" I yelled. "He would see this!"

She was silent.

And then it occurred to me.

That was her plan all along.

To hurt him.

Like he was hurting her.

He'd been cheating on her all my life.

But I never—never thought my mom would stoop to his level, to cheat on him back, to try to make him hurt so much. I never thought that she would be hell-bent on revenge in her quest to take him down—hurting me in the process.

"Thatcher . . ." Her voice was wobbly. "I'm so sorry, sweetheart, it's not what it looks like, it's only been a few times and—"

"Stop!" I yelled, backing up. "Just stop!"

I cut my parents off that very day.

Our family couldn't survive their selfishness. And I was the collateral damage.

I took out student loans and supported myself.

And didn't look back.

◆ ◆ ◆

"Thatch?" Austin's voice sounded in my dream. I blinked my eyes open at her worried expression. "Are you okay?"

"Of course," I lied. My heart was hammering against my chest, and I felt like I was going to break down any minute. They say the past always comes back to haunt you if you don't deal with it.

"You were yelling," Austin whispered. "Talk to me."

I wanted to.

It was on the tip of my tongue to blurt it all out—but it would destroy our happy moment, I just knew it. Sharing any part of that would be too much, and she'd be done with me.

And I wasn't sure I could emotionally handle having another woman I cared about hurt me—or what was worse, another woman that I loved not fighting for what we shared together.

"Go back to sleep." I reached up and kissed her forehead, my lips lingering on her skin before I flipped her onto her back and searched her eyes for permission.

"Whatever you need," she whispered, reaching up for me.

Her. I needed her.

I was just afraid that I was going to lose her.

That was it.

It was fear talking.

Nothing more.

Yeah, I was a shit liar.

Especially when it came to lying to myself.

I was inside her within minutes, driving away my demons the only way I knew how—sex.

Chapter Thirty

Thatch

"Let me get this straight." Lucas pointed at my black eye. "A panther ran out in front of you and you crashed a bike."

I bit out a curse. "Yes."

"A bike with training wheels?"

"Yes." Clenching my teeth hurt like hell.

"And this"—he held up fake air quotes—"'panther' escaped from the zoo."

"YES!" I yelled. "Look, all I'm saying is, I was having a nice leisurely training session with Austin, and she had to go to class, so I thought then why not practice on my own? So I grabbed my helmet—"

Lucas choked on his coffee.

"Whatever, why am I even defending myself right now?"

"A lot of good that helmet did. You still managed to get a black eye."

"I fell against the handlebars!" I showed him with my hands, not that it was helping. Swear it really was a panther or the largest cat I'd ever seen in my entire existence. "And you're a jackass—why did I even call you?"

"Oh, I don't know, because I'm one of the only ones who wouldn't make fun of you and take pictures?"

"You got out of the car with your phone already trained on me, and then asked how to do a live feed."

He grinned. "Look, it's not that bad, and I'm glad that in your moment of need, you know, mid–panther attack, you called me, not Austin."

"She's in class," I grumbled. And after sleeping like shit the night before, I'd decided to take the morning off. I cleared my schedule, hoping it would clear my head.

"Well, since the panther isn't anywhere to be seen . . ." Lucas stood, put on his sunglasses. "Should we go get lunch?"

"Fine." I started walking after him.

"Nope." He shook his head. "Helmet off, dude."

I rolled my eyes. "Hell, I may need it with the way you drive."

He flipped me off as I put the stupid Dora bike away in Austin's parents' garage and hopped into Lucas's car.

My car was back at my apartment, since I'd ridden with Austin and had planned on "practicing all morning."

I sent off a quick text that I'd crashed and was going to go day drink my sorrows away, knowing she probably wouldn't believe me, since I'd cleared my schedule for the rest of the day.

"So . . ." Lucas tapped his fingers against the steering wheel. "How's everything going with Austin?"

"Good." Just stick with short answers, nothing personal. I was too worried that he'd say something to Avery and it would get back to Austin.

"Interesting. Tell me more."

I gave him a look of disgust. "It's none of your damn business."

"You kissed another woman, broke up with Austin, then ignored her for a month, and now suddenly, what? You've had a change of heart?"

"What if I have?"

Lucas whistled. "Look, I've known you a long time. You don't do commitment, you sure as hell don't do relationships, and I've seen you do things with multiple women, multiple times, and not tire out."

I spit out a curse.

"The point is that suddenly you're . . . what? Settling down? Throwing around the *L* word?"

"Yes." I gulped past the giant baseball in my throat. "Why is that so hard to believe?"

"I'm sorry, did you black out when I was listing all your sins? Dude, a week after sleeping with her, you called me, panicked that she might want a commitment. You asked me to dump her for you."

I smiled at the memory. It had taken a week for Austin to completely consume me in a way so hellishly terrifying that the only option had been for me to break things off.

And then, I realized—I didn't want to.

It was fear talking.

Things had been perfect.

Until that night.

Hell.

It always came back to that, now, didn't it?

I was doing the right thing.

I was.

"Look," I said right before we pulled up to the little café, "all you need to know is that I love her. That's enough, right?"

He whistled. "Apparently, since you're learning how to ride a bike. If I see you adopt a frog, I'm going to be worried, man."

I laughed and then shuddered. "No, but I wouldn't say no to a dog."

He stopped walking. "But you hate pets!"

"And yet, I've taken care of you for how long?" I fired back.

"Touché," Lucas muttered under his breath as we made our way into the restaurant and sat in a corner booth. The waitress brought us menus and water.

I hadn't actually hung out with Lucas sans Avery in a long time. It was nice. Not that I didn't like Avery. I just hadn't realized how much I missed my best friend.

And baseball talk.

And everything that didn't have to deal with keeping lies and promises straight and a smile on my face even though the silence was eating me alive.

The waitress returned and took our orders and then brought us our sodas.

It was relaxing.

Just being with my best friend.

I was actually starting to relax.

The bell on the door clanged; both Lucas and I looked up.

My expression completely froze.

Lucas frowned. "Isn't that Mayor Rogers?"

"Yeah." Suddenly sick, I put down my sandwich and felt like I was going to barf.

"What the hell is he doing with your mom?"

Time froze. While I locked eyes with my best friend, my expression was a mixture of anger and irritation.

"Maybe you should start at the beginning." Lucas ran his hands through his hair.

It took me an hour to get it out.

And once it was out, I knew it was only a matter of time before my world shattered, taking Austin down with it.

Chapter Thirty-One

Austin

"I'm impressed." My professor actually said those words. They came out of his mouth, and I could have sworn he was smiling; I mean, his teeth were clenched, but the point? He said the word "impressed."

"Thank you." I grinned, feeling lighter than I had in weeks. "It's been really interesting." Images of Thatch on his knees in front of me, his hands clasped around my hips as he pressed hot kiss after hot kiss against my skin, flooded my head until a burning heat erupted like goose bumps all over my body.

"Has it, now?" He eyed me up and down. Yeah, I didn't like that look. I quickly put all images of Thatch on lockdown. The last thing I needed was for my professor to think I was hitting on him. "I have an idea of what you could do to make it better."

My eyes narrowed. If he said sleep with him, I would take an F and then punch him in the face.

Hands shaking with nerves, I put them behind my back and took a deep breath. "Okay, what's your suggestion?"

"Get one."

"I'm sorry?" A roaring sound exploded in my ears. "Get one, what?"

"A breast augmentation." He shrugged. "Imagine how many followers you would get if you blogged about it. Besides . . ." He stared at my chest longer than necessary before looking back at me. "It couldn't hurt."

It. Couldn't. Hurt.

I waited for him to say something more, rather than start organizing his papers on his desk as if expecting me to say, *Awesome, I'll get right on that.*

It couldn't hurt.

Well, something was going to hurt.

The feel of my sharp heel in his ass!

"Great suggestion." I tried to keep the venom out of my voice. "Although extremely sexual in nature, to the point where I'm pretty sure I could file a lawsuit against you and win—I'm going to have to reject that solid idea on the basis that I'm not a fan of going under the knife, and I'm happy the way I am."

The minute the words came out of my mouth.

I realized how true they were.

I was happy.

Actually happy with my body.

I smiled brightly.

My boyfriend was a plastic surgeon, he worshipped my body, he didn't tell me I had gained weight, and he encouraged me to have dessert.

He was perfect.

I'd dated guys like my professor all my life.

He and Braden would be great friends, wouldn't they?

"It was just a suggestion," he said in a clipped voice before meeting my eyes again. "You can go now."

Dismissed.

I bet if I had sex with him, I'd get an A.

Gross.

I nodded my head and made my way out the door just in time to see Satan in all his glory waiting by my car.

"Why am I not surprised to see you?" I was ten seconds away from slamming my books against Braden's face. "You're like a really, really, really, really, really—"

He sighed.

"Really," I added for effect. "Bad cold. Like the ones that kill a person dead."

"You done yet?"

"No."

"Whatever." Braden shrugged. "Your dad told me where I could find you, and we still haven't talked about the fund-raiser."

"So talk."

"It will look good for your father to have my family on his side. We have money, and money talks. All I'm saying is if you care about your father, you'll do it."

"Are you threatening me?" Who was this guy?

"No." He shrugged. "I just think that with everything going on, it would probably be best to show a united front."

"'Everything going on,' meaning the fund-raiser?"

He smirked; it was a cold look, one that chilled me to the bone. "Funny, and I thought you knew."

"Knew what?"

"Ask your boyfriend."

"How did you know I had a boyfriend?"

"Your father, how else?"

"You're not really making sense."

"I wasn't really trying to. We're going together, and that's final."

"Hmm, let me see. When hell freezes over, and even then, I think I'd rather freeze right along with it."

Braden towered over me. "You always were difficult."

"And you always were threatening."

"You'd think if you had a plastic surgeon as a boyfriend, he'd at least do you for free."

Okay, that was too many insults in one day.

I swung my arm back and punched him in the nose so hard I heard a crack.

Only it wasn't his nose.

It was my hand.

◆ ◆ ◆

"Austin!" Thatch ran into the ER, pulling back the curtain with one giant swoop. He kissed me on the mouth before I could get a word out, then lightly held my hand. "There's a lot of swelling, I can't tell if it's broken."

"You should see the other guy," I joked.

He swore as the ER doc walked in and shook his hand. "You must be Dr. Holloway, heard a lot about you." He grinned widely. "Looks like it's just a bad sprain with a pretty nasty-looking cut."

"Cut?" Thatch looked back at me. "How did you get cut?"

"I think the force behind the hit sent me to the ground, my other hand landed on a sharp rock, and it lodged itself in my skin." My lips trembled. All in all it had been a pretty traumatizing day.

Both hands hurt like the fires of hell; the knuckles on my right were all bloody and turning blue. And my left palm felt like I'd grabbed a sharp rock and had been forced to squeeze.

"Poor baby," Thatch said gently. "You're the only person I know who would actually punch someone in the face and walk away with more injuries."

I scowled.

"I'll treat her," Thatch said without looking away from me. His eyes laced with concern. "Can you release her?"

"Already done." The doc handed Thatch my papers. "I figured you'd want to do the sutures anyways, no scarring."

Thatch thanked him and then shook his head at me. "You ready for me to sew you up?"

"It sounds sexier on *Grey's Anatomy*."

He barked out a laugh. "Just call me Dr. McSteamy."

I shivered. He was way better looking, if that was even possible.

Chapter Thirty-Two

Thatch

I was just finishing up with my last patient when I got the call from Austin. I started running the minute she said "hospital." My heart had nearly stopped.

The fact that she was actually conscious and talking to me told me that she was alive, but that fear, that sinking feeling of loss, still clung to me with every step into the ER.

I felt sick to my stomach.

Nauseated.

I couldn't lose her.

Just the thought of not having her—of her even being injured—hell, it was a glorified paper cut, and I was ready to scrub in and save her life.

"Sit still," I scolded. "Or you're going to have zigzags on the side of your hand."

"Sorry," Austin hissed as I tugged the needle a bit harder, threading the sutures together. "It just feels funny."

"Don't puke," I said without looking up at her. "It's never the pain that gets people, it's the tug they feel when their skin's getting pulled and pinched together."

Austin sucked in a breath and whispered, "Yeah, I'm going to need you to stop talking."

I smirked down at my work as I made a final knot and cut the rest of the suture material. "Sorry." Not too bad, she only needed six stitches around the base of her thumb. The cut had been deep, probably from the force of her entire body landing on the sharp rock. "Well, I think you'll make a full recovery."

"I'll live?"

"As long as you don't get the hand wet," I said in a serious-as-hell voice. "So no showering, washing your hands, or eating."

"Eating?"

"Austin, we can't have you getting Mountain Dew in your cut, do you know anything? You could die!"

Eyes wide, she went completely pale. "But, but, that's how I deal with stress and—"

I burst out laughing.

She went from panicked to pissed. "You big jerk!"

"Whoa, careful there with that language." I winked.

She smacked me with her other hand, then winced and started shaking it, then blowing on it, like that was going to help.

I grinned and examined the other hand. There would be bruising, but she'd be fine. "Remember what happened last time you picked a fight."

"And I can have Mountain Dew? And take showers?"

I licked my lips and leaned in. "Sponge baths . . . but don't worry, I'll be very thorough."

"I think . . ." She met me halfway. "That you're full of shit.

"That's the drugs talking. Believe me, it's way easier if you just camp out at my place and let me take care of your . . . every . . ." I kissed her hard on the mouth. "Single . . ." Another kiss. "Need."

"You sure you can take care of all my needs?"

I gripped her ass and pulled her onto my lap, kissing her neck, inhaling her skin like a drug addict. "Pretty damn positive."

"Well . . ." Our foreheads touched. Already her breathing was picking up, her eyes having trouble focusing on mine. "I have MoonPies in my nightstand, how can you really compete with that?"

"Easy." I shrugged. "More MoonPies and a Mountain Dew trail to the fridge, where I'll stash extra chocolate milk."

She let out a little moan. "You know how I feel about chocolate milk, Thatch. Don't joke about something so serious. I may never leave your apartment."

I paused and then licked my lips. "Would you believe me if I told you that was part of my evil plan?"

Austin sighed and kissed my mouth softly. "Are you sure?"

I nodded. "I can't . . ." Shit, I needed to come clean. "I can't live without you in my life. Not only that." I gripped her face. "I don't want to."

Air whooshed out of her lungs as she kissed me hard, her body plastered against mine, her breasts sliding across my chest. I let out a moan as I returned her kiss and blocked out every single conversation I'd had with Lucas that day.

Why is he with your mom?

Why indeed.

The lie was on the tip of my tongue, but stole completely out of reach the minute my mom and the mayor grabbed each other's hands and then let go whenever someone looked at them.

One could never be too careful.

And he was starting to become careless.

I returned to the present.

To Austin.

To us.

To tomorrow.

She moaned as I started slowly dipping my right hand into the waist of her leggings.

I'll tell her tomorrow.

Chapter Thirty-Three

Thatch

"Just what do you think you're doing?" I asked a guilty-looking Austin as she drank directly from the chocolate-milk carton. She froze and then slowly put the carton on the kitchen counter and wiped her face with the back of her bandaged hand.

She had no idea how cute she was.

Or how aroused I was by just watching her drink out of the damn milk carton. The light from the fridge cast a sexy glow across her smooth skin and nest of dark hair as strands fell across her face and long neck.

She smiled, busted. "I was thirsty."

"And all the glasses were dirty?" I approached slowly, crossing my arms over my chest so I wouldn't reach for her.

Again.

Because a man needs sleep.

And ever since the day before—I'd been kissing her, taking her in the shower, and making sure that every single space in my apartment was christened with her presence.

Including the kitchen counter.

It still had remnants of chocolate sauce on parts of the granite. My blood heated at the memory.

"Yes," Austin finally answered. "Or, well, I didn't want to get another glass dirty, because I know how you hate dirty things."

"Do I?" Was she sleepwalking? When had I ever said that to her?

"Yeah." She nodded encouragingly and smiled. "You hate it when things get dirty, so much, in fact, that you have to get them clean right away."

Why the hell was I getting turned on again?

She reached inside the fridge, grabbed the chocolate sauce, and smiled.

"Austin—"

With a smirk, she held the bottle over her head and opened her mouth. I stared, slack-jawed, as she poured the chocolate syrup and gulped, only to have part of it spread down her chin and onto her white tank top, and farther into her cleavage.

Shit, it shouldn't have been hot.

It was messy as hell.

But she was right. I wanted to clean it up right away.

And yet, I couldn't look away.

My dick jumped when she licked her lips and sucked chocolate off her thumb, only to eye me up and down and say, "Want some?"

"Sure." I uncrossed my arms and made my way over to her, but when she handed me the bottle, I pushed it away and licked the sauce off her chin, moving down to her chest. Then I jerked her shirt over her head, sucking each nipple until she started panting.

"I didn't get chocolate there."

"My eyes were closed—I just wanted to be sure," I whispered hoarsely against her skin. "Look, more chocolate." I moved down her stomach and tugged her shorts to the floor.

She shivered. "Okay, now I know you're full of it, I didn't get chocolate anywhere near my—"

I licked, then I sucked until I could have sworn she orgasmed against my lips. "You were saying?"

"I was wrong." And then she was putting chocolate on her fingers and spreading it wherever she wanted me to kiss.

"A map, how thoughtful." I licked each spot.

"I'm a helper like that. Just think of me like your own personal compass."

I laughed against her skin, the vibrations making my lips buzz with each kiss and movement of my tongue.

"I love your mouth," she admitted, knees shaking together. "It's the perfect mouth, have I told you that before? I may build a shrine—and here we worship Thatch's lips, king of—"

"And here"—I flicked her with my tongue—"I worship yours."

"Clever."

I sucked harder. "Yeah, I thought so."

Her ragged breathing was making it impossible to think straight as I gripped her by the hips and stood, then kicked my boxer briefs down and off while she wiggled against me.

"I don't think I'll ever get enough of you," I groaned.

"Are you filing an official complaint?"

"Yes. And I'm charging you with making me lose sleep. Again. Death by chocolate . . ."

"Chocolate should always give orgasms, Thatch. You're a doctor, you should know these things."

"Yes, how silly of me to forget about that chapter during med school."

"That's why I'm here." She reached up with sticky hands and tugged my head down to her mouth. She tasted like chocolate and heat. "Take me."

"With pleasure," I growled, sinking into her heat and pushing away every shred of guilt I still felt whenever I took more of her—without dealing with the giant lie that separated us.

"Love you," she breathed against my neck as I moved within her. "So much, Thatch."

"I love you too." God, I was such a bastard. "No matter what."

I added that last part for myself.

Chapter Thirty-Four

Austin

Things were going too well.

And suddenly, that morning, I had that weird feeling where I could almost taste the tension in the air. Something felt wrong as I got ready for my last class to turn in my final assignment and found Thatch gone. I got the sense that the universe was shifting again and not in my favor.

It was the same feeling I'd had the night of our breakup.

He never left before me.

Except for that one time when he was helping his neighbor.

Concerned, I sent him a quick text and checked the time. The last thing I needed was to get docked points for being late to my final class, even though I'd completely killed that assignment.

Five hundred people had started following my journey into plastic surgery—though I think most of it had to do with Thatch just being that good-looking. I'd have been addicted to the blog too—and Thatch being Thatch, he didn't care that I added pictures of him to a few of the posts, as long as patients weren't part of them.

No text back.

I eyed the orange juice on the counter and took a swig.

Still cold.

So he couldn't have left that long ago, right?

Shrugging it off, I grabbed my backpack and keys and made sure to lock up the apartment.

I was so lost in my thoughts that I nearly ran into a man coming up the stairs. His eyes were bloodshot, and his hair was thinning near his very deep widow's peak.

"Oh, sorry." I smiled sheepishly. "I didn't see you."

He snorted and then looked at the door I had just come out of. "You another of his one-night stands?"

Bristling, I fought to keep myself from yelling at a stranger and said in a chipper voice, "Actually, I'm his girlfriend."

"Girlfriend." He crossed his arms. He smelled like whiskey and cigarettes. "He broke up with his girlfriend a few weeks ago."

And what? Got drunk with his neighbor and told him?

"Yeah, that's me." I nodded and backed away slowly. "Well anyway, have a great day."

The man snorted. "Haven't had a good day since that bitch ruined my life."

"Alright then." I waved. "Well, I'm sorry about that."

His eyes were furious. "You should be."

Okay, I needed either to get the hell out of there or call the cops.

"I have mace," I whispered, my hand on my cell phone screen just ready to swipe and dial 911.

He barked out a laugh and then another. "Don't judge a book by its cover, sweetheart. This"—he pointed at himself—"is your future, especially if you marry Thatch."

Yeah, I officially hated Thatch's neighbor.

"Sounds lovely," I said in a sarcastic tone.

His eyes narrowed. "You don't know shit. Then again, I imagine he's just waiting to drop the bomb on you like he did me—now look at me!" He flailed his arms wide. "Woke up in my own vomit."

"This has been a really great conversation, but I need to go." I backed away toward the door and then made a run for it down the street to my car. Once I got inside, I locked my doors with shaking hands and dialed Thatch's number.

It went straight to voice mail.

I started the car and headed toward campus, thankful that I could at least focus on something, no matter how irritating, instead of the creepy next-door neighbor.

I shuddered again and quickly turned off my car, then made a mad dash toward the business building.

Only to find a note on the door:

Email me your final thoughts on your project, what you learned, and how you can apply it, by five thirty this evening. Professor Asshole. Fine, so it didn't say "Asshole"; I added that part.

Ugh. Creepy run-in with the neighbor, and all for nothing. I could have slept in! Drunk all of Thatch's chocolate milk and then overanalyzed our relationship!

With a grimace, I stomped back to my car, got in, and checked my phone.

Still nothing from Thatch.

Should I be worried?

It just wasn't like him.

Not at all.

Finally, a bit of desperation kicked in and I called his office.

Mia answered in her usual cheerful voice. "Seattle Plastics, how may I direct your call?"

"Hey, Mia." I chewed my thumbnail. "It's Austin Rogers. Has Dr. Holloway come in yet?"

"I haven't seen him." I could picture her bright smile as she checked his calendar. "Looks like he doesn't have any appointments until this afternoon."

I sighed.

"Oh, wait!" The tap-tap of her fingernails was driving me a bit batty. "He did mention something about brunch when he called in this morning to double-check his one o'clock."

I swallowed the dryness in my throat. "Did, um, did he say where?"

"I wrote it down." She cleared her throat. "The Downtown Fifth Street Bistro, you know it?"

"Yeah." My stomach clenched. I knew it alright. It was one of my mom's favorite places to escape to, especially now that she was in the limelight so much. She loved the intimate atmosphere, and it was really dimly lit.

"Thanks, Mia!" I hung up and checked my phone.

Brunch.

But it was still a bit early for brunch. Maybe he meant to surprise me and just hadn't texted yet? Regardless, I really needed to grab some more clothes from my parents' place.

Decision made, I drove the short distance to my house, expecting it to be empty.

Instead, my dad was home.

He was never home this late in the morning.

"Hey, Dad." I walked in and tossed my keys on the table. "Everything okay?"

His shirt looked ruffled, and his eyes were a bit distant. "Is it true?"

"Huh?"

"Are you going to keep dating Thatch Holloway? I thought it wasn't serious?"

Taken aback, I didn't answer right away. Why did it matter? "Look, if this is about Braden—"

"Well, it damn well will be about Braden."

"Dad!" I never raised my voice at him. "What's going on?"

"Are you." He stood to his full height. "Dating him?"

"Well, yeah," I finally said. "I love him."

My dad's eyes widened a fraction of an inch before a cruel smile passed over his features. "I'm sure you think you do, but, honey, these things, they pass."

"Love? Passes?" I shook my head. "Are you even listening to yourself?"

"Are you?"

"Dad, what's this really about?"

"He's not good news," my dad said coldly. "I'm sure by now you know the whole story, his drunken father, his mom—"

"Whoa!" I held up my hands. "That's none of my business, and it's none of yours either!"

"Oh?" His eyes were like ice. Why was he acting this way? And what did it have to do with Thatch?

"You'll see for yourself. Love just opens you up to pain, and then, when you allow yourself to finally believe that everything's going to be okay, a bomb drops."

"Is this about Mom?"

"Your mom?" Dad repeated, his eyes a bit crazed. "Of course it is!"

"Do you want to talk about it?"

"She's cheating on me!" Dad shouted.

I gasped and covered my hands with my face. "Are you sure?"

He broke eye contact. "She hasn't been home."

"So you don't know for sure?"

"A cheater knows a cheater," Dad said in a hoarse whisper.

"Wait, back up, are you saying—"

Dad shrugged. "I'm not saying anything."

"But you just—"

"Austin!" He yelled my name, causing me to stumble away from the barstool. He never raised his voice at me. "Just do yourself a favor and break up with that boy before you get hurt."

"But I love him."

Dad nodded. "Does he love you?"

"YES!" Now it was my turn to yell. "Of course he does!"

"Have you met his parents?"

I gulped. "Well, no, but he's really private about family stuff."

"Uh-huh." Dad scratched his head. "And the reason you guys originally broke up? He just happened to have a change of heart?"

"Yes."

"And you still haven't met his parents?"

Why was he repeating himself? "His parents have nothing to do with this!"

"Oh, honey." Dad's smile was unpleasant. "I sometimes forget how young you are. Why, you're just a girl."

A girl.

Thatch said he wanted a woman.

My eyes stung with unshed tears.

That had been weeks ago.

And he'd only said it to be mean.

Right?

He said I was perfect.

Beautiful.

I couldn't stay in that house any longer. I left without saying another word, without grabbing any more clothes, and drove blindly toward the bistro downtown.

He was just having brunch.

Probably with Lucas.

They had bro dates all the time.

It was totally fine.

Everything was completely fine.

With a deep breath, I tugged open the door to the small restaurant and searched the sparse tables for him.

Sure enough.

In the back corner.

He was sitting, sipping coffee, his expression worried.

And then, a woman placed her hand on his; he squeezed it and hung his head; she stood and kissed him on the freaking forehead.

I let out a little gasp.

Just as the woman turned around and paled.

My mom.

And suddenly everything clicked into place.

He wanted the older version of me.

He wanted a woman.

She'd come to see him at his office!

Was I the way in?

Or just in the way?

Nothing made sense.

And in my pain and confusion, I turned on my heel and ran.

Past my car, down the street, in the rain, until the water from the sky mixed with my tears, and I cried until I had nothing left.

Chapter Thirty-Five

Thatch

That morning, I had left a sleeping Austin in my bed.

My warm bed.

She glowed, like an angel, her hair spread across the pillows while her arm was tucked under her head. She was peaceful, like she didn't have a care in the world. The last thing I wanted to do was leave.

God, I hated my life most days, but what was worse? The drama was so completely unnecessary! Dealing with our parents' messes was like babysitting grown children.

Austin's mom had given me a note with her phone number.

It sure as hell wasn't a booty call.

It was desperation.

And I'd refused to answer until last night.

Until I'd made love to Austin one last time, knowing that I couldn't truly love her if I kept parts of myself from her—parts of the truth from her.

So early that morning, I called her mom and told her to name a place. Not because I wanted to air out all the dirty laundry but because she deserved to know the truth about her husband.

And my mother.

Pain sliced through my chest. In all the scenarios I'd been faced with, I'd always chosen to protect myself, because I was selfish.

Until Austin.

And then everything was about protecting her from the truth.

And making sure she was okay.

But now I was in too deep.

And my father's threats were empty.

He said he'd kill himself if it got out in the open. He said that dating Austin was dangerous—it linked our families too closely together—he said it was only a matter of time before the news caught wind of it, ruined my career, and made us a laughingstock. He said it would destroy Austin in the worst possible way, just like how he and my mom destroyed our family.

And I believed him.

I believed him when he said it would all turn to hell.

I believed him when he said I was saving Austin by pushing her away.

Because it made sense.

And I'd been afraid.

So damn afraid about how I felt for her.

Afraid of what I would do for her.

Afraid of what she would do for me.

Afraid of what the information would do to us.

I wasn't her savior.

I was a coward.

"End it." Those had been his words months ago when he moved in across the hall, looking like hell had run him over and then done it again for good measure.

I lost my dad first.

But eventually, I lost them both.

And a part of me wondered if I wasn't destined to hurt those I loved, just like my parents.

A part of me believed him when he said I was just like him.

That was why I'd kissed Brooke.

Truth.

I was angry.

I was in too deep.

And I wanted to hurt Austin—to push her away from the clusterfuck that was our families.

She had no idea of what our parents were up to.

And I hoped to God it would stay that way.

Her mom was already waiting for me when I walked in, my shirt soaked through from the rain.

"He's with her again," she whispered in a gravelly voice. "I can smell her on him."

Hell. Med school had not prepared me for this.

"Look." I placed my hand on hers. "Mrs. Rogers. All I know is that the affair started three months ago, when my dad moved into my apartment building to wait out the divorce paperwork. Mom finally kicked him out, solidifying his worst fears that it wasn't just a fling but something more."

She swallowed and kept her eyes downcast. "Does Austin know?"

"Not yet."

Her head jerked to attention. "What do you mean, not yet?"

"She deserves to know. I've been waiting to say something."

"But . . ." Mrs. Rogers shook her head. "You don't understand! If you tell her, she's going to blame me and—" Austin's mom pressed a shaking hand to her face. "It's my fault. I drove him away. I didn't . . ." She bit down on her bottom lip. "I tried so damn hard. I just, I wanted to be perfect. I came to your office to see what you knew about the affair, and then while I was there, I realized, what if I just changed a few things, what if I was better, you know? If there was something I could fix or, you know—"

"I'm going to stop you right there," I said through clenched teeth. "Are you listening to yourself?"

Her eyes filled with tears.

"There is absolutely nothing you can do to yourself physically. Nothing. This is his choice, not yours. Sure, could you get Botox? Make yourself look younger? Absolutely. But what would it fix? Nothing. You'd still be miserable, and you'd be constantly on guard that he was still cheating. I'm going to tell you what I tell every person who walks into my office, alright?"

She nodded as a tear slipped down her right cheek, sliding over her deep-red lips. "Make changes for you. Never for someone else. If it's for someone else, you'll never be happy. When you change for a person, you start a vicious cycle of discontent." I sighed. "What do you see when you look in the mirror? A woman worth cheating on? Or a woman worth fighting for?"

"Right now I don't see much." She shrugged. "But . . ." Her eyes got that fiery look I was so used to seeing reflected in Austin's. "I'm worth a hell of a lot more than the way he's treating me, mayor of Seattle or not."

I smiled for the first time since I sat down. "I'd say I have to agree."

She clicked her nails against her ceramic coffee cup, then squeezed my hand. "You're a good man, Thatch Holloway."

My stomach sank. "Yeah, well, hopefully when I tell Austin the truth, she'll still think that."

"The truth."

"I was trying to protect her, from this, from . . . all of it actually, but originally I couldn't see past my own fear."

"You're allowed a moment of selfishness when it's something this big."

I nodded.

"It's only a matter of time before the affair leaks to the media."

"And how do you know that?" I tilted my head, suddenly curious.

"A woman scorned is a terrifying thing to behold." She smiled. "If you're going to tell her, just be sure to tell her everything. Part of me wants her kept in the dark. I don't want her looking at her father or me with disappointment. Know that I will fight with my last breath to preserve what is left of our family—Austin and me. I've let him control us too long. That stops now."

"Even if it's at the sacrifice of your own perfect world? Because the easy thing to do would be to just let him do his thing and keep pretending."

"I'd be living a lie. And I'm tired of living in a world where all people see is what we allow them to see, so yes, even then."

She stood and kissed me on the forehead.

I had to smile.

No wonder Austin loved forehead kisses.

My anger quickly dissipated, and then I realized I'd wronged her by trying to control the situation, and by protecting Austin, I'd done exactly what her parents had done to her all her life.

Controlled her.

I glanced up to say one final thank-you and felt like I'd just been kicked in the gut.

Austin was standing in the open doorway, her expression horrified.

I did a quick calculation of what she probably saw, her mom kissing my forehead, us sharing coffee, hardly anything bad. But she looked so pained, as if she could barely breathe.

She ran out of the restaurant like someone was chasing her.

Mrs. Rogers cursed under her breath.

"Shit!" I quickly pulled a few bills from my pocket, tossed them on the counter, and ran after her.

"Austin!"

She ran by her car.

And into the street. A few horns honked at her as she stumbled to the other side and continued running, until, finally stopping to catch her breath, she bent over and pressed her hands against her knees.

I caught up to her.

And heard nothing but broken sobs coming from her lips.

"Austin." The wind roared in my ears as cold wet rain pelted against my cheeks. "Baby, I have no idea what you think you saw, but I can guarantee you it's not that."

"Leave me alone!" She made a weak effort to shove me away.

Yeah, I sure as hell wasn't having any of that.

I grabbed her hand and tugged her against my chest, locking her against my body with my arms. "Why are you crying?"

"Because," she sniffled, "my mom's cheating! My dad alluded to that much this morning when I saw him. He was so upset, and he said, he said—"

"Your dad's a fucking liar," I interrupted with barely restrained anger. "And your mom was just asking me if it was true."

"If what was true?"

"I can't do this here." I looked around the busy street, at the people scurrying beneath colorful umbrellas as they passed us by.

"Well, this is your only choice or I walk!"

"Damn it, Austin, why do you have to be so stubborn!"

"Tell me!" She shoved against my chest. "Are you . . . ?" Her lips quivered. "Why was she in your office that day? Why was she kissing you!" She spit out the last part like I'd done something unforgiveable. And maybe I had.

"It's not what it looks like." I reached for her, but she jerked away. "We were just talking."

"Oh, that's rich. Just talking. You were just talking and holding hands." Her look went from pissed to horrified. "Was that it? Was that the reason? You were using me to get to my own mother!" She stumbled backward. "She gave you something in the office that day, and you said, you said . . ." Her eyes filled with more tears as they spilled over onto her cheeks. "You said I was a girl and you wanted a woman—" She hiccupped.

I kissed her roughly across the mouth.

She beat me on the chest and then sank into my hungry kiss.

"Austin, I love you. YOU."

"But—"

"Stop talking and just listen, think you can do that?"

"No."

I sighed. "Well, I tried."

She glared at me even though I could tell the corners of her mouth twitched to lift into a smile.

"Let's go." I tugged her hand toward the Starbucks across the street and ordered some hot Pike Place Roast for both of us before leading her to a table in the corner.

"Why would you be meeting my mom?" Her eyes held so much hurt, and I was about to make it so much worse.

"Your dad's cheating."

Her shoulders slumped as she went completely still and then whispered, "That doesn't explain why you'd be meeting with my mom."

I sighed, feeling like pouring hot coffee all over my face to at least give me a brief reprieve from the cold rain before I confessed all my sins.

"Your dad's cheating on your mom . . ." I cleared my throat and made sure to look directly into her eyes. The bomb was about to drop. I hesitated. Because what type of person wanted to have this conversation? "With mine."

She frowned. "Your what?"

"My mom."

"Huh?"

"My mom," I said slowly. "Your dad."

Austin's jaw dropped a few inches. "What?"

"This has been going on for three months," I ground out. "I found out about a month after we started dating."

"How?"

"My father found out and ran to tell me he had proof . . ." And here came the really uncomfortable part. "He had pictures of our parents together. And said he was going to go to the press, was going to finally ruin my mother and 'show the world what a slut she is.' Mind you, my father's a raging alcoholic, so I'm not even sure he'd make it to the news station without stopping at the nearest bar and getting drunk off his ass." I paused. "And then . . . he saw you. Put two and two together and . . . well . . . suddenly it was like I was nineteen again, walking in on my mother with our gardener. My father blaming her for ripping apart our family even though he'd made the first mistake." I ran my fingers through my hair. "Damn it, Austin, I didn't want you to know this way. I didn't want you to know at all. I thought if I just pushed you away . . ." I didn't want to keep talking. At all. It hurt finally telling her the truth, because every word caused her to flinch like I was delivering a physical punch to her gut.

Finally Austin asked, "Where are the pictures now?"

"I have them." I shifted uncomfortably. "In my apartment."

"You have pictures of your mom and my dad . . . naked?" she hissed.

I groaned into my hands. "It's not like I'm keeping a sordid private stash, Austin!"

Her eyes welled up with tears and then narrowed. "When did you say you found out?"

I was silent and then said, "I was angry at you. But it was misdirected, the anger. I was angry at myself. At my family for ruining one more good thing in my life—you."

Her expression almost killed me, so lost, so full of hurt and pain, pain I had caused.

"I was angry at your dad, angry at my mom, and even angry at my dad for telling me that I was just like them. Both of my parents are cheaters. And it scared me, scared me that he was right. And the closer we got, you and I, the more panicked I felt. What if I was capable of that? And when I finally realized I wasn't, that I wanted to be with you, I realized a relationship was impossible. It would destroy you."

Austin looked down at the table. "So you did exactly what they did, right? You became the man you never wanted to turn into—and cheated."

"I kissed Brooke. I didn't like it. And it was enough to make you so angry that you'd break up with me, or so I thought—and then you came back, and I almost told you the truth. But my father, he opened his door just a crack and—"

"Whoa, whoa, back up. He was in your apartment?"

I frowned and then tried not to wince. "No, he uh, he lives across the hall."

"Creepy neighbor man is your dad?"

"Smells like whiskey?"

She nodded.

"Looks like hell?"

Another nod.

"Probably him."

She reached for my hand, but I jerked away. I didn't want her pity or her sadness, not right now. I still had more to say.

"I broke up with you to protect you. Eventually, the affair will come out. They're careless, our parents. And you'll be caught up in all of it." I stood and backed away.

"Thatch." Tears filled her eyes as she clenched her jaw. "Thatch, what are you doing?"

"What's best." I almost couldn't find my voice. "Weathering this storm together is always an option. Or I could leave."

"No," Austin growled. "You don't get to decide for both of us. That's not how these things work." Her eyes flashed as she shoved against my chest and then gripped my shirt between her fingers, pulling me close. Her eyes glittered with anger. "Did you ever consider that I would want you by my side when the scandal came out? That I would need you to survive it? All of it?"

She shoved me away.

I let her.

And stared in shock.

I blinked and opened my mouth but didn't really know what to say. Because in every single scenario, I'd never thought of this one, the one where the girl wants to be by my side come hell or high water.

Because my mom had chosen to hurt my dad.

My dad had chosen to hurt my mom.

All I had seen in their relationship was pain.

I never saw love.

I never saw them look at each other the way Austin was looking at me right now. The way I'd always wanted to be looked at—with complete trust and confidence that no matter what, we'd still be holding hands in the end. And as if to prove her point, she reached for my hand and squeezed it hard.

"Are you going to go kiss someone to piss me off again?" she asked in confusion.

"What? No. Why the hell would I do that? I love you."

"Then that's really all I need to know." She held out her hand. "One step at a time."

"Austin, I don't think you've really thought this through, all of it, what it will look like."

"Funny you should say that"—Austin wiped at a few escaped tears—"since this really smart doctor once told me that it's how you feel about yourself that defines the person you are, not what others say. He also said this really awesome thing about eating all of your dessert."

"You would fixate on that part."

"He buys me MoonPies."

"Because he loves you."

"And he lets me drink Mountain Dew."

"And he prays every night it won't kill you."

She smiled and walked into my open arms. "I love you. Let's just . . . wait and see what happens. Let me talk to my mom and . . . well, the good news is this. I'm on Team Mom, and I know a thing or two about revenge."

"Believe me, I know, but you can't just go keying your dad's car."

"Um, yeah, I can."

"Austin—"

"I know a really easy way to slit his tires."

"I'm not helping you commit a crime."

"Fine, I'll just call Avery."

I jerked the phone out of her hand and shook my head. "I refuse to bail you out of jail. If you want to get even, I think I have a great idea, but let's just . . . wait and try to get through the day for now, alright?"

She nodded and kissed me softly on the lips. "Thank you for telling me."

"Thank you for not being angry."

"Oh, I'm angry as hell that you thought by breaking my heart in a million zillion pieces, you'd be fixing things for me—"

I backed up slowly.

"But I also know angry sex is the best kind, so you'll just do hard time in the bedroom, plus I had my eye on that stethoscope of yours. Think you could bring it home?"

"Something's wrong with you."

"Or very right?"

"No." I shook my head. "Just wrong."

"You love me."

"I do." I kissed her again. "Let's go."

Chapter Thirty-Six

Austin

A loud knocking sounded on Thatch's door.

I opened it and took a step back as Avery held her hand in the air and then sucked in breath after breath before finally stumbling into the apartment. "Hold . . . just one sec . . . can't breathe."

Lucas followed and shook his head slowly. "She ran."

"She needs to start power walking or something," I mumbled, biting off a huge piece of a Twizzlers licorice.

"Heard that," Avery said on another wheeze. "And I was worried, okay? You texted me a picture of two MoonPies, a Snickers bar, and a six-pack of Mountain Dew! It wasn't Diet, Austin."

"Gross, Diet?" I scrunched up my nose. "And why would that freak you out?"

"Need I remind you of last time?" She threw her hands in the air. "I had to rescue you from your own filth!"

I waved her off. "Well, I'm not in need of rescue, though Thatch did the honors at least a few times this afternoon."

Avery made a gagging noise and then looked around the apartment. "Where is good Thatcher?"

"On his way home." I shrugged. "Why?"

"Are you living here?"

I tried to find the right words. Technically I was about to. Thatch and I had at least come to that conclusion on the way back from the restaurant. I was to move into his apartment away from the crazy that was my father as soon as possible.

"Kind of." I needed to tell her about my parents, but I wasn't really sure how not to make it sound like a bad soap opera.

If that weren't bad enough, Braden had been trying to call me all day as if we even had something to talk about. I assumed he got my number from my dad.

And suddenly everything made sense.

My dad had wanted me away from Thatch.

He had been worried about his affair being made public.

And he was so selfish, he was willing to put a psychopath in my way.

Asshole.

I chewed the licorice harder while Avery quietly slid the tub close to me and nodded in encouragement.

I'd been hungry for the last six weeks for junk food—more than my usual, which just meant the stress was getting to me!

It's probably why I hadn't started my period.

The piece of licorice got stuck in my throat.

I started coughing.

Lucas slapped me across the back. "You gonna make it?"

"No." My eyes filled with tears. I'd been emotional too. Really emotional. More than usual. I covered my face with my hands and then started counting backward on my fingers, and when I ran out of my own fingers, I had Avery and Lucas hold up theirs.

Clearly they were good enough friends to just do it and not question my sanity.

My numbers counted back to the day before Thatch and I had broken up for good.

But that would mean . . .

I looked down.

And back up at my friends. Several times. Up, down, up, down.

"Is she having a seizure?" Lucas whispered under his breath.

"I don't know, check her pulse," Avery encouraged.

I slapped his hands away. "You guys would literally die in the wild. That's not how you check for a seizure! And if I was having one, I'd be on the floor."

Lucas held his hands back. "Whoa, just trying to save your life."

"If that was you trying . . . I would have been dead. But thanks." The tears kept coming.

"Honey"—Avery grabbed my hand—"you're freaking us out on game night."

Since when did it turn into game night?

"I, uh . . ." I licked my lips. "I think I'm—"

The door opened, Thatch strolled in, looking handsome as sin. His muscles bulged beneath his black button-up, and his gray slacks slid against such thick thighs that I found myself staring like I hadn't seen him in years.

The final piece clicked together.

I'd been unbelievably horny.

As in, ready to jump his bones for offering me the newspaper and a piece of bacon.

"Turn on the news, now!" Thatch demanded.

I was still in shock while Lucas and Avery ran over to the couch. Lucas found the remote first and flipped to the local news.

"Breaking news out of Seattle. Pictures of the mayor's wife, Shana Rogers, and her young lover have recently surfaced. The pictures show the two holding hands and talking closely. Mayor Rogers has released a statement asking for privacy at this heartbreaking time."

The screen switched to a photo.

It was Thatch.

And my mom.

It was bad timing.

And suddenly I wasn't sure about anything.

With a heave, I placed my hand over my mouth and barely made it to the bathroom before puking up way too much licorice and Mountain Dew.

"Austin?" Thatch was immediately knocking on the door, then jerking it open. And then I was being pulled into his arms. "I'm so sorry. I know it looks bad." He felt my forehead. "What's wrong? Is it the news? Do you have the flu? I can prescribe something for nausea, just give me a min—"

"I think I'm pregnant."

The phone slipped from his fingers and dropped onto the bathroom tile with a clang.

Yeah. So write that, Hollywood.

My dad set up my own mom.

With my boyfriend.

Whose child I was carrying.

Kill me now.

◆ ◆ ◆

Avery went to the store with me.

I told Thatch to stay with Lucas, plus it wouldn't be good for him to be seen. His name wasn't ever given, but it was impossible not to notice the high cheekbones and ever-present blond man bun. Besides, he was on buses, park benches—the guy was well known. And I was pretty sure that within the hour, news would break that Dr. Holloway—you know, my possible baby daddy?—was the home wrecker.

I groaned.

I was so angry at my dad, I wanted to give him a black eye—he wasn't the best dad, but at least he'd always protected me, kept me safe.

Put a roof over my head. Made me believe that no matter what, we'd stick together, even if it was all a front. I never thought he'd actually throw me under the bus—or Thatch for that matter. Not to mention my mom. The woman he supposedly loved enough to marry.

I knew I needed to confront him, but the very idea that he would set up our family like that had me reeling. I wasn't even sure what I would say, but *I hate you* was item number one on the list.

"You okay?" Avery rubbed my leg. "I mean, I know this is all a bit much, but it's going to be fine. Right?"

"Totally fine," I said through clenched teeth as we made our way through Walgreens and grabbed a few different pregnancy tests. Avery bought them.

For obvious reasons.

All of them pointing toward breaking news. No way was I going to add any fuel to the flame.

When we were back in the car, I started to cry again.

"Why can't we do anything normal?" I asked the universe. "Remember? White picket fence? One dog? A kid AFTER you get married and have the perfect job? And the perfect family reunions where both sets of parents hang out and aren't cheating with each other!" I yelled the last part.

"Okay," Avery said slowly. "First off, it's just your dad and his mom, it's not like everyone's swapped. Second, that's not real life." Right, because that made everything better.

"This, this isn't real life!"

"Actually, it is." Avery shrugged. "Life is messy. It's chaotic. And I hardly doubt you'd want perfect. I mean, have you ever even seen a picket fence? You have to paint that shit!"

"Avery." My eyes welled with hot tears.

"You can't even watercolor!"

Woman had a point.

"And one dog? Who gets one small, tiny, annoying little dog? You're more of a big-dog girl, and even then, have you seen Thatch with animals? He tried to pet a turtle once and was so rough, the little thing nearly drowned!"

I burst out laughing as I wiped away a stray tear. "That's true—he's only good with people."

"Not creatures. And I'm sure all pet owners everywhere say a thanks to God that he didn't decide to become a vet."

"True."

"The point is this," Avery said softly. "It's not always going to be how you planned it—but is love ever planned? Do you think I wanted to fall for my sister's ex-fiancé? The one who cheated on her? That sure as hell wasn't in my life plan!"

"Yeah, but your story is romantic!"

"Right, and so is yours, just in a different way, Austin." She rolled her eyes as she pulled out of the parking lot. "Sheesh, remember when you guys met? And you were all stumbling over to him and he couldn't take his eyes off you? And the man was a certified man whore, ask Lucas!"

"I don't think I like that part of the story," I admitted.

"Right, but the minute he found you, he changed his ways. Bam!" She slammed the steering wheel, causing me to jump a foot. "And now, look at you guys. Basically cohabitating and ready to have a baby, and—spoiler alert—the baby is going to be so beautiful! And healthy. And have a doctor as a dad!"

"And the story just got better, but we don't even know if I'm pregnant."

"You're over two months late," Avery said, then just had to add, "If you aren't pregnant, we really need to talk about your stress levels, or maybe it's just the Mountain Dew finally going radioactive in your system and changing you into a superhero! If that's the case"—she winked—"I say wait for Captain America."

"Good talk." I gave her a high five before grabbing the Walgreens bag and making the trek back up to Thatch's apartment.

Chapter Thirty-Seven

Thatch

"What does a nervous breakdown feel like?" I kept checking my watch, and every time I checked, only a minute had gone by. Walgreens was two blocks away.

Two!

"What the hell? Did they stop to feed the ducks or something?" I paced in front of Lucas while he devoured half a bag of potato chips. "And why aren't you saying anything?"

"One." He held up a finger. "Because you'll just tell me to shut the hell up." He crunched down on another chip. "And two, because I'm ninety percent sure if I say something, no matter how helpful, you'll just take out your pent-up aggression on me and punch me in the face, and I like my nose. I'm attached to it, literally. So I've got nothing."

"I wouldn't punch you."

"Admit it, you want to punch something."

"Because I don't know what the fuck to do!" I yelled. "I'm pretty sure Austin's dad wants to start a smear campaign in order to protect his own ass, and if Austin's pregnant . . ." I sat and groaned into my hands.

"And if she is?" Lucas asked.

A buzzing sensation washed all over my body. "I'd be stoked," I finally admitted. "It's not like I'm getting any younger."

"Saw a wrinkle near your lip, man, I'd fix that shit."

"You have smile lines too, dumbass."

He grinned. "Mine make me look sexy, since they're paired with this cleft right there." He winked. "Yours make you look old, ergo, congrats on the baby."

I tried to tamp down my excitement.

But it was impossible.

So when the door opened and Austin held out about six different types of pregnancy tests, I was ready to give her as much water as necessary so she could hurry the hell up and pee on the damn stick.

Austin walked toward the bathroom and closed the door. I sat on the edge of the recliner, then stood, then sat again.

"Just sit the hell down." Lucas placed his hands on my shoulders to make sure I didn't move and then went to help himself to a glass of wine before pouring me a shot of expensive whiskey and bringing it over. "Here."

It burned all the way down.

And threatened to come right back up when two minutes later, Austin walked out of the bathroom.

I couldn't read her expression.

I could always read her expression.

The room was completely silent.

I held my breath as she slowly walked over to me and pulled the little stick from behind her back and held it out.

I looked down.

"Holy shit." Tears filled my eyes. "You're pregnant."

She nodded and then wrapped her arms around me. I was afraid to squeeze her too tight. "I'm so sorry!"

"Wait, what?" I gently pushed her away and kissed her wet cheeks. "Baby, why are you sorry?"

"I know it's not part of your plan, and you're paying off school loans and—"

I silenced her worries with a kiss and lifted her into the air, twirling her around a few times before setting her back on her feet. "I'm a doctor, I think we'll be okay."

She huffed. "No, I know that, but then, my dad, and your picture, people are going to recognize you and—"

"Let's worry about that later."

She nodded and then a beautiful smile spread across her face. "I'm excited, why am I excited? I'm barely graduating with my MBA, and I don't even have a job."

"Hi." I kissed her nose and then tapped my chest. "Doctor. Not that you have to stay home. You've worked your ass off to be in the business world. What I'm saying is, you've always set your mind on a goal and achieved it, and this is no different. Plus, we have each other."

"Sorry, I'm just—there's a lot of things going on."

She was right about that.

I'd already fielded two phone calls from a partner at the firm who'd seen the photos on the news and was wondering what the hell was going on. The last time a scandal had hit our office, one of the doctors was asked to take leave for two months.

But I had a baby coming.

Two months?

No chance in hell.

I needed my job.

Because I wasn't going to screw up again.

And I refused to let this affect Austin. Again.

I *needed* to keep my job.

Which meant I needed a plan.

I thought back to the pictures I had stashed in my room. A twinge of remorse hit me square in the chest. A sick feeling washed over me as my stomach clenched. I wasn't sure if they would fix everything; I wasn't even sure if they would make things worse. But I had to try, right? Wasn't that what family did? They tried? They sacrificed?

I knew in that moment. I would do anything for her.

Give up everything.

To keep her safe—to keep my new family safe.

Chapter Thirty-Eight

Austin

We celebrated all night, and Thatch told us part of his plan before disappearing with Lucas for a good hour while I hung out with Avery and tried my best to come up with more ways to take my dad down.

Everything Avery and I came up with fell short.

Because really, who would believe my mother over the mayor? Especially with proof? People loved a good scandal, and even though Thatch wasn't actually kissing her, it looked like she was going in for a kiss and they were holding hands. It looked bad. I mean, I knew them, and I'd suspected the worst.

The answer came easily enough.

In fact, the answer came when *Zootopia* popped on and Avery made us pause for the Shakira song.

"I would kill for a carrot recorder pen." I yawned and then shared a look with Avery before grinning up at Thatch.

"That look scares me." He scooted away and then narrowed his eyes. "Just what's going on in that pretty head of yours?"

"The fact that I'm brilliant."

"I agree with that if I can add in 'terrifying' before the 'brilliant' part." He scooted back toward me. "Now, what's your idea?"

"Braden." I nodded. "He knows what's going on. I'll bet money my dad asked a favor for a favor. Date me, take me to the fund-raiser, make us look good, and pull me away from Thatch, and he'd put in a good word. Braden wasn't that good of a student that he'd get a high-paying lawyer job right out of college. He used to cheat off my papers all the time. I mean, the guy's smart, but I guarantee he struggled with his classes."

"No." Thatch shook his head. "Absolutely not. You're not talking to that dipshit, besides, last time he saw you, you drew blood."

"Right." I rubbed my hands together. "But if I tell him I saw the news and I'm confused . . . and sorry . . . I just bet he'd confess that my dad got him a job in exchange for dating me or at least distracting me. He always likes to sound like he's smart, like he knows everything. He's too arrogant not to say something."

"I still don't like it," Thatch said.

Lucas nodded. "I'd have to agree with Thatch on that one, you're carrying his child."

I crossed my arms. What the heck? What does a baby have to do with it! "Guys, it's not the seventeenth century, you know this, right?"

They both ignored me, and then Avery piped up.

"Honestly . . ." Avery shrugged. "The easiest way for you to talk to him without making it look like you're crawling back is to pretend like you're a woman scorned, a woman cheated, a woman needing to get even."

The room fell silent again.

"What?" She popped an almond into her mouth. "You said he's arrogant—he'll love that you came to him. And boom, he'll be eating out of the palm of your hand. Just bring your carrot recorder pen and you're golden."

"Or iPhone, that's always a solid option too," Lucas joked.

"Please." I gripped Thatch's hand. "I want to fix this, I—I want to move past all of this crap. I don't want the white picket fence and dog and two perfect kids!"

"Huh?" Thatch asked the room. "Is this normal for pregnancy?"

Avery patted my back. "What she's saying in her own weird way is she wants to start fresh, and have a family, and be happy, with you, not with the *idea* of what was pumped into her when she was little about happily-ever-afters. Get it?"

Both men nodded.

While Avery and I rolled our eyes and began to plot.

◆ ◆ ◆

"I see you've come to your senses," Braden snorted over a martini. Ah, even the way he drank made me want to smack him on the head.

It cheered me up that, while fading, the black eye I'd gifted him with was still visible, though my money was on cover-up making the purple look more of a muted yellow.

"Yeah, well." The waitress appeared at the table, and I ordered a drink but knew I wasn't going to touch it. "I'm pissed. He cheated on me, freaking cheated. Again!"

Braden rolled his eyes. "Stop being so dramatic. You know it was a setup, right? Your dad just wanted me to keep Thatch away from you so your dad could continue screwing Thatch's mom without you finding out or ruining it for him. I asked for all the gory details, especially since I was really happy with my last girlfriend. Then again, she couldn't get me into the best law firm in town. So, I did what I could."

Wow, that was almost too easy.

"Yeah, well." I drummed my fingertips on the table and tried not to shift too much since my phone was on "Voice Record." "I'm still pissed."

Braden tossed back the rest of his drink. "All I know is that your father's up for reelection next year, and he'd do anything—*anything*—in order to get it. You know he wants to run for Senate next."

I fought the urge to gag.

I loved my dad.

I did. He was my dad.

He would always be my dad.

But sometimes he was just too much. And ever since the shit had hit the fan, I noticed how that love between us had always been one-sided. I did things for him, and if I did them well, he gave me love.

If I did them poorly?

I was ignored.

Ugh, no wonder I dealt with so much insecurity where Thatch was concerned.

"He'd be a great senator. Aren't they known for cheating?"

Braden smirked over at me. "Someone's still bitter. Look, from what your dad said, they've been hooking up for a few months."

I thought about Thatch's dad. About the smell of whiskey, the way he leered at me, the language Thatch said he used in reference to what was happening.

And his mom.

The woman I had yet to meet.

Sighing, I stood. "Thanks, Braden. You still need a date for that fund-raiser?"

It was an olive branch.

I didn't want to go with him.

But I also wasn't sure what was going to happen to him when my dad discovered that he was the source.

"You punched me in the face last time we talked," he said drily. "And don't take this the wrong way, but you really are putting on weight. Maybe up the cardio, huh?"

My fingers itched to hit him again.

Instead, my anger was quickly replaced by happiness. "I have noticed. And I'm okay with it." Baby's gotta eat! "Good-bye."

"Wait!" He stood. "That's it? I thought you wanted to hook up or something?"

Hah. No. Just no.

"Sorry." I shrugged. "I'm feeling a bit sick now."

I smiled the entire way out the door.

Chapter Thirty-Nine

Thatch

"If we didn't need that bastard, *I* would have punched him in the face," I said through clenched teeth as we slowly got ready for bed. The bathroom was large enough for both of us to move around each other, and I kind of hated it, because I liked feeling her warmth around me, knowing that if I reached for her, she'd be there.

I'd turned into a complete sap.

And I'd never seen it coming.

Austin put her hands on her hips and shook her head at me. "You've said that . . . at least five times."

"It was true the first time, true this time too." I looked down at my shaking hands and clenched them into fists. "The fact that he ever kissed you, touched you—"

"Whoa there, cowboy." Austin was suddenly in front of me, tugging me by my hair in a way that drove me wild, pulling me into her arms and kissing my mouth, her delicious tongue sweet on my lips. "I'm yours. Plus . . ." We both looked down as she placed my hand on her stomach. "Now we're going to be a family. Every time you touch me or kiss me, it feels like I'm ready to jump out of my own skin. I love you.

This, what we have, it's worth fighting for, even if it means we fight our own blood."

My entire body trembled.

I wasn't really sure what that looked like.

The only model my parents had set up for me was "cheat or be cheated on."

And although I knew a part of them did love me, they just chose to love me from afar.

While I rarely saw my dad, the few times our paths crossed publicly, he said he was proud of me in front of others. But in private? That was a completely different story. He was constantly upset that I didn't follow in his footsteps and painfully vocal about my field of choice.

And my mom stopped answering my calls the minute she discovered good old Dad had moved across the hall from me and blurted out her dirty secrets. Even though I had distanced myself from my mother, I still called her on holidays. I called when I got a job. I called and thanked her for at least showing up to my college graduation. But because my dad moved across the hall, I'd apparently "picked a side." And now she cut me out of her life. Completely.

The point? I felt abandoned by her, yet again, and it wasn't fair. The entire situation with my parents was ridiculous. And I was finally over it.

Sighing, I kissed Austin softly across the mouth, my hands spreading across her flat stomach. I wondered if the baby could sense me, feel me, know that even now I loved it more than anything in this world.

Tears pricked the back of my eyes.

I'd never been an overly emotional guy, especially considering that I thought emotions showed weakness, and both of my parents were emotional terrorists in their own right, throwing atom bombs at each other without caring who was caught in the crossfire—or that the person getting injured the most was their only son.

"Thatch?" Austin said softly.

"Yeah?"

We pulled apart.

"I want to talk to my dad before everything happens."

Everything in me wanted to shout, *No!*, to tell her that he'd try to manipulate her like he did everything else—like he had her entire life—but I was at a loss. He was her father, and I didn't have a leg to stand on other than being her boyfriend, and a protective one at that. Besides, Austin was tough.

I nodded once. "If that's what you need to do."

"I just—" Tears filled her eyes. "I want him to come clean. Maybe if he admits the affair and says he'll fix the media shit storm, we won't have to go to all of this trouble, you know? I just feel like I'm handing down a life sentence without actually seeing if he'd be willing to plead guilty."

She was right, damn it. It wasn't fair to blame him for everything without even talking to the man. I knew firsthand where a fucked-up family got you.

Lonely.

Desperate.

Lonely.

Lonely needed to be said twice for obvious reasons. I'd almost lost her and would have been living in my own personal hell right now if she hadn't kicked me in the ass and made me see reason.

"You know, I hate admitting when you're right, but . . ." I grimaced. "You probably are."

She grinned. "I love hearing that from your mouth."

"Don't get so used to it," I muttered. "Want me to go with you?"

"Maybe just, I don't know . . ." She shrugged. "Hang out in the car? Just in case he freaks out and we need a getaway vehicle." If the man touched a hair on her head, I was going to have a hell of a time staying out of prison.

"Man the vehicle." I nodded. "Got it."

I had no idea what her dad was going to do, though I was pretty positive that there would be yelling and hurt feelings—but I couldn't go and ruin the man's life, even if he was trying to ruin mine, without giving him a shot at redemption.

Right? It was only fair that Austin give him a chance. One I never gave my own parents.

"Hey." Austin wrapped her arms around my body. "I don't like that look. Want a Mountain Dew?"

"Seriously? Is that how I'm going to feel better?"

She nodded emphatically. "Or a MoonPie, I have a stash of those too."

"Oh, yeah?"

"Pickles!" she shouted directly in front of my face, then whispered, "Oops. I mean, pickles, I heard they're good and um—"

"Is this your way of asking me to go get you pickles and MoonPies, because you know we don't have any of those in the house, right?"

She grinned. "Good doctors take care of their patients."

"You realize I'm not that kind of doctor, right? I don't fluff pillows and give you junk food. Furthermore, you should know that, since you spent the last three weeks shadowing me. Just what was in all those notes you were taking for those blog posts?"

"Really accurate pictures of your ass." She winked. "And oftentimes, I'd doodle 'Austin loves Thatch' and then write little hearts around our names. When things didn't go my way, I finally just danced around your apartment naked when you weren't home and cast a love spell on you."

I fought an eye-roll. "Not weird at all."

"I'm so glad you agree." She started kissing my neck, making it impossible to think straight, and then my shirt was over my head, my pants were hanging from the door, and I was getting completely seduced and assaulted by a pregnant lady with a one-track mind and a really wicked grip.

"Austin." I jerked against her.

"I'll take care of that." She bent down.

"No, you're pregnant and—"

Just kidding.

All conscious thought left my system at the feel of her mouth, my body, her heat, her tongue.

I gripped the sink with one hand while she continued torturing me, and when I didn't think I could take it anymore, I pulled her to her feet and pressed her body against the door, taking her mouth over and over again until she whimpered beneath me.

"My turn," I whispered hoarsely across her neck as I shoved her shorts to the floor and found her center.

Hips bucking, she smacked my hand and let out a soft laugh. "You're killing me."

"All's fair." My answer before opening the bathroom door and carrying her to the bed, sinking into her the minute her back kissed the mattress and staring down at the gorgeous girl I wanted to spend the rest of my life with.

The thought hit me like a semitruck.

It had nothing to do with the baby.

And everything to do with her.

I'd wanted her from the beginning.

And impossible as it might sound, I wanted her more now.

Her soft moans as I made love to her were the only thing keeping me sane, keeping me from jumping off the cliff, falling to my knees, and proposing.

It wasn't the right time.

That seemed to be the new motto of my life.

But in this moment, it wasn't because I was afraid of what my words would do.

Until Austin, I never realized how much beauty could be found in the mess.

We had survived this mess.

The least I could do was give her a perfect proposal.

Chapter Forty

Austin

I didn't want to dance around anything, so when I walked up to my house—the house that I was going to be moving out of as soon as this all blew over—I felt empty.

Kind of like, the home I'd grown up in hadn't really been a home, just a place to put my things. I'd always felt empty in this large house; I just never realized how empty until now. I expected some sort of sadness, another emotion, something. Instead, it was like I was walking up to a stranger's house.

Thatch's apartment felt more like a home, and for the first time since finding out about my dad and his mom, I was justifiably sad.

Sad that my dad had done this to our family.

Sad that he felt the only way to cover his ass was to blame someone he should be protecting—my mother.

And just sad all around that although I was bringing a life into the world, as far as I was concerned, if he didn't apologize, he wasn't going to share a part in it.

By the time my hand reached the doorknob, I almost itched to knock. I knew he was home, because I'd texted him earlier and told him I wanted to talk.

Mom was gone—I was meeting with her later. All she'd done was cry on the phone and apologize—like it was her fault.

We'd talked for two hours, during which she confessed that she'd suspected my dad was having an affair for a while. And whenever she would finally work up the nerve to confront him, my dad seemed to have a sixth sense that something was wrong and would come home and bring her flowers or take her out to dinner and make everything better. She had convinced herself that he was just going through a phase.

Poor Mom. She cried harder when she said she'd even followed him one day to his meetings.

Ah, the apple really doesn't fall far from the tree.

I finally realized, in that moment, that my mom kept her façade up not because she actually liked living the life where everything was a perfect illusion, but because she wanted to protect me.

Just like Thatch.

But sometimes, love isn't enough. Her love for my dad wasn't enough to keep him from cheating.

And maybe the sick part was that my dad loved us in his own way, just not enough to put our needs above his own. I refused to love that way, with only a part of my heart. Maybe that's why I refused to let Thatch go—he'd stolen my heart and never given it back. So I fought him for it, and I'd like to think we both won.

I turned the knob and shivered as I took a step inside my house and saw my dad sitting at the breakfast bar, sipping coffee and reading the newspaper.

How many mornings had I woken up to this?

And how many mornings had I woken up to a note saying he was already out?

Not enough mornings where he was sitting at the table.

And too many mornings to count—where he was absent.

"Dad," I croaked.

He turned. His eyes were sad, and then a steely resolve replaced whatever else had been present. "You knew better."

"Wow." I held up my hands. "I love you too?"

"I told you that boy was trouble. Now look at him, sleeping with both my wife and my daughter."

It was a lie.

I knew that.

And so did he.

"I know everything." I reached for his hand.

He jerked it back. "I don't know what you're talking about." He checked his watch. "Now, I have a meeting in a few minutes. Was there anything else you needed?"

I took a deep breath. "Tell me the truth. That's all I need."

He looked down at his coffee, then stood. "The truth is that your mother isn't being faithful."

"Dad." I felt my entire body tense, though I tried not to show it. "She isn't cheating. You know that."

"No." He shook his head wildly. "She is, that's what everyone believes, and that's how it's going to stay."

He started walking away.

"Is it worth it?" I said to his back. "Is being mayor? Running for public office? Is it worth losing your family over?"

For a brief second he hung his head, and then his back straightened as he called over his right shoulder, "I do love you, baby."

"Prove it," I whispered.

His only answer was silence, and then the front door clicked shut. I didn't cry. I wanted to. But I didn't feel like giving him my tears.

Instead, I waited in the tense silence and then, very slowly, went into my room and started numbly putting things in boxes.

My childhood felt shattered and I had no idea why; it wasn't like I had this perfect upbringing and now the rose-colored glasses had fallen to the ground and got crunched beneath his boot or something.

A deep sadness filled me.

And then determination.

To be better.

To not cheat my child out of a life full of love and happiness. I wasn't going to give my kid gifts when I worked too late, or fun trips with his or her friends because I couldn't take time off for a family vacation.

When I looked around at all the pictures in my room, it was oddly reassuring that in almost every picture I was with Avery, and some even with Lucas.

And then there was Thatch.

The missing piece.

I picked up an old teddy bear and tossed it in a Goodwill box.

And then I grabbed another box that I'd been keeping in my room for when I eventually moved out, and slowly started tossing in shoes, clothes, pictures, pieces of my life that seemed worth rescuing and keeping for later, for my new life with Thatch.

I didn't realize I was crying until strong warm hands wrapped around my middle and tugged me down to the carpeted floor.

Thatch held me in his lap for at least a half hour while I cried out the rest of the tears my dad had caused. When I blinked up at him, his face was soft, so beautiful.

Let it be known that you can meet the love of your life after a one-night stand and a crazy game of Mario Kart.

"I'm sorry." He kissed my forehead softly and then pulled back. "Why don't we just grab what you need, and you can finish up later."

Nodding, I took his hand as he helped me stand up.

With a sheepish grin, he took a look around my room and then burst out laughing.

"Hey! What's so funny?"

"You liar!" He charged toward one of my poster boards. "You knew who Enrique Iglesias was!"

I gave him a wide-eyed innocent look and then said, "Who's your hero, baby?"

"That's it." He charged after me and then picked me up in his arms and started tickling my sides. "You said you didn't know the song!"

"I wanted to see," I said, laughing, "if you would sing it!"

"I was drunk!"

"You were adorable."

"I puked all morning."

I scrunched up my nose. "Yeah, well, maybe not that part."

"You're a horrible human being, you know that, right?" He set me down, still grinning as a piece of surfer blond hair fell across his high cheekbone.

"You love me anyway."

"True."

"And you really are my hero."

"No." His face sobered as he brushed a kiss across my lips and then touched my stomach. "You're mine."

Chapter Forty-One

Thatch

"I think I may puke," Austin said at my side. She was dressed in a gorgeous black gown that hugged her every curve. It was lacy, and it was really messing with my head, since the lace gave glimpses of her creamy skin. If our driver stared at her one more time, I was going to punch him in the face.

I'd gotten really territorial all of a sudden.

Hell, I'd always been territorial where Austin was concerned; I'd just never wanted to act on the feeling as much as I wanted to right now.

"You look awesome," Avery encouraged. She was sporting a short red dress that kept hiking up enough to cause Lucas to have trouble breathing every few seconds when he looked down and did a double take.

We decided to rent a limo to drive us to her father's fund-raiser. Rather than hide out while news went wild. It only made sense to show our unity and strength.

It had been a week since the news hit about me and Austin's mom, and the fervor hadn't died down, but without any more proof, it was all about speculation, which I'm sure was exactly what Austin's dad wanted.

Just enough speculation to make his wife look bad. And for him to look like the wounded party and sail into reelection.

I patted my suit jacket for the second time that night, just to be sure what I needed was still there, and smiled when I felt the familiar shape.

Tonight was going to be epic in more ways than one.

The minute I helped Austin out of the limo, cameras flashed like lightning and reporters shouted questions, trying to figure out what we were doing together.

I ignored their questions and chose to kiss Austin full on the mouth before kissing her forehead twice and looping her arm in mine.

The cameras flashed even more.

Avery and Lucas brought up the rear of our small group, and when we finally made it inside, I felt like a five-hundred-pound brick had been lifted off my shoulders.

Austin's mom was waiting for us, champagne in hand. She looked beautiful, but she wasn't Austin. She smiled at both of us and then walked right up and linked arms with Austin as if to say, *We're a team.*

I was afraid Austin was going to cry. Instead, she held her head high as we made our way to our table.

Where, wonder of all wonders, Austin's dad was talking business.

He looked ready to puke when his eyes fixated on his wife with me and Austin in tow.

But I think the best part, the truly best part of the night, was the moment when Austin's mom said aloud, "Honey! This is Dr. Holloway. You know, the one you sent me to for that surgery you wanted me to have?" She was talking so loudly, it was impossible not to hear her over the soft music playing. She turned toward me. "It was so kind of you to make an out-of-office visit, since I had so many privacy concerns."

"Any time." I nodded. "And I have to thank you too."

"Oh?" Her eyebrows arched. "For what, dear?"

"Giving me permission to date your daughter."

The look on Mayor Rogers's face was absolutely priceless as his expression shifted from rage to a forced smile as he nodded at his wife and said, "Oh?"

"Well . . ." She winked at both of us. "When you said you loved her, I was so excited that she'd finally found someone like you."

We had a captive audience.

One that was eating up every word.

And there wasn't a damn thing Mayor Rogers could do about it.

Lucas coughed behind me.

"Oh, sorry, we're going to go grab a glass of champagne." I leaned in and kissed Austin's mom on the cheek. "Thank you."

"Mayor." I nodded toward him and held Austin as close as physically possible. "Have a good night."

"Oh, I intend to." His fake smile perfectly poised, he looked ready to take another picture for the newspaper.

"If I were you, I'd enjoy this moment." I tilted my head to the side. "You never know what tomorrow may bring, am I right?" I forced a smug laugh while Austin's father's mouth twitched into what could have been mistaken for a slight frown.

Honestly, in that moment, I felt sorry for him.

What good was having money and popularity when you didn't have anyone to go home to? When the reputation you'd spent your whole life building disappeared overnight? When you lost the job you'd sacrificed your family for and were left with nothing?

He had a grandchild on the way.

And he didn't even know.

And my suspicion was that even if we told him—he'd use it as a way to gain more attention and divert focus from the impending scandal.

He whispered something in his assistant's ear.

It didn't matter if he found out tonight what was going to be in the papers tomorrow. They were already printed.

When we were out of earshot, Austin finally said, "You didn't do it."

"What?" We stopped walking while Lucas and Avery slid past us to grab something to drink. "What are you talking about?"

Austin's blue eyes locked on mine. She was so pretty, it hurt. "You had everyone eating out of the palm of your hand, plus you had the pictures and the recording in your pocket, and you could have destroyed him." She poked me in the chest and then frowned. "Or I mean it was right there earlier, because you kept checking your pocket, all paranoid, and then—"

I dropped to one knee.

Austin gasped.

Avery held up her phone to record the whole thing as instructed while Lucas had champagne ready for our little celebration—though Austin was getting sparkling water.

Lots and lots of water.

And if she said yes, maybe a sip of Mountain Dew. God save me from a child as addicted to sugar as its mama.

"Austin . . ." I reached into my jacket, slid my hand past the next day's newspaper spilling all of the mayor's dirty deeds to the public, and grabbed the small velvet box. "I have something to say."

A crowd slowly started gathering around us.

Out of the corners of my eyes, I saw cell phones lifted, people grinning from ear to ear, and Avery either ready to pee her pants or so excited she couldn't sit still.

"You do?" Austin's eyes shone with tears.

"Yeah." I kept the box in my hand. "But I'm a bit terrified you're going to tell me it's a horrible idea, that you've known me only three months, that we're rushing into things. So I thought I'd tell you all the reasons you shouldn't say yes first."

She frowned.

"When I get drunk, I sing Enrique Iglesias. It isn't pretty. But I swear, I really do want to be your hero, every single day of my life." She wiped a tear. "I can't stand soda, and every time you buy Mountain

Dew, I swear somewhere in my body a very healthy cell just gives up and dies." She covered her face with her hands and giggled. "I didn't even know MoonPies existed until you—and now, whenever I look up at the moon, all I see is you. It's a horrible idea, trying to make me so clearly obsessed with you that everything reminds me of you." It wasn't really a reason, but it needed to be said. "We've known each other three months, three whole months, part of that time we spent apart, and it was the worst four weeks of my life. I think I'd die if I ever had to endure it again." I sighed and then kissed the palm of her hand. "I work. A lot. I argue. I hate messes. And I'm stuck in my bachelor ways." She nodded. "I can't ride a bike." Someone gasped. "And yes, I really do hate ice cream."

Another gasp. Really, people?

"If you want a pet, it's going to have to be either an app on my cell phone, or it will probably die because I'll forget to feed it."

"That's true," she whispered.

"And most important. I broke your heart. I made you think I didn't love you when the exact opposite is true. My heart had trouble working properly without you, and I can't imagine a life where I'm not able to hold this hand and wonder if our son or daughter's hand will be exactly like it." Tears fell freely from her eyes. "I'm hoping that my love for you trumps all the reasons we shouldn't do this, so that when you say yes, you mean it, and then won't overanalyze all the no's, because I already did it for you."

"Yes."

"I wasn't finished."

"You're finished." She tugged me to my feet and kissed me hard on the mouth. People applauded, and I still hadn't even shown her the ring. "I love you, Thatch Holloway."

"I love you too, Austin Rogers." I swallowed the lump in my throat as champagne was thrust in my face and water in Austin's.

"Ring." Avery took a large sip from her glass. "Show her the ring." She sighed. "It's gorgeous."

I held out my right hand and then opened the box with my left, revealing a simple sapphire-cut two-carat diamond on a thin white-gold band.

Austin's eyes about bugged out of her head. "That's—" She covered her mouth with her hands, and then I was tugging her left hand down and slipping the ring on.

"A perfect fit," I whispered.

She nodded and then hugged me tightly. "When did you plan all of this?"

"When you were in your bedroom crying, and your dad was being an asshole, I decided that it was best we start our lives together now, the right way. I love you. You love me. There was no reason not to. Besides, what better way to stick it to your dad, not by stooping to his level, but by fighting his ugly . . . with our love."

"You know, you're a brilliant man." Austin laughed.

I raised an eyebrow. "You should probably marry me so we'll have smart kids, and they can take care of us when we're older."

"Because that's why you get married," came Lucas's reply.

I elbowed him in the ribs.

I knew it was only a matter of time before he popped the question, mainly because I'd hijacked his ring-shopping time in order to find something for Austin.

But what Avery didn't know wouldn't kill her.

"This is perfect." Austin sighed. "All of it."

And it was.

Chapter Forty-Two

Thatch

I was too excited to sleep.

By the time eight a.m. rolled around, Austin was still sleeping, and I was trying to make coffee without dropping cups and running into walls. I was dead on my feet and so thankful I had taken the day off.

With a yawn, I was just getting ready to grind some coffee when a hard knock sounded at my door.

I knew that knock.

Just like I knew who would be on the other side.

And suddenly the tension was back in my shoulders as I rigidly made my way toward the door and opened it, expecting to see the usual—my father, red-rimmed eyes, swaying unsteadily on his feet, smelling like whiskey, and shouting about how my mom and I ruined his life.

Instead, I found my dad.

Completely.

Stone-cold.

Sober.

Showered.

Dressed.

He looked like the dad I remembered. His hands shook as he held out a newspaper and pointed at it. "You did this?"

Shit.

"Yeah." I swallowed the guilt and pushed it away completely. "It needed to be done."

"Closure," he said after a few minutes. "I finally feel like we have closure. I thought—" His eyes watered. "I was so angry for so long. I pushed for the divorce and settlement, thinking it would make her realize how much she needed me, needed us. Then I thought if I protected her, she'd come back, she'd see that I didn't expose her, that I was better for her and that he was using her." He choked on a sob and then shook his head. "It doesn't matter. It's done."

"It is," I whispered. "It's finally out in the open."

"I shouldn't have cheated on her. I loved her. I was . . ." He locked eyes with me. "Thatch, I'm a weak man. I can't promise to be better, but I'm going to try."

"Care to start now?" a soft voice said from behind me.

Austin looked gorgeous in a soft white silk robe and her pinstriped shorts with one of my old V-neck shirts just barely covering her breasts.

My dad nodded and then spoke a simple "Yes."

"We're pregnant," she said immediately. "You're . . ." Her eyes glowed. "You're going to be a grandpa."

I'd never seen my dad cry. But the old man broke, there was no other way to put it, as he fell to his knees and sobbed.

Maybe because the situation was so close to him.

A family.

One that wasn't broken, but was getting a fresh start.

And me, a carbon copy of him, so close to the man he could have been.

The father he could have been.

When he wiped his tears, he got to his feet and asked, "If—if I get better, would it be possible to help deliver your baby?"

"Of course," I said without asking Austin. I knew she wouldn't want it any other way.

"I think we'll have to ask the hospital, though, just to make sure." Austin smiled brightly.

My dad let out a low chuckle.

I followed.

And then we were both laughing.

I'd forgotten how private I'd kept my life, from everyone, but especially from her.

"Baby, you're looking at the former surgical director of neonatal research at UW—there's a wing dedicated to my dad at the U hospital. He retired last year."

Austin's jaw dropped. "You're, but you're—"

"It was a rough year," my dad finally said, then mumbled, "Hell, it was a rough ten years. But I could deliver a baby with my eyes closed." He glanced at me. "Then again, so could Thatch. The only reason he went into plastics was to piss me off."

"Partial truth," I corrected. "I like plastics. It's always interesting, and I'm not owned by my job the same way you were."

"And you like pissing me off." The old man wrapped an arm around Austin. "He was at the top of his class at UW, primed and ready to go into neonatal just like his old man, but one day he came home, and all you need to know is, I think what he saw pushed him over the edge . . ." My dad's voice softened. "Well, it was just as much my fault as his mother's that he wanted nothing to do with us."

Austin listened while I went to make the coffee I had started brewing before we were interrupted.

I don't even know how long they talked.

But when my dad finally left, saying that he needed to go think, it was close to noon.

"So?" Austin's eyebrows shot up. "Where do you want to start?"

I sighed and leaned back against the couch. "I didn't want to take his money. It felt like hush money or something you give someone instead of love because it's easier, which is horrible, right? It was easier for him to write a check than give me what I'd always wanted, a hug, a high five, anything that said he was proud of me, or that he cared. But he was so stuck in his own misery, and I didn't want to follow in his footsteps because his being a cheater was what destroyed my mom, our family. I just—I wanted something different."

"You wanted boobs," Austin said in a serious voice. "Admit it."

I burst out laughing. "Yes, Austin, I wanted tits, and to think all this time, I would have been satisfied with just yours! Would have saved me a lot of money."

"I'm sure you'll be just fine." She winked.

I tugged her foot and pulled her over to my side of the couch. "Maybe, but I should probably take a look at them just in case. You know, nipples can be very sensitive during pregnancy. I would hate for you to . . . suffer in silence."

"I'm not suffering."

"I think I see a tear." I ignored her. "Baby, just let me take care of you."

"You're full of shit."

"Acting out is another symptom of nipple tenderness, it's in the manual."

"Hmm, is it right next to a picture of Enrique?"

"Low blow!" I started tickling her.

She started singing at the top of her lungs, and I silenced her with a deep kiss. "Are you going to kiss away my pain?" she belted out the second I drew back.

I pressed my hand across her mouth. "That's enough."

Naturally, she just kept singing against my fingertips.

"Want a MoonPie?"

She stopped singing and then narrowed her eyes and gave me a thumbs-down when I pulled my hand away. "Well played, fiancé, well played."

Fiancé.

I grinned so huge, I probably looked terrifying.

Austin crawled into my lap and straddled me with a knee on each side of my body. "You sure look pleased with yourself."

"I'm seventy percent pleased."

She frowned. "Why only seventy percent?"

I ran my hands up and down her sides, then very slowly started peeling down her little shorts until my thumbs reached her hips. "I think you know why."

"Nope. No idea."

"You're killing me here." I moved my hands beneath her shirt and groaned when I came into contact with her breasts. Perfect. So damn perfect.

Her moan joined mine as she ground against my erection.

"Fine, you win." She peeled her shirt over her head and then stood and tugged her shorts down.

"Wow." I stood, already jerkily removing my clothes. "That was easy."

"Yeah, well." She lifted a shoulder. "I know how much you like to see tits, remember? I figure if you're always looking at mine, when you touch others, it will be like feeling up a nice old grandma."

"Let's leave grandma talk out of naked time, yeah?"

She nodded and then crooked her finger at me. "You know, I think your dad's going to be okay."

"Yeah," I agreed, glancing at her stomach. "I think so too."

Chapter Forty-Three

Austin

His mouth.

Why would I ever want a job?

Sex with Thatch. That was my new job title.

He was probably just trying to distract me from watching the news, since my dad's face was all over it right along with his mom's.

Every time I tried to reach for the remote, he slapped my hand away and started kissing me.

"Focus on us. Focus on this," he'd say over and over again, loving me with his mouth, holding me, touching my stomach. So I listened.

But it was time.

And it was like we both knew we needed to face it, to watch the news and see what happened once the story hit.

I grabbed Thatch's hand and rose from the bed, leading him out into the living room and pointing at the remote.

"They're still our parents," I whispered.

"Yeah, they are," he echoed, and then hit the power button.

It was breaking news alright.

But it wasn't as bad as I'd thought.

I mean, it wasn't like he was guilty of embezzlement. Speculation said that the affair had been going on for years.

I knew the truth, just like Thatch, but it wasn't our place to correct anyone. There were several pictures of his mother and my father together.

And it made me sick to my stomach when, in one of them, he was kissing her on the mouth and laughing.

That could have been Mom.

We should have had a happy family.

He broke that.

And for what?

I still didn't get it.

"Why?"

I didn't realize I had said it out loud until Thatch hit "Mute" on the remote and grabbed me by the hands.

"Sometimes people do stupid things, make the wrong choice out of boredom, revenge, pride." He shrugged. "You may never know why, and I know that kills you, because when I broke us—" I opened my mouth to correct him, but he shook his head. "When I broke us, I didn't tell you why—I thought I was protecting you, now I know the truth. You may never know the truth about my mom and your dad, but know this—you won't ever be cheated on again."

Tears welled in my eyes. "I know."

"I'm serious, Austin." His grip was firm, solid on my fingertips. "I will never cheat on you. I want this relationship to be one of communication, I want a real family. I want love."

"Me too." I nodded. "And I promise, I won't ever cheat on you."

He sighed.

"Unless cheating means I can beat you at board games, or if we race and I trip you beforehand, or if I cheat with calories on a non-cheat day, or—"

He kissed me.

I giggled against his solid chest.

"I love you," he murmured, "and I always will."

"Good, because you're stuck with us."

"Thank God," he whispered reverently before kissing me again. And then once again, helping me remember why we were so good together. Because our love was shared equally, because it wasn't about obsession, or even lust, but about that very real thing that was shared between two people who got it. Who understood the sacrifice it took for something to work—and were willing to make it.

We were cheated.

But we weren't cheaters.

And it felt good to say it.

Epilogue

Austin

"You're doing so well." My father-in-law winked at me and moved around the bed to grab my hand. "How are you feeling?"

"Oh, you know." I clenched my teeth. "Like I'm giving birth to a ten-pound gorilla, but other than that, splendid. Hey, where are we on those drugs?"

He grinned, and his expression reminded me so much of Thatch.

Over the past few months, father and son had mended their relationship so much that we had family dinner nights, and he'd even paid off every cent of Thatch's student loans so we could start fresh. The divorce settlement had gone through, and the very first thing his father wanted to do with his money was take care of us.

Thatch said no.

But his father said it was necessary, and said if we didn't take the money, he'd just set up a trust fund for the little boy we were about to have.

So Thatch took it, and later that night, cried in my arms.

Three hundred and fifty thousand dollars' worth of loans.

Gone.

Forgiven.

Funny how the minute he was able to forgive both his mom and dad—his dad was able to forgive himself.

"Ahhhh!" I shrieked as my belly tightened and a giant invisible vise squeezed me like a tube of toothpaste. "This isn't natural!"

Thatch was calm.

He *would* be calm.

Weren't dads supposed to pass out?

"STOP BEING SUCH A DOCTOR!" I snapped at him when he was ducking his head under the sheet and discussing God-knew-what about places that should never be discussed or looked at by a father-in-law and sexy husband!

"The drugs are here!" Avery announced.

Lucas chose to wait in the waiting room.

Smart man.

Avery held out a MoonPie. "You can have this once you push super hard."

"I hate you, I hate you so much."

She dangled the MoonPie in front of me.

"No solids!" The elder Dr. Holloway wagged his finger at me.

I flipped him off in response.

Thatch burst out laughing. "You okay, baby?"

"You're never touching me again. I'm joining a nunnery, how's that for okay?"

"You're just in a lot of pain."

He nodded toward the door as another man in scrubs walked in and said, "Someone need an epidural?"

"ME! Yes! I volunteer!" I shouted as Avery, watching me, winced when another contraction hit.

I reached for her hand and grabbed the MoonPie by accident, smashing it into tiny bits before dropping it on the floor.

"No! My MoonPie!"

"I have more." Avery patted my shoulder. "So, you good here? I think I'm just going to go . . . back to my husband and . . . pray . . . for you! Not for me. I'm fine."

She wasn't fine. She was twelve weeks pregnant.

"This is your future!" I yelled after her.

"Austin," Thatch snapped. "Is that really necessary?"

"Oh, I don't know, is THIS necessary!" I pointed at my belly and made a face.

He smirked. "I love it when you're feisty."

"Get it out!" I said with a snarl. "It hurts."

"Drugs." Thatch kissed my forehead, my utter weakness, and then nodded to a doctor who looked too young to be holding a needle so big.

"Hi, Austin. My name's Ben. I'm going to make this feel like a cake walk, alright?"

I sniffled. "I really like cake."

"Great." He winked. "Now, turn on your side and grab your knees and hold still. The minute your next contraction hits, I want you to take a few deep breaths, and once it ends, I'm going to put in the epidural.

"Okay? You'll feel a slight sharp pain and then some pressure and we'll be all done. You can't move though."

I nodded. I was sweating and freaking out. I hated needles.

Thatch was immediately on the other side of the bed. "Let's just fight through this next one together, alright?"

I couldn't speak; the contractions were getting worse. I clenched my eyes shut and waited for the torture to end.

And then I heard Ben's voice. "That was a big one. Alright, let's go."

I tried not to tense, but like I said, the needle was huge and it was getting placed in my spine, of all places. Already woozy, I waited for my legs to go numb and was pleasantly surprised when the pain started to dissipate and, within five minutes, went away altogether.

"It's a miracle!" I could talk and function like a normal human being. "What's in that thing?"

"Fentanyl," Thatch answered with a smirk. "There's no chance in hell you should feel any pain, and if you do, just click this handy little button but not too often, 'kay?"

He handed me a magic button.

And suddenly I felt powerful again.

And like myself.

"I'm going to rock this." I nodded.

Thatch rolled his eyes. "Yeah, I think it's safe to say she's got drugs in her system, since a few minutes ago she was flipping everyone off."

His dad smiled, and they started chatting about the football game while I was busy trying to figure out why the little guy hadn't decided to make an appearance yet.

A half hour went by.

And then a full hour.

I was restless, reading a magazine, when Thatch's dad checked me again and smiled. "You ready?"

I knew everyone was restless, and eager to see the baby. My mom was in the waiting room with everyone else, most likely pacing away the carpet.

"YES!" I threw the magazine on the floor and waited. "Do I push now or—"

"Patience." He chuckled. "We don't want to stress the baby." He glanced at the monitor. "At the height of each contraction, I want you to grab behind your knees and use that to help you push from your stomach, alright?"

I nodded.

And during the next contraction, I pushed as hard as I could.

Thatch was on the right side of the sheet, holding my hand and squeezing with each push.

"Two more and I think we got it. You're born to do this, Austin."

"I am," I said more to reassure myself. "I am. I've got this."

"Love you." Thatch squeezed my hand tighter as I pushed again.

"I see baby's head," Dr. Holloway said hoarsely. "One more, honey."

I pushed again.

And then all the pressure was gone.

And a warm, wailing, tiny, wrinkly little thing was placed on my chest.

I burst into tears.

Thatch was already there, helping the nurse clean up the little guy while his dad did whatever he was supposed to be doing down there.

"This is going to hurt a bit." He looked up. "We need to get all the fluids out along with the embryonic sac. You ready?"

I nodded and held my baby tight while he pushed down on my stomach. I was seriously going to puke if he didn't stop soon.

Thatch was staring at the bundle on my chest with tears streaming down his face.

"So beautiful," Dr. Holloway said. "The way the body creates another precious human." He held up something bluish and gross looking, and I about passed out.

"Thank you," Thatch whispered in my ear. "You did wonderfully."

"I don't really hate you," I said, suddenly exhausted.

"I know, baby."

"And I don't want you to jump off a cliff."

"I'm aware."

"And I really do want you to touch me again," I whimpered. "Maybe just not tonight."

He smirked. "Austin?"

"Yeah?"

"I love you."

"Love you too." I kissed him on the mouth and felt full, so full, I thought I would explode.

A family.

Who would have thought that saying yes to a hot doctor at a bar would lead to this?

Not me.

It was the perfect ending.

Acknowledgments

I still pinch myself. I love my job; it's my passion. And I'm so blessed to be able to do it, and so thankful to God for allowing me to do it and putting me on the right path so that a dream could become a reality.

To my amazing husband and son, who put up with my late nights and constant craziness over book deadlines—I love you guys. Nate, you are truly the best book boyfriend EVER, only you're real . . . Wait, you are real, right?

Melody, thank you for all your hard work with this manuscript. Courtney, thank you for always being so up for whatever crazy ideas I have and going, "Okay, yeah, let's do it!" So honored to be a part of the Skyscape team!

Erica. Best agent EVER! Thank you for pushing me, and always being such an amazing friend and agent. I love you!

Jill—you literally make sure everything is perfect before publication. Thank you for keeping me sane and making sure that every *t* is crossed and every *i* dotted. I don't know what I would do without you as family and as a friend!

Liza, Kristin, Jessica, best beta readers ever! Thanks for loving this book as much as I did and for helping me when things got a bit sketchy!

To Rachel's New Rockin' Readers, GAH! I love you guys, and I know I say this basically every single day on Facebook, but we really do have the best, most supportive group ever!

Bloggers, Readers, I love you guys hard. And words will never be able to adequately express how thankful I am that you stick with me or that you even pick up one of my books. I'm fully aware I would not be where I am today without you guys!

If you want to stay in contact, follow me on Instagram @RachVD or you can join my totally awesome group on Facebook, Rachel's New Rockin' Readers. To be kept up to date on future releases and all the stuff in between, just text MAFIA to 66866 to be added to my newsletter!

HUGS!

RVD

About the Author

Photo © 2014 Lauren Watson Perry, Perrywinkle Photography

A master of lighthearted love stories, Rachel Van Dyken has seen her books appear on national bestseller lists, including the *New York Times*, the *Wall Street Journal*, and *USA Today*. A devoted lover of Starbucks, Swedish Fish, and *The Bachelor*, Rachel lives in Idaho with her husband, son, and two boxers. Follow her writing journey at www.rachelvandykenauthor.com.